SHATTERED LINKS

SHATTERED LINKS

The Cari Turnlyle Series, Book 8

by Leslie A. Piggott

INDIES UNITED PUBLISHING HOUSE, LLC

Dedication

To Brad, Abby, and Simon: Life is the best with you in it.

Table of Contents

Chapter 1

The billboards for Jackson's Used Cars boasted it had the largest selection of used cars in the tri-county area. Krystal Covington smirked as she looked across the enormous lot. Maybe they had the largest selection of Toyota Corollas, but forgive her if she wasn't excited to get one of those.

"Krystal, over here!" her boyfriend, Tate Sundrick, called out from across the lot.

"Coming," she said under her breath.

She walked between the rows of cars, only partially paying attention to the giant prices painted onto each of the windshields. The wind gusted and blew her blonde hair into her face for the eighty-fifth time that morning. Tate told her it was fun to shop for a used car and initially, she'd been excited. February in New York was not pleasant outside. It was bitterly cold and windy. She felt silly for thinking she'd spot the perfect car for her as soon as she arrived. It's not like they were at the animal shelter looking at the adorable dogs who wanted to be adopted. It was just row after row of brightly painted metal with wheels. She wished she'd taken Tate up on his offer to pre-shop and give her the rundown of which cars were best for her budget and needs.

"Where are you? You've got to see this one!" Tate yelled.

"I'm almost there!" she shouted back.

Krystal estimated he was still four rows of cars away from her. She could see his head peeking out from the line of sedans. He had on a bright red beanie, so it was easy to spot him from a mile away. Tate was about as far away from the office building as you could get. Only one or two rows of cars were behind him. The sun was high overhead and she'd forgotten her sunglasses, so she watched her feet while she walked rather than squint in the light. Whoever Jackson was, he kept the lot pretty clean. She didn't see any dirty oil spots on the pavement or weeds growing along cracks. She was almost to Tate's row when a stain on the concrete caught her eye. She stopped and looked closer. At first, she thought it was an oil stain, but then she realized the color was off for that. It wasn't a brownish oily spot; it was still wet and dripping from the trunk of the car. She bent down closer.

"Krystal!" Tate yelled just as she figured out what she was staring at.

She screamed as the realization hit her. "Tate!!!! Tate! Tate! Oh my god, Tate!!!"

Tate rushed to her side. "Stop screaming. I'm right here. What happened?"

Krystal's hand was shaking as she pointed at the puddle forming under the trunk of the car. "Just look," she hissed. "It's blood. I think there's a body in that car."

"Stop being dramatic. There's no way there's a body—" Tate suddenly stopped talking. "Get your phone out. Call 911."

Krystal pulled up the hem of her long coat and fished her cell phone out of her back pocket. She didn't know why Tate couldn't get his phone out. She touched the phone icon on the screen and punched in the three numbers.

"9-1-1, this is Monica, what's the emergency?" the operator asked.

"Hi, uh, this is Krystal Covington. I'm at Jackson's Used Cars over on Broadway…um, I think there's a body in the trunk of one of the cars," Krystal told the operator.

"Can you describe what you're seeing?" Monica asked.

"Uh, there's a dark blue Corolla and it has something dripping from the trunk. It's something red. It smells bad too," Krystal added. She hadn't noticed the smell at first, but now she was close to gagging.

"Krystal, are you by yourself?" Monica asked.

"Uh, no. My boyfriend is here," she paused. Where did Tate go? "Well, he was just right here. Oh, there he is. I think he's going to get the car lot owner."

"I'm in touch with dispatch. They're going to send some officers your way. Are you safe?" Monica asked.

Krystal looked around the vast lot of cars. Everything suddenly felt menacing. She frowned at her chicken-heartedness. There might not be a body in the car. It could be spoiled food or…something less terrible. She took a deep breath and let it out.

"I'm okay," she answered finally.

"I'm going to stay on the line with you until the officers arrive. Can you describe yourself to me?" Monica asked her.

"Sure. Uh, I have wispy blonde hair that's a mess because of the wind. I'm wearing a white puffy coat. It's long, but without a hood. I'm about five-foot-seven. Uh, the car is on the far right-hand side, um…the right side if you're looking at the lot from the road. It's in the fourth row from the end."

Krystal had no idea if she was on the east side or the west side. It could even be north or south. She wished she were better at directions.

"Okay, perfect. The officers should be there any minute. Are you still doing okay? Is your boyfriend back?" Monica asked.

Krystal looked toward the office. She couldn't see Tate anymore. "Uh, no. He must still be tracking down the owner. I'm still okay."

* * * * *

"I was really hoping to stay inside today," Detective Alex Runimoss grumbled to his partner.

"Something new and different," Detective Genevieve Viacorte teased him. "Turn right on the next street."

"Why are we getting called out for this? Don't we have some patrolling officers who can take this call?" Alex asked for at least the third time.

"Grusky wanted us to handle it because it sounds like there's a dead body in the trunk," Genevieve reminded him of their lieutenant's words.

"It better not be a dog. Or some wild animal," Alex whined some more.

"A dead *person* is preferable to a dead animal?" Genevieve questioned him. "I said turn right here."

Alex cranked the wheel and just barely made the turn without hitting anything. "Sorry, I was caught up in your philosophical question. And, I know where the lot is. You don't need to give me directions."

"Clearly," she smirked.

Genevieve decided to stop razzing Alex and watch the other businesses roll by her window. The wind looked to be extra strong. She wondered if it was blowing in a snowstorm. She finally spotted the large sign with bright red letters on a yellow background with the words "Jackson's Used Cars" in a Comic Sans font. She'd always thought it was an eyesore for Brenington, but she knew it was a popular location. She saw a blonde woman holding a phone to her ear and figured that was Krystal Covington.

Alex pulled into the entrance. Small arrow-shaped signs directed them to visitor parking on the left side.

"I saw our caller on the far side. Dispatch mentioned her boyfriend was trying to track down the owner. Why don't I go speak with Ms. Covington while you go to the office…in case he tries to run or something?" Genevieve suggested.

Alex turned the cruiser off. "Works for me. You're pretty fast, for a girl, but the caller would probably rather talk to you than me."

"For a girl? I can keep up with you any day of the week, old man," Genevieve said as she took off her seatbelt.

"Old?! I'm barely forty-five," Alex argued. "I'm at least a foot and a half taller than you. You'd never keep up with me."

"That sounds like a challenge," Genevieve said and opened her door.

"Just go talk to the woman. I'll holler if I need help with the owner," Alex grumbled.

Genevieve heard him muttering something about being old as he walked away. She held back a laugh. It was fun to get under his skin. She looked across the lot. It was at least a quarter mile long. The wind blew wisps of her dark brown hair into her face. Most of her hair was pulled back into a bun at the nape of her neck, but the strong wind had tugged a few strands free. She pulled her hat out of her coat pocket and tugged it onto her head. She could straighten up the bun later if she needed to.

The used car dealership ran frequent ads on the local TV stations. Just seeing the billboard had brought their jingle to mind: *Come to Jackson's. Your future ride is waiting for you.* She hurried past row after row of cars to the Covington woman. Genevieve saw the woman look toward her and wave. She waved back. Only a few more rows until she reached her. The wind seemed to be gaining in strength as she got closer. She could feel herself leaning into it as she walked through the lot. She was still about three rows away when the smell hit her. The wind must have carried it her way. She cringed. Whatever was in that trunk was definitely dead. She adjusted her direction so she was two cars over from where the woman stood. It made the smell less noticeable. Covington took the phone from her ear and touched the screen when Genevieve walked up.

"Brenington PD? You're a police officer?" Covington asked Genevieve.

"Detective Genevieve Viacorte," Genevieve replied and held up her badge. "Ms. Covington?"

"That's me…and this is the car," Covington replied and pointed at the dark blue Corolla.

Genevieve saw a drop of what definitely looked like blood drip from the trunk and splat into a dark puddle on the concrete. She had to agree with the woman. The odds were high a dead body was inside that trunk. She pulled out her notebook and pen.

"I know you told the 911 operator some of what happened already, but can you tell me what led to your discovery here?" Genevieve asked her.

"I'm right then, right? It's a body? You can smell it, right?" Covington asked. Her pale blue eyes were barely visible as she squinted at Genevieve.

Genevieve nodded. "It's pretty bad. What time did you get to the lot today?"

"Krystal!" A man's voice startled Genevieve.

"That's Tate. Looks like he found the owner…uh, and your partner, maybe?" Covington explained.

Genevieve turned toward the voice. A lanky man with a bright-red beanie walked with Alex and another man dressed in a suit and tie. The suited man had on sunglasses, but even with his eyes covered, Genevieve could tell he was upset. His lips were pressed into a thin line and his nostrils were flared. His face seemed a bit red too. She wondered if his tie was too tight, but thought it was equally possible he was just out of shape. Alex's long stride was a challenge to keep up with and the used car dealer was a few inches shorter than the tall detective. At six-foot-six, Alex was at least a few inches taller than almost everyone.

"Detective Viacorte, this is Rutherford Jackson, the owner, and Tate Sundrick, a witness. Ms. Covington, I'm Detective Alex Runimoss, with two esses," Alex introduced himself. "Mr. Jackson, could you pop the trunk please?"

"Please, call me Jet. Rutherford is so formal," the owner complained.

Jackson wiped a hand across his forehead first. Genevieve found it odd he was sweating when it was so cold out. The man pressed a button on the fob in his hand and the trunk of the neighboring car flicked open.

"Sir?" Alex asked with his eyebrows raised.

"My apologies. I seem to have grabbed the wrong keys. Let me radio one of my guys to bring the right ones over in the golf cart," he offered and pulled a walkie-talkie from his suit coat. "Coop, I need the keys to the new Corolla. The blue one…No, the other one. Fine, I'll just get them myself."

Alex gestured for him to do so. Genevieve gave Alex a curious look. Something was off and it wasn't just the possibility of a dead body in the trunk.

"Should we call Dr. Green and CSU out?" Genevieve asked Alex.

"Not yet. If it's just a raccoon or a dog or something, we'll be wasting their time. If the owner doesn't come back with the right set of keys this time, I'm popping it open with a crowbar," Alex told her.

"Couldn't we pop the lock on the driver's door more easily?" she asked.

"Possibly, but then the window seal gets messed up. That's a pain for future owners," Alex explained.

"Right, because someone will totally buy this car once they learn there was something bloody and dead in the trunk. Ups the resale value in unbelievable ways," she retorted.

"I'm going to go get the crowbar from the trunk of the cruiser. I'll be right back," Alex said and took off for their cruiser.

Genevieve decided to talk to the two witnesses while she waited. "Ms. Covington?"

The blonde woman looked her way. "Just Krystal, please."

"You noticed the blood?" Genevieve asked her.

"It's blood? For real?" Krystal asked.

"I can't say for certain, but I've seen a lot of blood and it looks like blood to me," Genevieve explained.

"Yeah, I saw the *stuff* dripping from the trunk," Krystal answered.

"What time did you arrive at the lot?" Genevieve asked for the second time.

"Right after it opened," Krystal said.

"Nine-ten or so, like ten after nine o'clock," Tate Sundrick responded. "We wanted to get an early start."

"Have you seen any other shoppers today?" Genevieve asked.

"Are you wanting to know if we saw someone stash a body in the trunk? Because, no, we didn't see that happen," Tate said and rolled his eyes.

"I'm just trying to get a feel for how many people were present when the blood was first observed," Genevieve told him plainly.

"I think there were a few groups of people. I didn't really pay attention," Krystal admitted.

"There were maybe five other people wandering around, but they were all on the other side. We were the first ones over here," Tate expanded on Krystal's response. "No one drove any vehicles onto the lot after we arrived. This was here when we got here."

"Got it," Genevieve said and made a note. Her fingers were starting to ache from the cold. "Have you shopped here for cars before?"

"My first time," Krystal answered.

"Same," Tate said.

"Did you touch the car?" Genevieve asked.

Krystal recoiled. "Of course not. Gross."

"I don't think I touched it. I started by looking at the cars closer to the office building and then made my way over here. Those are usually the nicer ones and can be seen on their surveillance cameras. The ones they don't care about as much are further out," Tate told Genevieve.

"Good to know. Let me get you a card and get your information too," Genevieve replied. She pulled out a card from her messenger bag. "Here's my card. If you think of anything else, please give me a call."

"We can go?" Krystal asked.

"You don't want to shop anymore? I bet we can get a great deal today. Like hazard pay because of our negative experience," Tate told Krystal.

"Gross. I just want to go home," Krystal said with a frown.

"I just need both of your names and contact information. I have a tablet you can enter it into in my bag. Just a moment," Genevieve told them.

She pulled out the tablet and unlocked it. Then she opened the witness information form and handed it to Krystal. "Just enter your information and then Mr. Sundrick can do the same."

Krystal peeled off one glove and quickly typed in her information. She handed the tablet to her boyfriend and he did the same. Genevieve heard footsteps and looked over her shoulder. Alex was back with the crowbar.

"I got their statements and information," Genevieve told Alex. "They're entering contact info now."

"Cool. I'm wagering we're going to need to use this guy in just a minute," Alex told her.

The couple turned to walk toward the building. Krystal stopped and looked back at Genevieve. "We're going to see if they have anything warm to drink like cocoa or coffee," she explained.

Genevieve nodded and watched them walk away. "I don't know how you could drink either of those after seeing blood drip from a trunk. Weirdos."

"Here comes Mr. Jet himself," Alex said as though Genevieve couldn't see him.

Jet Jackson jogged over to the car again, if you could call it jogging. He clicked another fob and the Corolla's lights flashed.

Genevieve watched Jackson's face. She saw relief wash over him when the lights of the correct vehicle flashed. The wind shifted and he caught a whiff of whatever was hidden in the trunk. His face contorted and Genevieve was certain he was about to vomit. The dead body smell was growing stronger by the minute as the temperature increased. It was cold and windy, but the sun was out, so the body was warming up. Jackson backed up a few steps.

"Do you need me to witness this?" Jackson asked and choked back a gag.

Alex shrugged. "Suit yourself. I'll take the keys now."

Jackson hesitated. "Uh, I unlocked it. You can pop the trunk from the dash now. Why do you need the keys?"

Alex snorted. "We have to conduct an investigation here, Sherlock. Hand over the keys."

Jackson sighed and dropped the keys into Alex's outstretched hand. Alex looked at the fob and pressed a button. The latch released and the trunk popped open. The smell intensified.

"Oh, no. Not good," Jackson said and stepped back several more steps.

Genevieve had to agree with him. The Corolla's trunk was home to one very dead white male. His face was smashed and covered in blood. Both detectives turned toward the owner.

"We're going to need everything you have on this car," Alex said firmly. "Stay here with us until our CSU team arrives. Sorry to make you suffer in the cold, but we don't exactly trust you anymore."

* * * * *

The dry cleaner's was busy when Cari arrived with Bob's suit on Wednesday morning. He'd told her he had been called to testify in court on Friday and needed to look professional. He'd worn his suit to the delayed rehearsal dinner almost two weeks ago and Joel had spilled soda on him. They'd kind of forgotten about it between moving into the new apartment and helping get Bea and Robby's family around, as neither was cleared to drive for over two weeks. Luckily, Robby could take a rideshare to the subway to get to work and their kids rode the bus to and from school most of the time. Cari stepped up to the counter after waiting in line for several minutes.

"How soon do you need it back?" the clerk asked as Cari entered her information into the keypad.

"Tomorrow?" Cari asked hopefully.

"It should be done by the end of today, but definitely by the start of business tomorrow. You'll get an email with the tag receipt," she explained. "Next."

Cari refreshed her email and saw the receipt show up. She exited the store and got back in her car. The wind felt extra cold and blew some of her curls into her face. She'd wrestled her hair into a messy bun that morning after waking up a bit later than she'd intended. The newspaper building was just a few blocks away. She turned on her radio and tapped her thumbs on the steering wheel to the beat as she drove.

Her boss's car was already in the parking garage when she arrived a few minutes later. He seemed to be working longer and longer hours ever since they'd restructured the business almost six months ago. She rode the elevator up to their floor and went directly to the break room for some coffee. She'd forgotten they were out of beans when she put in their Instacart order on Monday, so she and Bob were both stuck with office coffee for the week until one of them made it to the store. She fixed her coffee and then sat down at her desk to see what was on tap for the news day.

"Turnlyle!"

The outburst surprised Cari and she had to use her left hand to steady the coffee cup in her right. She'd been a journalist at the Brenington Beagle for a few years and her boss, Mr. Ollaman, still sometimes managed to startle her. She set her coffee on her desk and grabbed her messenger bag off the back of her chair. Ollaman's office was just thirty or so feet away from her cubicle. She quickly marched over and peeked her head into the room.

"Yes, sir?" she asked with a smile.

Ollaman's bald head was red and shiny. He was staring at his cell phone screen, which was dark. She could see something had upset him. She'd already turned in her articles for the week, so it wasn't a late deadline issue. He looked up from his cell phone and grimaced.

"Take a seat and get out your notebook," Ollaman ordered her.

Cari quickly picked up a stack of newspapers from the only other chair in his office and set them aside. She sat down and got her notebook ready.

"My friend Jet Jackson, that's J-E-T," he paused and ran his hand over his bald head.

"You have a friend named Jet Jackson?" Cari asked. She felt like she remembered watching a TV show with a similar name as a child, but maybe the alliteration was just striking her funny.

"It's more of a nickname, though he might have changed it to give himself more, uh…pizazz when he opened the used car lot here," Ollaman explained.

"Oh, *that* Jackson," Cari realized.

"He just called me and needs our help. He's one of my oldest friends. Apparently, someone stashed a dead body in the trunk of one of his cars. The police are there and he's having a hard time convincing them he doesn't know how it got there," Ollaman told her. "I know used car salesmen have a rep for being sleazy, but he's a great guy. He'd never be involved in something like this. Go over there and talk to him. You have a detective friend. Pump her for information. Go!"

Cari scribbled the snippets of background information into her notebook and then stuffed it back into her messenger bag. She nodded her goodbye to Ollaman and exited his office. While she didn't want to put her friend Genevieve in a bad spot, the whole case sounded rather intriguing. Obviously, Jackson could be lying through his teeth, but finding a body in a used car lot? This was a first for her. She double-checked that her keys were in her bag along with her cell phone. Before rushing to the elevator bay, she retrieved her coffee from her desk. She'd barely had a drink of it before Ollaman beckoned her to his office.

Bryson Millar stepped off the elevator just as she reached it. He was the other investigative journalist for the newspaper, but preferred to cover city politics more than crime and actual investigations. Cari was happy he liked that side better; she found it horribly boring.

"Leaving already?" Bryson quipped.

"Ollaman's got me chasing a story. Dead body at Jackson's Used Cars," she told him. "And watch your words: Ollaman knows the owner. He's pretty torn up about the whole thing."

"Thanks for the tip!" Bryson called out as the elevator doors closed.

Cari rode the car down to the parking garage and hurried to her vehicle, a tan Toyota Camry. She unlocked the driver's door with her fob and tossed her messenger bag into the passenger seat. If they'd found a dead body at the lot, then the odds were high two of her favorite people were at the scene: her husband of ten days, Bob Hursley, and her good friend, the detective. She didn't want to interrupt either of them while they were at a possible crime scene, but she hardly ever drove anywhere without calling someone. Her grandmother's health had been weighing heavily on her mind since her wedding weekend. Grandmother had been Cari's closest family member her entire adult life, but it seemed like her health was declining rapidly. The wedding had been chaotic and didn't leave time for her to talk with her grandmother about her new symptoms. The used car lot was about ten minutes from her office, so she called her grandmother using her car's Bluetooth feature.

"Cari, Cari, married lady, how are you, sweetheart?" her grandmother's voice sing-songed in her ear.

"Hi, Grandmother," Cari responded. "I'm headed out to a crime scene at a used car lot. How are you?"

Her grandmother coughed twice before she answered. "Right as rain, my dear."

"We still haven't talked about why you're coughing and short of breath," Cari reminded her.

"What kind of crime scene?" Grandmother asked, dodging the question.

"I'm not certain, but I'm serious!" Cari said almost laughing at her paradoxical language. "You never answered me before."

"Oh, Cari. I'm not going to live forever. You know that, right?" Grandmother asked and cleared her throat.

"Have you seen your doctor since you got home?" Cari asked with concern.

"I told you at the wedding, I go to my doctor regularly. I'm in good hands, Cari," Grandmother assured her.

"But…" Cari prompted.

"You're right, or your smart husband was right with his hypothesis," Grandmother confirmed. "I have congestive heart failure. It's a tricky thing to treat."

Cari swallowed. "I've been avoiding reading about it…sort of hoping you just had a cold or something."

"My heart is getting tired. It's worked hard for a long time," Grandmother said gently. "But I'm not dying any time soon. I'm trying some medications and altering my diet a bit. They took away my salt shaker."

"What?" Cari asked in surprise.

"Well, not really, but they might as well have. I'm not supposed to add salt to anything anymore. It's all incredibly bland," Grandmother complained. "But I've had worse things. It's okay. Now, tell me about your new story."

"Well, I honestly don't know much. I guess they found a dead body in the trunk of a car at one of the used car lots in town. My boss knows the owner and said I have to help clear his name," Cari told her. "Hopefully, I won't have to disappoint him."

"Stick with the truth and you'll be fine, my dear," Grandmother replied.

"I'm just pulling into the visitor lot now. Maybe I could come visit for a weekend sometime soon? Are you busy?" Cari asked.

"Talk to Bob first before you make plans with your old granny," Grandmother teased. "Now, go find that bad guy."

"I will. I love you, Grandmother," Cari said.

"I love you more."

Cari ended the call and turned off her car. She could see the medical examiner's van over on the opposite side of the lot. She figured they probably wouldn't let her get too close to the scene, so she decided to go inside and look for the manager or owner first. The wind almost ripped the car door from her hand when she opened it. Her messy bun got messier and she tried to tuck the loose curls back into place. She needed another hair tie to secure everything better. She picked up her messenger bag and rummaged through it for a hair tie, but came up empty. She knew there was one in her car somewhere. She leaned back inside and popped the console open. Several napkins from fast food restaurants spilled out. She tossed them aside and sifted through the other items. Finally, she felt the elastic band at her fingertips and pulled it out of the compartment. She hurriedly secured her wild curls into a bun and then locked up her car.

The tall glass doors had brightly colored numbers and words painted all over them. The lot was having a twenty percent off sale this week. She wondered how they made money if everything was always discounted. She pulled open the door and looked around for the office area.

"Can I help you?" a woman near a red sports car called out to Cari. The woman was fairly tall with dark curly hair and dark skin. She wore a light grey pantsuit with a pale pink shirt.

Cari walked over to her. "I'm looking for Mr. Jackson. He should be expecting me. Tell him Mr. Ollaman sent me."

The woman frowned for a moment before smiling again. "I'll go get him for you. Ollaman, right?"

"Yes, Ollaman," Cari repeated.

She watched the tall woman walk away, her high heels clicking on the linoleum. Cari decided to straighten up her hairdo while she waited. She removed the hair tie from her hair and ran her hand through her dark curls. Her wedding ring snagged on one strand of hair and tugged it. She carefully untangled the jewelry and teased the snaggles from her hair. Then she wound all of her hair into a messy bun with the hair tie. She figured it still looked frightful, but at least it wasn't in her face.

"Ms. Turnlyle? Or is it Hursley?" a voice spoke from behind her.

She turned around. "Mr. Jackson?"

He stuck out his right hand. "Yes, ma'am. So, is it Hursley now? I heard you recently got married."

Cari found it odd the man wanted to know her marital status while the police were investigating his place of business as a possible murder site. She tried to give him a friendly smile. "Uh, I'm still Turnlyle. I'm kind of known by my name, but it's only been ten days. I can still decide to change it at some point later. Mr. Jackson—"

"Please, call me Jet with one T," Jet interrupted.

"Right. Mr. uh, Jet, I understand they found a dead body in one of your vehicles?" Cari asked.

The front door chimed and they both looked toward it. Two men entered, one of whom looked to be the father and the other the son. Cari assumed they were car shopping.

"Allison, could you, uh…?" Jet gestured toward the duo.

"I got it, Jet," Allison assured him. "Gentlemen…"

Her voice trailed off. Jet watched her walk away and then turned back to Cari. "Why don't we talk in my office? The police will probably want to speak with me again soon. I have my business lawyer looking for a criminal attorney for me right now."

Cari tried to keep her face neutral. "I understand."

He escorted her to his office and unlocked the door. "Have a seat. What did Ollie tell you?"

Cari almost laughed at the nickname. She'd only heard one other person call her boss Ollie and she knew it embarrassed him. She looked around the office. It was completely in order, which surprised her. She half-expected files to be sticking out of drawers and cabinets, his desk to be a mess of paperwork, and keys to be lying about in random places. Instead, his desk only had three items on it besides the computer: a bin with signed documents, a ballpoint pen, and a telephone.

"He said a dead body was found in the trunk of one of your vehicles," Cari explained.

Jet opened his mouth and then closed it. "Uh, well, um, yes. That's the short version."

"What else can you tell me?" Cari asked.

"Ollie assured me you won't try to double-cross me. You're not going to burn me in the news, right?" Jet asked with trepidation.

"Mr. Ollaman asked me to help clear your name. I'm here to investigate…as a journalist," Cari said matter-of-factly.

"That wasn't really an answer, but I guess Ollie is the editor and he won't burn me. Part of the problem for me is…well, you see…" Jet squirmed in his chair, crossing and uncrossing his legs. "I wasn't able to produce the title to the car. I did have the keys, so it's just a matter of time until I locate the title."

"But it is one of your cars?" Cari asked in confusion.

"Um, it's on my lot…so…yeah?" Jet didn't really claim ownership.

"Do you have a record for the car at all?" Cari asked, trying to understand how he'd have a car without papers for sale.

"Not exactly," Jet confessed.

"Mr. Jackson, uh, Jet, how do you typically acquire cars for your business?" Cari asked.

He smiled. "A myriad of ways. Sometimes, they're trade-ins from other purchasers. Other times, we buy them from a dealership if they're trying to clear out inventory."

"When did this car arrive on your lot?" Cari asked and jotted down some notes.

"It was earlier in the week," Jet said vaguely.

"Don't you have a record of it?" she asked in confusion.

"I wasn't able to locate it yet," Jet replied.

Cari could feel his anxiety escalating. "I feel like you're hiding something from me. You asked for my help, but you won't answer my questions fully. What's really going on here?" Cari demanded to know.

"I honestly have no idea. I promise you. I have no idea how that body ended up in that car."

Cari stared at him in disbelief. Jet fidgeted with a pen on his desk and refused to look her in the eye. Beads of sweat lined his receding hairline and she could see spots of wetness dotting his stomach too. The desk phone rang. He looked down at the caller ID and started to shake his head no. It was as though she could see his train of thought. He seemed to remember he wasn't alone. He punched a button on the keypad and the ringing stopped. She sat taller in the chair so she could read the caller ID if someone called again.

"You're worse than the cops," Jet grumbled. "They gave me the third degree too. I thought they were going to arrest me at one point."

"Jet, where did the car come from?" Cari asked.

He gulped and bit his lip. "Uh, I was looking for the paperwork earlier…um…everything is on file, of course."

A knock sounded on the open door. Cari glanced over and saw Genevieve's partner, Alex, stick his head in.

"Mr. Jackson, we're going to have more questions for you in the coming days. Please don't leave the area. If you have travel planned, it's probably best if you cancel it now," Alex instructed him.

Jet nodded. Cari thought his face seemed paler. She still had virtually zero details about the car, the body…all of it. Alex turned around without speaking to Cari. *Not surprising.*

"Jet, I'm still on page one over here. As in, I was told there was a possible dead body in the trunk of a vehicle on your property. I don't know how it got there, or who it is, or where the car came from. Why am I here if you aren't going to tell me anything?" Cari asked, her voice laced with frustration.

Jet stood up and closed his office door. He raised his hands in surrender. "Okay, okay. I'll tell you what I've told the police. A couple was here earlier and the woman saw what turned out to be blood dripping from the trunk. They freaked out and called 911. For some reason, BPD decided to send its best detective squad over. Have you met the female detective? She has these eyes…like she is staring into your soul, daring you to lie so she can call you out on it. Terrifying."

Cari simply nodded. Now that he was talking, she didn't want to interrupt and make him stop. His phone rang again. She watched him look at the caller ID and then punch a button on the keypad again. She had only seen part of the name and committed it to memory rather than draw his suspicion by writing in her notebook.

"Let's see, so the cops showed up. The *detectives*, sorry. I only made that mistake once. That ogre of a detective; he's just as intimidating as the tiny one. He's like seven feet tall…I'm getting off track, sorry. I brought out the keys to the car, but it was the wrong set of keys," Jet explained. "I had to come back in and get the right set. Thankfully, I knew right where they were."

Cari tried to keep her face neutral, but she knew Alex and Genevieve's hackles would have been sparked by that mistake. She didn't believe he accidentally grabbed the wrong set of keys.

"I was just trying to locate the title when you arrived," Jet told her. "Like I said, it's one of our newest additions to the lot."

"Got it," she replied and underlined her note from before.

"The big detective got out a crowbar and was going to force the trunk open if I didn't find the keys the second time. That would have really damaged the vehicle. I would have had to have it repaired before I could sell it…" Jet trailed off. Cari gave him a pointed look and he started talking again. "The body in the trunk…"

Jet gagged and looked around the room. Cari grabbed the small trash can and offered it to him. He waved her off.

"I must have set my water bottle down somewhere. It's fine. I'm okay," Jet assured her. "Do I need to describe the body?"

"Just do what you can," Cari suggested.

"So, it was bad. It was definitely a guy. No woman is that tall. Muscular. Probably dark hair, but it could have been dark from the…" Jet gagged again. "Blood. His face was smashed and like…mottled? Is that the right word?"

Cari stared at him. "I didn't see the body, Jet."

"Right, well, it was discolored in a weird way. Like bruised, but grey and one eye was open, the other…I can't. Sorry, it was gross. And the smell," he added and gagged a third time.

"Did they find any identification on him?" Cari asked.

"No, his pockets were empty. The whole car was empty except for the body. Even the glove box. It usually has an info sheet from us…uh…I guess we put it out on the lot too soon," Jet remarked quietly.

"Just to clarify, the police weren't able to identify the body?" Cari asked.

"Not that I heard," Jet responded.

"Walk me through the intake of a vehicle to your business," Cari requested.

"I mean, we follow all the state laws and policies. We take possession of the title and get it inspected by a third party. If the vehicle needs repairs, we leave that up to the new buyer in most instances. If the needed repairs are excessive, we just sell it to a scrapyard for parts," Jet explained as his phone rang again. He immediately pressed the button to silence it.

"Do you need to get that?" Cari asked.

"No," Jackson said in an irritated tone.

"How long does that usually take? Does it usually get a new license plate while it's in your possession or keep the old one? Pretend like I'm a new buyer and don't have any idea what to expect," Cari said.

"No, once we buy it from the previous owner, the plates are dead. We register the VIN and keep it in the file along with any repair needs," Jet said.

"Okay, so who did you buy this car from?" Cari asked.

Jet looked at the ceiling. "I told you. It's new, so it's still being processed. It shouldn't have been out in the lot yet."

"Do you have security cameras, Jet?" Cari asked.

"Of course…that's where the detectives are now. I can probably get you a copy if you think it will help," Jet offered.

"That would be great," Cari said excitedly. "What else can you tell me?"

Jet shook his head. "That's all I know for now. Do you have a card? I can send you a link to the video footage. The detectives seemed pretty certain the guy died sometime in the last twenty-four hours."

Cari fished a card out of her messenger bag and stood up. "Thanks for the information. Can I talk to the person who does the intake for all new vehicles now?"

Jet's face dropped. "Seriously? Did the police send you a list of questions to knock me over the head? It's me. I process the new cars. It's my business."

"Then, why don't you know where this car came from?" Cari asked.

Jet looked miserable. "I'm working on it, okay? Once I figure it out, I'll give you a call."

Cari set her business card on his desk. "Thanks again for your time. I'll see myself out."

She exited his office and looked around the building. Everyone seemed to be pantomiming busyness as though they were watching the meeting in the office until the moment she stepped out. She paused in the hallway before walking away. She was betting he was going to return that call and wanted to know who it was. She could hear the beeps from him pressing buttons on the phone. She stood as still as she could and listened for him to speak.

"…-orge…not to call me…" Jet hissed. "…call…I can."

She heard the receiver slam back onto the phone set and quickly walked away. Jet knew more about that car than he was letting on. She needed to get the VIN for it, but wasn't sure if it was new enough to have it etched on a window like hers did. She stepped outside and looked in the direction of the car. The ME's van was still in the lot, which meant the CSU team was still around too. They weren't going to let her look at the car. She'd have to get her hands on the VIN some other way.

Chapter 2

Genevieve tapped her pencil on the desk. The used car guy had been honest about one thing: the edge of the lot with the blue sedan didn't quite make it into the camera frame. The parking lot lights helped some. They were able to see the shadow of the car appear, so they knew what time the vehicle arrived at the lot. Unfortunately, they couldn't really see who was driving it.

"There's a traffic cam on the intersection right before the lot. We can access it at the station and see who drives through it near the time in question," Genevieve told Alex.

"Is CSU still out with the car and the body?" Alex asked.

"Check the camera feed. You'll be able to see the ME's van," Genevieve told him.

"You check it. I don't know how to switch from playback to live," Alex said and shrugged. "Do not call me a dinosaur."

She snorted. "Okay, old man." She reached over and clicked on the screen with the mouse. The live feed came back up. "Looks like they just got the body into the van. The tow truck should be here any minute to take the vehicle."

"Are they towing it to the state lab?" Alex asked.

"I guess they have to. We don't have a garage to store it in, and we don't want to leave it to the elements and lose more evidence," Genevieve said. "I can't believe the VIN was removed...I know this is a used car lot and maybe places like this aren't known for their sterling reputations, but still. That's really suspicious."

"Keep it down. I'm sure they're listening to our conversation," Alex reminded her.

"Yeah, they have surveillance of their surveillance room," Genevieve said in a mocking tone.

"I meant outside the door, Sherlock," Alex mocked her back. "At least we know it's a 2017. That can help narrow it down."

"Well, we've got to identify the body or we're never going to figure out who killed him," Genevieve said. "Having a VIN could have really helped."

"Maybe someone reported him missing. He looked like he was in pretty good shape before he got his skull bashed in," Alex observed.

"I guess we're done here then," Genevieve remarked.

"Yep," Alex agreed and opened the door.

As Alex predicted, the person usually tasked with watching the surveillance footage was standing right outside the room. He was staring at his phone.

"It's all yours," Alex told him. "Here's my card. Please call if anything else happens or if you remember any details about the car."

"Today is the first day I saw that car, detective. I have nothing else to remember," the man told Alex.

Genevieve smiled at him as she exited his office. "Thanks again for the help. Just out of curiosity, has a car ever just *shown up* overnight like this before?"

The man looked toward his boss's office and grimaced. "I really just watch the feed here. I don't get involved with sales and stuff."

"That wasn't a no," Alex remarked.

"Honestly, I have no idea and I need this job. One of the salespeople might know more," he told them.

"We'll be talking to them too. See ya around," Alex said and walked down the hallway.

Genevieve hurried to keep up with him. "Who do you want to talk to first?"

"Let's get a list from the person answering the phone. Then we can just check them off one by one," Alex suggested.

They walked back to the front of the building. A young man was seated at the desk nearest the entrance. He had on the same red polo as the surveillance guy. He was Latino and wore his hair on the long side. His dark, wavy hair looked like it was styled with gel or some other hair product. Genevieve could see a silver chain around his neck and wondered what sort of charm was hidden under his shirt. He had a phone receiver up to his ear. They waited for him to finish his conversation. His name plate read "Corey Ardring".

"Detectives. How can I help you?"

"Mr. Ardring, we need a list of all the current employees, please," Genevieve told him.

The young man's eyes widened. "Are we all in trouble here?"

"No, sir. We just need to talk to everyone and get a feel for how things work. Standard with any investigation," Genevieve explained. "Do you have a minute?"

"Until the phone rings again," Ardring replied.

"Your boss had a hard time locating the information for the vehicle in question. Does that happen often?" Alex asked.

"Uh, well, I've only worked here a few months, but I don't remember it happening before," Ardring told him.

"We saw the car just show up in the middle of the night. Has that ever happened before?" Genevieve asked.

Ardring swallowed hard. "I don't think so, but I don't get involved with the car processing part really. I mostly just answer the phones."

"Besides the owner, who does process the cars?" Genevieve asked.

"Uh, I mean, ultimately, I think everything goes through Jet, uh, Mr. Jackson," Ardring informed them. "Here's the employee list."

"Got it. If you think of anything else, please don't hesitate to call," Genevieve told him and handed him her card.

A saleswoman was just waving goodbye to a father and son. Genevieve gave Alex a nudge and looked in her direction. He nodded.

"Excuse me, ma'am?" Alex called out.

She turned toward them. "Yes?"

Genevieve hurried to catch up with Alex. His long stride carried him to the saleswoman in just a few steps, while she needed about twenty to get there.

"We have a few questions if you have a moment," Alex told her.

"About the…" she cringed. "Body?"

"More or less," Genevieve replied. "How long have you worked here?"

"Just a few months. I was going to do real estate now that my kids are all in school full-time, but I saw the post looking for a salesperson here. I have some experience in sales from my college days and thought I'd give this a try first. Plus, I don't have to take a class to get a license or anything to work here," she said.

Genevieve looked at her nametag. "Is it okay if I call you Allison?"

"Of course," Allison responded.

"Allison, has a car ever shown up without warning like the blue sedan from this morning?" Genevieve asked.

"Gosh, I don't think so, but I don't do intake on vehicles. I just make sales," Allison said and flashed them a smile.

Genevieve nodded. "We've been hearing that a lot. Does Mr. Jackson handle the intake for every vehicle?"

"Hmm, I guess so?" Allison answered as if she were asking a question. "Someone who's been here longer might know."

"Who might that be?" Alex asked. Genevieve saw the muscle in his jaw clench and knew he was getting frustrated.

"Uh, let me think. Dave!" she called out to a man entering the building.

Dave was tall with blond hair and a muscular build. He turned toward them and smiled broadly. Genevieve wondered if a broad smile was a prerequisite for selling cars. He was wearing the red polo and khakis. It reminded her of the State Farm ads.

"Dave, is it?" Alex asked when he reached them.

"That's me," Dave remarked. "What's up?"

"Allison, thank you for your help. If you think of anything else…" Genevieve handed Allison a card.

"You got it," Allison said and walked toward the front entrance. Genevieve watched her pull a parka from the coatrack and then exit the building.

Genevieve waited until she was outside to ask Dave a question. Normally, they'd question people in an office space with some privacy, but they were just trying to get the lay of the land.

"Dave, how long have you worked here?" Genevieve asked.

"I'll be at a year next Friday," Dave said and grinned.

"Is there a lot of turnover with employees here? Has anyone been here more than a year other than the owner?" Alex asked pointedly.

Dave raised his eyebrows. "I'd never really thought about it. People come and go, I guess. I've never heard of someone being fired. I'm hoping to stick with the place for a while. I've done well for myself so far."

Genevieve smiled. "I'm sure you saw the whole circus surrounding the vehicle near the edge of the lot. It seems like it just showed up overnight. Has that ever happened before?"

"Oh wow. Hmm. I can't think of it happening before, but we have a lot of cars. I try to keep track of new arrivals so I can talk to potential buyers about them, but we sell cars here every single day. We definitely have a lot of inventory turnover. It's hard to keep up with it," Dave admitted.

Genevieve made a note. "Has your boss ever struggled to find the keys or paperwork for a vehicle of interest in the past?"

"No way. That was a huge shock this morning. Jet is incredibly organized. He always knows where everything is, well, until today, I guess," Dave told them.

"Do you work every day?" Genevieve asked.

"Not on Tuesdays. That's my day off," Dave responded.

"How many employees have today off?" Alex asked.

"I have no idea. Corey should know," Dave answered and pointed back at the desk.

"Thanks, we got an employee list from him," Genevieve explained. "How many salespeople work here?"

"Let me think. Me, Allison, Coop, Steven…uh…I think Eddie got a new job, so he isn't here anymore. Maybe that's it," Dave told them.

"Are Coop and Steven here today?" Alex asked.

"Coop is probably taking a smoke break out back," Dave replied. "Steven…hmm…maybe he's off today?"

They heard the bell sound over the front entrance. Genevieve looked and saw a short man with a large gut walk inside. He had on everyone's favorite red polo. It seemed like everyone but Allison was wearing it. Genevieve wondered if she found it too unstylish and hindering to her car-selling tactics.

"Oh, there's Steven now," Dave observed. "Guess he's working today after all."

Alex flagged Steven down. "Thank you for your help, Dave. Detective Viacorte has a card for you. If you think of anything else, please don't hesitate to call."

Genevieve gave him the side-eye after handing a card to Dave, who walked outside, ostensibly to replace Steven on the sales lot.

"Why can't you give someone a card?" she hissed at him before Steven reached them.

"I don't like talking on the phone," Alex grinned. "I'm out. I forgot to refill my wallet before we left this morning. Sorry."

"Detectives. Crazy morning, huh?" Steven quipped. "I hope the tow truck gets that bloody car out of here soon. It's really putting a damper on sales."

Genevieve looked outside. The tow truck had arrived and was loading the blue car onto the trailer bed.

"I apologize for any inconvenience. I'm sure you realize we needed to secure the scene and keep the public from contaminating it. Anyone who wasn't already here couldn't be allowed inside," Genevieve told Steven.

"Let me guess. You want to know how long I've worked here," Steven hypothesized.

Alex nodded, but remained silent.

"I've been here almost as long as the big man himself," Steven told them.

"Dave?" Genevieve asked.

"No, the jefe, the owner himself. Jet," Steven clarified. "After he bought this place in the nineties, I was his first new hire."

"Was it just the two of you until the last year or so?" she asked.

"Oh no, but no one has staying power like Steven," he said proudly. "Jet and I see eye to eye on a lot of things. We work well together. Plus, the money isn't bad. You have to earn your keep, but I'm good for it."

"We checked the security footage. It seems like someone just ditched the car here last night. Has that ever happened before? A car just showing up unannounced?" Genevieve asked.

"No. People like to get paid for their property, duh," Steven rolled his eyes.

"I understand that. Is the lot not locked after hours?" Genevieve asked.

Steven chewed the inside of his cheek. "That's on me. I was on closing last night. I'm supposed to check both gates, but we didn't have anything new come in yesterday. The back gate shouldn't have gotten unlocked, so I didn't check it. It's a bad habit. Most people don't even know we have a back gate. I'm really lucky nothing was stolen. Even Jet wouldn't have let me get by with that."

"Do you ever do intake on new vehicles here?" Alex asked.

"I mean, I know how, of course, but Jet likes to keep his thumb on everything. It is his place, after all, so I get it," Steven said. "Every now and then, I'll enter a car or two for him, but he's the brains and brawn of this place. I used to hope he'd take me on as a partner, but none of my strengths outweigh his. He's got the mind for business and the salesman personality to go with it. I'm just easy-going Steven."

"Here's my card, Steven. If you think of anything else, please give me a call," Genevieve requested.

"Will do, girlie," Steven responded.

"Detective," Alex growled at him.

"Easy, chief. Just being friendly," Steven begged.

"Try being respectful," Alex said and motioned for Genevieve to join him.

Once they were outside, he pointed at the tow truck. "Let's go talk to the CSU guys. I want to make sure they dusted that back gate for prints."

Genevieve nodded. "How likely do you think it is they'll get something usable?"

"Fifty-fifty, maybe? It's a padlock, so we might get one on that. It has a nice flat surface. There's a chance for a palm or something on the gate itself. The chain is a waste of time. It's not wide enough anywhere to get a decent print," Alex told her.

"Always a chance they wore gloves too," Genevieve proposed.

"Let's hope they aren't that smart," Alex replied. "Bob, Chris, got a minute?"

The two men turned and looked their way.

"Did you get any prints off the back gate?" Alex asked.

"A treasure trove of prints, Runimoss," Chris answered. "Two palm prints on the cross bar, an amazing thumbprint on the lock, a whole set of fingers on the cross bar in two places…the gate was covered in prints. I'm about to go inside and scan everyone's prints as deletions or whatever."

"Great, let me know when you run them," Alex requested.

"Will do," Chris assured him.

Chris walked toward the building with his tablet. Genevieve felt a wave of frustration. This case was starting out messy.

"Something is really bothering me," she told Alex.

"Just one thing?" he smirked.

"Shut it," she grumbled. "Why did the owner act like he recognized the car if it didn't have a VIN? And we have video proof it showed up overnight?"

Alex nodded in agreement. "I'd like to know that too. He really faked being familiar with the car until we realized the VIN had been removed. I don't see another vehicle like it in the lot, do you?"

"I see other Corollas," she said with a shrug.

"Not from the same year and definitely not the same color," he argued.

"I can't tell one year from another. They all look the same," she admitted. "I think we need to ask for an inventory list and compare it to the vehicles in the lot."

"Let's do it," Alex said and pointed at the building. "I think Turnlyle is gone, so he's free."

"Hey, you didn't call her the journalist chick. Look at you," Genevieve observed.

"Don't push your luck," he retorted, but she could see the smile in his eyes.

* * * * *

Cari waited for the couple who found the bloody trunk in the visitor parking lot. She positioned herself between two SUVs to help block the wind. She wanted to find out what they'd heard from the police as well as get their firsthand impression of the scene. When she walked outside after talking to Jackson, she saw them with the CSU team. She guessed they were getting fingerprinted in case they put a hand on the car inadvertently. She was too far away now to see what they were doing.

Jackson hadn't been forthcoming at all. She didn't understand why he'd called Ollaman for help if he wasn't going to tell them anything. It made him look really guilty and she was sure both detectives picked up on the behavior too. The man didn't strike her as a killer; he was jovial and friendly, almost light-hearted. She heard footsteps on the gravel and looked up. The couple was finally headed her way. She stepped forward and waved.

"Hi! Excuse me, hi!" she called out to them. The blonde woman's head whipped her way.

"Are you talking to us?" the woman asked and looked around.

Cari stepped closer. "Yes. I'm Cari Turnlyle. I work for The Beagle and wondered if I could speak with you for a minute."

The couple exchanged a glance and shrugged. "Sure, but make it quick. We're really cold," the man said. "Uh, my name is Tate and this is my girlfriend, Krystal."

"That's Krystal Covington and Tate Sundrick," Krystal clarified and got an eye roll from Tate. "What? If she writes about us, she needs our real names."

"Thanks," Cari replied. "I understand you were the one who saw the blood first?"

"Yes, that was me," Krystal raised her hand.

"You're such a…like, Girl Scout. Raising your hand. Wow," Tate mocked her.

"And you're rude," Krystal hissed at him. "We were car shopping and I saw this stuff…*blood* as it turns out, dripping from the trunk of a dark blue Corolla. It smelled terrible. I gagged a few times. It's the worst thing I've ever smelled and I've worked at a daycare center."

"I heard it was pretty bad," Cari remarked.

Krystal gulped and Cari almost stepped back, but the woman didn't gag. "Sorry. I feel like I can still smell the body. They found a man with his face bashed in! No one knows who it is. He didn't have a wallet or anything," Krystal told Cari. "And they can't figure out anything about the car either. The VIN was scraped off!"

"Scraped off. Duh. You can't scrape off a VIN, Krystal. It was etched off," Tate interrupted.

"She knew what I meant," Krystal growled. "Can you stop being so mean? What's your deal?"

"I'm cold. I'm sorry, babe. I am being a huge jerk," Tate grabbed her hand and squeezed it.

Cari almost looked away. She had the distinct feeling he was about to start kissing her, but Krystal tugged her hand free.

"Not right now, Tate. I'm almost finished," Krystal rebuked him. "The police took our statements and our fingerprints.

Hopefully, they can find some decent leads. I heard one of them mention finding fingerprints on the back gate."

Cari raised her eyebrows. "Interesting. I didn't realize there was a back gate."

"Same, girl!" Krystal said with a grin. "Well, I can't really think of anything else to tell you. Do you need my phone number for follow-up questions?"

"That would be great, thanks," Cari responded.

Krystal pulled out her phone. "What's your number? I'll just text you with my name."

Cari recited her number and waited while Krystal punched it into her phone. "Okay, got it. Thanks again for your time."

"You're welcome!" Krystal smiled again and waved goodbye.

Cari watched them walk away and then made her way to her Camry. She'd learned more than she expected from the witnesses. The car no longer had a visible VIN. She had a feeling Jackson knew that, but didn't want to reveal it for some reason. She remembered the phone calls he silenced while she was in his office. She unlocked her car and tugged the door open against the wind. When she was safely inside, she pulled out her notebook and wrote down what she had seen on the caller ID screen. *SAMSON*. Now, to figure out who Samson was and why he kept calling the used car lot owner. She thought back to the conversation Jackson had after she left his office. He'd said a name: "-orge"…*George!* Cari felt confident she knew the caller's name; she needed to find out why he'd been calling the used car lot repeatedly.

Chapter 3

The office felt stuffy. Genevieve didn't like the way the owner grinned at her like they were playing a game. She felt pretty confident he hadn't killed the man in the trunk; he was too awkward. He had done something else, and she hoped he'd do some more talking this time around.

"Mr. Jackson," she started to say.

"Just Jet, please," Jackson interrupted and smiled.

"Right. Jet. We want to know more about this car you're pretending to be familiar with, but somehow know nothing about."

He swallowed. "I know. I haven't had time to track the info down for you yet. I was speaking with the journalist and my phone was ringing off the hook. Obviously, I've been distracted by many things."

"Ringing off the hook? Who was calling?" Genevieve pressed him.

His face paled and then relaxed to its normal color. "I mean, who didn't? News outlets were looking for interviews and people call all the time to ask if we have this make or model on the lot."

Genevieve felt certain he was lying. "The press called, wow. Which stations?"

"I mean the newspaper woman was here, so the Beagle, obviously," Jackson said and flashed his goofy grin again.

"Yes, but she came in person. You said people were calling," Genevieve reminded him.

"Yes, that too," Jackson confirmed. "All the major news stations."

Genevieve decided to drop it and try a different tactic. "Jet, it seems obvious to everyone except you, that the car isn't one of yours. Someone left it here in the middle of the night."

"Allegedly," Jet countered.

"We saw it on the security video, man," Alex inserted. "You should be relieved. Why aren't you?"

"I think I'm in shock. I've never seen a dead body before," Jet answered.

Genevieve started to ask another question, but Jet's face became contorted and pale. She realized he was about to vomit. She grabbed the trash can and shoved it in front of him.

"I'm fine," he hissed and then gagged again. "I'm—"

"Not at all fine," Alex remarked as the owner hurled into the trash can. "I think Jet's had enough for today."

"Agreed," Genevieve said with a nod. "Jet, we still need to chat about this. We'll let you take some time to get through the day, but please don't go out of town."

He put up his right hand while he hugged the trash can to his chest with his left. "Thank you. I never go out of town. I have to keep up with the business."

"We'll be in touch," Genevieve told him.

He gave her a thumbs-up.

"We'll see ourselves out. Take care, Jet," Genevieve said and turned toward the door.

Alex pushed the office door open and held it for her. She waited until she heard it click before she spoke.

"That was foul," she said to Alex.

"Yeah, I feel like he forced himself to do it to get us to leave," Alex said with a disgusted look.

"He's a bit of a weasel. I don't know what else we're going to get out of him, but I'm tired of getting the run around already. Let's head back to the station. Maybe our CSU team will have some names for us from the prints," Genevieve suggested.

"Works for me," Alex said and started to button his coat.

Genevieve followed suit and then tugged her beanie onto her head. She could hear the wind howling outside and pulled her gloves on too. Alex was already at the exit. She hurried to catch up with him. He leaned into the door and pushed it open despite the strong wind. He had to keep a tight grip on the handle so it didn't slam back into the building and break the hinge. Genevieve ducked under his arm and stepped behind him so he could push it closed again. It seemed like the wind had gotten quite a bit stronger since they'd gone inside. She jogged to the cruiser to keep up with Alex. He unlocked the doors and they climbed inside.

"That wind is intense," Alex remarked. "Glad to be out of it."

"Same," she agreed. "We agree, Jackson…sorry, Jet knows something about how that car showed up in the lot. I think he was genuinely shocked to see a body in the trunk, but he's trying to hide what he knows about the car. Why not just plead ignorance, which is completely believable?"

"He has a ton of employee turnover except for that Steven guy, who is super weird," Alex observed. "All the employees seemed happy for their short time there, so why are people quitting or getting fired so often?"

"Good question," Genevieve acknowledged. "I'm making a note to review employee records and find some recent former employees."

"Once we get back, I'm getting another coffee," Alex told her. "Mostly to warm up my hands."

"Luckily, it's a pretty short drive. Does the heat work in this cruiser or what?" Genevieve asked.

"It takes a few minutes. The engine has to warm up first," he explained.

"Well, apparently, it takes longer to warm up than it does to drive to the station," she replied. "We're only two blocks away."

The heat finally started to come out of the vents. She stuck her hands in front of them. Alex alternated his hands from the steering wheel to the vents. Once he pulled into the parking spot, she grabbed her bag and unbuckled her seatbelt.

"See you inside!" she yelled as she jumped out of the cruiser and ran for the entrance.

Alex beat her to the door. "I'm still faster."

"Sign up for a real race and prove it," she challenged him.

"I don't run long distance, Smalls," he scoffed. "I sprint. That's it."

He opened the door and they pushed inside together. Dana, the gatekeeper of the precinct, gave them a quizzical look. Genevieve laughed.

"It's cold, so we're being childish," she explained.

Dana raised her eyebrows and went back to typing on the keyboard in front of her. Genevieve and Alex entered the detective bay. Lieutenant Grusky was waiting just outside his office. The overhead lights glared off his bald head. He motioned them over.

"Detectives. I'm ready for an update," Grusky said when they reached him.

"We don't have much," Genevieve told him. "Dead body in a trunk. The car's VIN was etched off the windshield and removed from the driver's door. The body didn't have a wallet. The owner is acting oddly."

"How so?" Grusky asked.

"He acted like he knew something about the car, like it was one of his," Alex told their boss. "At first, he couldn't find the keys to the car and he never did find the title. The security video showed someone smuggling it into the lot last night, which would take him off the hook, but he didn't seem relieved. He kind of acted like he didn't want us to know how the car got there."

"He's smuggling cars into his used car lot?" Grusky asked with a confused look.

Genevieve shook her head. "No. I don't think that's it. I think he has something going on with used cars on the side and he doesn't want us to find out what it is."

"Let's get a warrant for his finances. I'll write it up and get it to a judge," Grusky said and nodded toward their desks. "Go find a usable lead."

Genevieve took off her beanie as she walked with Alex over to their desks. She shoved it into a pocket along with her gloves. They both shrugged out of their coats and draped them over the backs of their chairs.

"It's going to take Dr. Green most of the day to do the autopsy. Identifying the victim is going to be a struggle unless someone reports the guy missing," Alex pointed out.

"I'll check the missing persons list and see if there's anyone who fits the description. I think our vic is probably thirty to thirty-five," Genevieve offered. "You call down to CSU and see if they have anything for us yet."

"You might want to widen that age range," Alex suggested.

"I'm good at reading people's ages," she argued.

"Let's check the traffic cam first," Alex said. "Maybe we'll be able to see who was driving."

She motioned for him to take the lead on the search. "Pull it up."

Alex sat down in his chair and used his index fingers to enter his login information. The screen came to life and he opened a browser window. He logged into the traffic camera database and typed in the intersection of interest.

"Okay, what time did we see the car roll into the lot?" he asked her.

Genevieve checked her notes. "1:27 a.m."

"I'll start it at 1:20 and put it at double speed," he told her.

He continued to hunt and peck at the keyboard to enter the needed information. He clicked play and they could see the tree branches blowing in the wind. The minutes ticked past, but no cars went through the intersection. Genevieve checked the clock.

"It's past 1:30 now. I don't think he accessed the lot this way. He must have known about the camera," she remarked.

"Do you know where they towed the car?" Alex asked as he picked up the phone. "I'll call down and see what Green can give us as far as a description goes for the vic so you can enter it into your search parameters."

"Wherever the nearest impound lot for the state is…you'd have to look it up or ask CSU when you call them. They'll know," Genevieve reminded him.

She unlocked her computer and opened their database. The missing persons log was a fairly fluid list. People frequently filled out reports for their loved ones, only to discover they went on a road trip on a whim or fell asleep at a friend's house. She filtered the list for white males, thirty to thirty-five years old, with brown hair. She paused at eye color.

"Hey, do we know the vic's eye color?" she asked Alex.

He shook his head. She clicked enter and watched the number of results tick up higher and higher. Over fifty names met her criteria for the tri-county area.

"Ugh," she groaned. "Looking at the images of people on the missing persons list is useless. Our victim's face is unrecognizable. We need to get his height and approximate weight from Green."

Alex nodded, but was still on the phone. She rolled her chair closer to hear what he was saying. He took the hint and put the call on speaker.

"…definitely brown hair and brown eyes. I estimate his height to be just over six feet. Muscular build. This guy definitely did a lot of heavy lifting. He weighed about one-eighty-five give or take," Dr. Green informed them.

"Were you able to estimate the time of death?" Alex asked.

"My best estimate is around eight or nine on Tuesday evening," Green responded.

"What about fingerprints?" Genevieve asked.

"Hello, Detective Viacorte," Dr. Green greeted her. "Fingerprints for the vic or from the facility and car?"

"Both," Genevieve and Alex answered in unison.

"The victim isn't in our databases, so I can't help you there," Green replied. "However, we got some interesting prints off the steering wheel, the door handle on the driver's side, and the gate."

"What about the rest of the car?" Alex asked.

"Wiped clean," Green remarked. "Kind of odd, but some people clean their cars inside and out fairly regularly. I'll send the fingerprint information to you now. One final item of note: we recovered a pottery shard in the cuff of the man's left pant leg."

"Color?" Genevieve asked.

"A dark turquoise color. It doesn't have any insignia or design on it. I bagged it in case you can find something to compare it to. Any other questions?"

"What about dental records? Could we ID the vic that way?" Alex asked.

"I'm afraid several of his teeth were knocked out and his jaw was broken," Green lamented. "Whoever hit him, didn't want him to get back up ever again."

* * * * *

Back at her office desk, Cari opened up LexisNexis and entered the name Samson into the surname field and George as his first name. She decided the person must be local or, at the very least, a New York resident. She left the city field blank, but selected NY for the state. She clicked on the search button. George Samson was a fairly common name and almost one hundred people in the state had it. She needed to narrow her search parameters some more. She decided to use the local county in hopes the man lived near Brenington or maybe even in Brenington. This dropped her results to just three names.

She looked at the ages of the three people: seven, forty-four, and ninety-one. Bingo. George number two had to be her man. Cari pulled out her phone and entered his home address into her maps app. Then she clicked on his name from the LexisNexis result to see where he worked. He'd worked for an autobody shop a decade ago, but was currently unemployed. In the photo George Samson had dark hair with a receding hairline, dark eyes, and a pudgy face. His profile said he was Caucasian, five-foot-eight inches tall, and almost two hundred pounds.

"Turnlyle," Ollaman's voice startled her. "Who'd you find?"

She looked up at her boss. "Hi, Mr. Ollaman. I'm not sure, yet. While I was talking to, uh, Jet, he got a few phone calls and he silenced them. I could tell it really frustrated him that the person kept calling."

"You make it sound like he was doing something shady. I've known him for years. He's an honest man," Ollaman argued.

"I'm not trying to accuse him of anything, sir," Cari explained. "Jet was…scared about something."

"Scared? Not Jet!" Ollaman laughed. "What did he tell you? The police found a body in one of his cars. That would unsettle anyone."

"I don't think he was scared about the body exactly. That grossed him out. He was really hesitant to talk to me," Cari told Ollaman. "He definitely didn't want to talk to this person on the phone while I was in his office."

"Maybe it was his mom or his wife. His wife is a bit of a harpy," Ollaman told her flippantly. "I silence calls from my wife all the time."

"I don't think the caller was his wife," Cari responded and explained what she'd seen and heard.

"George Samson?" he asked in a confused voice. "Is that who you looked up?"

She rolled her chair over a bit so he could see the computer screen too. "Yes. I'm not sure who he is, but Jet called him after I left his office. He told him not to call the office again, or something like that. I couldn't hear everything clearly."

"Are you going to go interview this person?" Ollaman asked.

"I just entered his address into my phone, but I haven't had a chance to think through the questions I want to ask him. He's probably not going to just out and out tell me why he was calling the owner of a used car lot if he's connected to something involving that car," Cari hypothesized. "I could ask him if he's ever bought a car from the lot. Or what connections he has to the used car place. I'd like to do a little more research on him first. All I know right now is he used to work for an autobody shop."

"Maybe he breaks cars down for Jet," Ollaman proposed.

"Why would that sort of call be something Jet would want to hide?" Cari challenged.

"I don't know. Go talk to him and find out," Ollaman encouraged her.

Cari looked at the screen again. Samson didn't look too menacing. She could definitely outrun him if he tried to chase her. She was torn. "I need to look into his background some more. I think it might be wiser to call him than to show up on his doorstep."

"Keep me posted," Ollaman said and walked back to his office.

Cari read through more of Samson's LexisNexis entry first. Samson hadn't graduated from high school and there was no record of a GED either. She scrolled down further. He'd been arrested for petty theft twice in his life, but only had to do community service hours as punishment. She wasn't able to see what he'd stolen and thought about calling Genevieve to ask her to look it up. That would mean divulging the name before she knew the connection. Something told her if the police showed up at Samson's residence, he'd try to run and no one would learn anything from him. It was better if she talked to him on her own. First, she wanted to see if she could find a connection between him and Jackson.

She opened a new tab and entered Jet Jackson into the first and last name boxes, along with Brenington, NY. The search returned zero results. Cari frowned. She double-checked the spelling and confirmed everything was entered correctly. She started to call Ollaman to ask where his friend lived when she remembered him saying Jet was a self-created nickname, not a legal name. She deleted all of the fields and searched for the used car lot business instead. *Bingo!* Jet was really *Rutherford* Jackson. She clicked on his name and scanned his information. He attended Green Mountain High School and graduated in 2001. Samson hadn't graduated from high school, but she couldn't remember where he'd attended. She switched tabs and looked at Samson's information again. Green Mountain High School: dropped out in 1999 at age sixteen. She wondered if she could access an online copy of their sophomore yearbook. It was so long ago, she wasn't sure if they'd have a digital version.

Cari opened a new tab on her internet browser and searched for Green Mountain High School and yearbook. Every link gave her information about how to order a new yearbook or when the yearbooks would be available. None of them mentioned a digital copy. She located the school's phone number and dialed it on her desk phone. The call rang twice before someone answered.

"Green Mountain High School. How may I direct your call?" a woman's voice said.

"I'm not sure. This is Cari Turnlyle with the Beagle. I was hoping to talk to someone about old yearbooks," she told the woman.

"Transferring you to the librarian," the woman responded.

The call beeped twice and then made the ringing sound again.

"This is Ms. Williams. How can I help you today?" The librarian sounded like an older woman, but Cari couldn't be sure.

"Hi, Ms. Williams. This is Cari Turnlyle. Is there any chance you have a copy of the 1998-99 yearbook?" Cari asked her.

"Definitely. You're with the Beagle, right?" Ms. Williams asked.

"Yes, ma'am," Cari answered.

"I thought I recognized your name. Is there something specific you're looking for in the yearbook?" she asked Cari. "That was my second year working here, so I remember some of the students."

"Well, I was hoping to see if Rutherford Jackson and George Samson ran in the same circles," Cari told her.

"George Samson. I haven't thought of that child in ages. I tried really hard to talk him out of quitting school," Williams reminisced. "He'd gotten certified as an autobody tech and got a part-time position at one of the local repair shops. They paid him minimum wage, which he thought was a king's ransom. It was nothing, but having his own money made him think he didn't need a high school diploma. He could get more money if he worked full-time, so why did he need to learn algebra or history or how to write properly?"

Cari was glad the woman remembered Samson. She hadn't answered her question about the possible friendship though. "And was George friends with Rutherford Jackson?"

"Rutherford…oh, you mean Jet!" Williams said with a laugh. "Jet tried out several nicknames in his years here. Ford, Jack, Jax…he had to work pretty hard to get Jet to stick."

Cari tried again. "And was Jet a friend of George's?"

"Oh, sorry. You asked me that already. Let me think. You know, I think they lived near each other. They rode the same bus. I remember them walking into the school together the first two years of high school, before George quit."

Cari felt a spark. "Were they in any classes together or activities?"

"Hmm…" Williams clucked her tongue. "I'm not sure. George often came to the library to avoid getting in trouble in his classes. He didn't want to be in any of them, so he'd ask for a pass to "study" in the library. The teachers were happy to see him leave their classroom rather than spend the period disrupting it…well, except for his automotive classes. He loved those. Goodness, thinking about him has me a little choked up. He was a sweet kid, even if he didn't always behave properly for his teachers. He was always polite to me. Just one of those kids who marched to a different beat."

"Thank you, Ms. Williams. I really appreciate your help," Cari told her.

"If you want to come by and look at the yearbook, you'll need to register as a volunteer first. They'll do a background check and then you can sign in at the office as a library volunteer," Williams explained. "You can't just visit schools anymore these days."

"I understand. I think I got what I needed by talking with you. Thanks again," Cari replied.

"Happy to help. Good luck with whatever story you're working on. I always enjoy reading your articles," Williams said.

"Thank you. I'll let you know if I need anything else," Cari said and hung up the receiver.

George and Jet were friends, or at least connected in high school. Cari felt confident about asking George about his interactions with the used car lot owner now. She found his phone number in his LexisNexis file and lifted the receiver from the cradle of her desk phone. She punched the number into the keypad and waited for it to connect.

"Hello?" a gruff voice answered.

"Hi. I'm Cari Turnlyle with the Beagle. I'm looking for George Samson," she explained.

"I'm George," he confirmed.

"Great. Do you have time for a few questions?" she asked.

"Questions about what?" he barked.

"Jet or Rutherford Jackson," Cari responded, offering the salesman's legal name too.

"Who says I know him?" Samson asked.

"Just a hunch," Cari replied. "Are you a friend of his?"

"I knew him once. In high school. He finished. I didn't," Samson told her.

"Have you seen Jackson recently?" Cari asked.

"No. I haven't seen him in years," Samson said glibly.

Cari hesitated. "Mr. Samson—"

"George."

"Apologies, George it is. Do you still work on cars, George?" Cari asked.

"I'm kind of between jobs right now, but I do a little solo work from time to time," Samson answered.

"What do you mean by solo work?" Cari asked.

"I can fix pretty much any vehicle problem, assuming it is fixable. Air conditioners, oil changes, busted tires, windshield repair…I do it all. People call me sometimes," Samson told her. "I can also inspect a vehicle someone's wanting to buy. Let them know if it's everything the seller says it is."

"Do you ever do that for your friend Jet?" Cari asked.

"I told you. I haven't talked to him…in a long time. A really long time," Samson reiterated.

"I have reason to believe you called him today," Cari challenged the man.

"Jet? *I* called Jet? Nah. He's a tier above me. He doesn't want to associate with the likes of me," Samson retorted.

Cari thought about the used car salesman. He probably didn't want people to know he interacted with someone like Samson, but Cari was certain the two men were still acquainted.

"Do you have any other questions or can I get back to what I was doing?" Samson grumbled.

"No, that's all for now. Thank you for your time, George," Cari said sweetly and ended the call.

She wondered what Samson had been working on before she called him. Something told her he was connected to the mysterious car at Jackson's lot, but she couldn't prove it. The librarian's words echoed in her mind. She'd referred to Samson as a sweet kid. Cari recognized the fondness in the woman's voice. Williams had tried to be a positive guide in young George's life, but he hadn't listened. She thought about Samson's claim about inspecting vehicles for new buyers. It sounded probable, but if Samson was so qualified with cars, why wasn't he employed? Samson had implied he was an aide to buyers, not sellers. Cari wondered if the buyers he was helping were associated with illegal chop shops. She didn't know how many cars were stolen in their area each year, but her gut was telling her the car with the dead body was stolen.

* * * * *

Bob stared at the disheveled stack of boxes in the corner of the primary bedroom. Cari had promised to unpack them over the weekend, but instead, she'd been picking her way through them and getting what she needed as she needed it. Clothes hung from the edges of two boxes, a stray washcloth was on the floor next to another box, and two hadn't even been opened.

He sighed and squeezed past the clutter to get into the closet. He slipped off his loafers and slid them under the shelving they'd purchased for all of Cari's shoes. As he squeezed past the boxes again, he heard a key in the door.

"Cari?" he called out.

"It's me," she responded.

He heard her drop her bag onto the sofa and kick off her shoes. Bob smiled. He knew she was messy when they started dating. It would take some time to adjust to her habits and maybe compromise on a thing or two.

"How was your day?" he asked once he was out of the bedroom.

Cari was perched on the edge of the sofa, typing on her laptop. "It was busy. Ollaman knows the used car guy. I'm not sure how, but he's certain Jackson isn't involved with the dead body in any way."

Bob sat down next to Cari. "That's surprising. I wouldn't have pegged Ollaman as a used car man."

"I'm not sure that's how he knows him. He didn't elaborate," Cari explained. "I kind of have a lead on another *friend* of Jackson's. This guy was calling Jackson repeatedly while I was trying to interview him. It really got under his skin."

"Do you think the friend knows how the car got on the lot?" Bob asked. "Jackson told Gen and Alex it was one of his cars, he just couldn't find the title for it."

"That's my suspicion. I called the guy and he refused to admit he called Jackson today. I'm going to try to interview some of his neighbors tomorrow. Maybe they can tell me more about him or if they've seen him with Jackson," Cari told Bob.

"Sounds like a plan," Bob responded. "What should we make for dinner? I think we have some ground beef in the freezer, but it will take a bit to get it thawed." His stomach growled loudly.

"I can hear your hunger starting to shout," Cari laughed. "What about breakfast for dinner? I'm pretty hungry too. I'm glad we're back to just the two of us, but it was kind of nice having family in town to plan dinner every night."

"It was almost like being on vacation; we went out to eat every night last week. At least someone else was paying for it," he chuckled.

Cari set her laptop aside and stood up. "Eggs and bacon or pancakes tonight? Or, we could try making waffles on our new waffle maker…?"

"I like the sound of that," Bob said as he got up too. "I'll have to let Alex know we took it for a spin."

Bob grabbed Cari's hand before she could walk into the kitchen. She turned back to look at him and he pulled her in for a kiss. She leaned into him and wrapped her arms around him for a few seconds before pulling away.

"That's never going to get old," Bob said with a smile.

"What?" she asked.

"You being here with me every night. I still can't believe we're actually married sometimes," Bob told her. "The whole weekend felt like a whirlwind…somehow, we've already been married over ten days."

She squeezed his hand and smiled. "I think our wedding planner was starting to regret working for us at one point."

"She definitely ended up doing more than expected. Robby wasn't able to get the flowers because of his concussion and head injury. Bea couldn't drive. Genevieve missed the entire rehearsal dinner after completely disrupting it with news of the car wreck…it was a circus," Bob agreed.

"I think my parents are glad to be home. They are not a fan of cold weather. Once Bea assured them the two of us could cover their family's driving needs, I think my dad had their stuff packed up and ready to go within an hour," Cari laughed. "They were booked on the next flight to Florida."

"So…waffles?" Bob asked.

"Waffles," Cari agreed.

Chapter 4

Genevieve had spent the previous evening going through the list of former employees from the used car lot, as well as the list of reported stolen vehicles. None of the stolen cars matched the Corolla that showed up at the used car lot. She had a hunch the vehicle was stolen, but apparently it hadn't been reported yet. She also had no way of knowing which county the car was registered in, so the list was incredibly long.

"Regardless of what Green said, I think it's weird the car was wiped clean. Jackson knows something about that car. I don't believe for a minute that it's part of his inventory, but he knows who brought it there," Alex said to Genevieve.

"Do you think he's smuggling cars through his lot for parts?" Genevieve asked.

"That's an interesting theory," Alex acknowledged. "You said you worked on two things last night. What else?"

"I looked at Jackson's Used Car Lot's employment history. I've never seen more turnover at a business. I can't tell if someone was terminated or quit; I can only see how long they worked for the business," she told him.

"I have no idea if that's typical for a used car lot or not," Alex admitted. "I'm going to ask the internet and see what it tells me."

"Because everything you read on the internet is true," Genevieve remarked and rolled her eyes.

"AI says it's typically less than two years," Alex informed her. "Maybe there's nothing weird about the short time periods for Jackson's staff."

Genevieve's phone pinged with a text. She pulled out her phone and glanced at the screen.

"Let me guess. Turnlyle," Alex said with a smirk. "Oh wait. Is she Hursley now?"

"I don't think she's changed her name, but you're right, it's Cari," Genevieve told him. "She's on the same wavelength."

"How so?" Alex asked.

"She wants to know how many cars are reported stolen in this area every year," Genevieve explained.

"Call her. See what she knows," Alex said with his eyebrows raised.

"I'm so proud of you, Alex. You've come a long way from calling her the newspaper chick to actually encouraging me to collaborate with her," Genevieve beamed at him.

"Don't push it," Alex grumbled.

Genevieve unlocked the screen and hit the phone icon next to Cari's name. Her friend answered immediately.

"I didn't expect you to call me so quickly," Cari said when she answered.

"We're curious about what led you to ask about stolen cars," Genevieve told her. "I have you on speaker."

"I was looking into…people acquainted with the used car lot owner," Cari answered.

"Anyone in particular?" Genevieve pressed her.

Cari sighed into Genevieve's ear, but didn't answer. Genevieve looked at Alex. He was only half paying attention to the phone call. He had the list of names from the fingerprint analysis pulled up on his computer. He snapped his fingers and pointed at the screen. Genevieve took a step toward the monitor.

"Any chance it was George Samson?" Genevieve asked.

"You found him too?" Cari confirmed with a question.

"His name has come up," Genevieve responded. "What do you know about him?"

"He knew Jackson in high school. I talked to the librarian from their school. She described Samson as sweet and polite. I know he has a record, but not for violent crimes," Cari pointed out.

Genevieve looked at Alex. He rolled his eyes at Cari's mention of Samson's record. She put her finger up to her lips and hoped he wouldn't say anything rude.

"We haven't gotten that far into his history yet," Genevieve admitted. "What makes you think he stole the car?"

"I didn't say I thought he was a car thief," Cari countered. "I am aware that if a vehicle has its VIN etched off, it probably didn't pass from one owner to another in the typical way."

Alex used his two index fingers to type in Samson's information into their database. Genevieve smirked at his rudimentary typing skills. Samson's record appeared on the screen. She skimmed it. Two petty theft charges. No jail time. Alex started making the 'kill it' sign with his hand across his throat to signal he wanted her to end the call.

"I'll get back to you with the stolen vehicle numbers," Genevieve offered.

"Or you could call the station. They can look it up too," Alex said gruffly.

"Wait," Genevieve interjected.

"Yes?" Cari asked.

"Don't go interview this guy, Cari. I know the librarian thought he was a nice guy, but that was decades ago. Like you said, he has a record," Genevieve reminded her.

"Don't worry. I already called him," Cari replied.

Alex's eyes bugged out of his head. Genevieve put up her hand. "What did he tell you?"

"Almost nothing. He claimed he hasn't talked to Jackson in years," Cari told her. "He's lying."

"You can tell he's lying over the phone?" Genevieve scoffed.

"I'm pretty certain. Get his phone records. They'll prove it. And, don't worry Alex. I'll call the station for the stolen car stats. Talk to you guys later," Cari remarked.

The call ended and Genevieve gave Alex a look.

"Let's look him up and see if he's ever owned a Corolla," Genevieve suggested.

"Go for it," Alex replied.

She logged into the system and typed the man's name into the search bar. His driver's license appeared on the screen as well as his driving record and vehicle ownership history. She skimmed the list.

"He owned a Corolla a couple decades ago, but it was white. I suppose he could have repainted it, but this says he sold it about five years ago," Genevieve read from the screen. "His current vehicle is a 1997 green Ford Ranger pickup."

"I think it's time to go interview Samson. We've got his prints on the gate and in the car," Alex told her.

"How could she know he's lying?" Genevieve wondered aloud.

"Who knows? She was in Jackson's office yesterday. Maybe she saw something while she was in there," Alex suggested.

"Maybe so," Genevieve said.

She stepped toward the wall to grab the keys to the cruiser, but Alex beat her to them. She glared at him.

"I'm pretty sure it's my turn to drive," Genevieve said firmly with her hand out.

"I didn't realize we took turns. Grab your coat. It's still cold out there," Alex reminded her.

They shrugged back into their coats and gloves. Genevieve could feel her adrenaline rising. Samson seemed like a solid lead. She wasn't sure how Cari came up with his name in the first place.

She didn't buy Cari's story, but the fact was they both found the same person of interest.

"Ready?" Alex asked, pulling her from her thoughts.

"Yeah. Unlock the car from here if you can. Then we can just hop in when we get to it," Genevieve suggested. "I can hear the wind from inside."

"One step ahead of you, as usual," he teased her.

She rolled her eyes and pushed in her desk chair. "Lead the way, smarty-pants."

They reached the cruiser and got inside quickly. It somehow seemed colder inside the car as though it had frozen overnight. Genevieve rubbed her hands along her arms as Alex started the car.

"To the trailer park, east side of town," she directed him.

"I'm familiar with it," he said. "I've lived here longer than you have, remember?"

"Drive, Jeeves," she commanded him.

"Hilarious," he responded, but put the vehicle in reverse.

"Are we bringing Samson in for questioning or just having a chat with him?" Genevieve asked.

"I think we have to bring him in. His prints are on the gate and the car with the db. We need to record it and have it be official," Alex said. "Unfortunately, we don't have an arrest warrant, so he's going to have to agree to come in and give a statement."

"I seriously doubt he's going to do that," Genevieve said. "Maybe he'll run or something."

"Why would you wish for that? Now he's totally going to be a runner. It's too cold out for running," Alex whined.

"Cold weather is the best running weather," she said with a laugh. "Take a right at the next light."

"I know where I'm going already," he reminded her.

Genevieve got out her notebook and looked over her interview with Jackson. "Jackson was adamant he had that car title somewhere. He just needed more time to find it. You know what else?"

Alex didn't respond. She glanced out the window and realized he was parking the car along the curb. No other vehicles were parked at the entrance to the trailer park, so he didn't have to parallel park. He put his hand on the keys and looked her way.

"Did you ask me something?"

"Yes, I was reading through my notes on Jackson. He knew before we looked at the surveillance video the Corolla wouldn't be in it. Does he just know his lot that well, or is he oddly aware of blind spots in his surveillance setup?" Genevieve asked.

"Good question. The car was just barely out of range. He's owned the lot a long time. It might not be so amazing for him to know where the blind spots are," Alex surmised. "Ready? Samson's trailer is the third one to our left after we walk up the dirt path."

Genevieve looked to her left. She could see the trailer in question. "Ready."

They got out of the car. Genevieve was relieved to discover the wind had died down some. She had been shocked when she looked in the mirror when she got home the night before. Her cheeks were red and a bit chafed from the wind at the used car lot. She watched the windows of each trailer as they passed. The blinds split on the window nearest the front door of the second trailer. They snapped back closed almost immediately. She nudged Alex.

"I saw it," Alex responded.

Genevieve heard boards creaking and the click of a dead bolt disengaging. Her eyes snapped to Samson's trailer. The door swung open and a portly man with a large belly rushed down the steps. He had a large bald spot amidst dark curly hair. Alex grunted and took off at a sprint. Genevieve was close on his heels.

"Brenington PD!" Alex shouted. "Stop!"

Genevieve saw the man grimace and realized his feet were bare. He wasn't wearing a coat either. An old green pickup was parked in front of the trailer. The man ripped the door open and hefted his girth into the driver's seat. He slammed the door closed with his left hand while turning the key with his right. Alex ran around the back of the vehicle as the man tried to start it. The engine groaned, but didn't turn over. Genevieve could hear the engine grinding as she reached the passenger side of the pickup.

"Mr. Samson. Step out of the vehicle," Alex demanded.

Genevieve pulled out her cell phone. "Should I call for backup?"

"No, we've got this. He's unarmed and slow as molasses," Alex remarked.

She shoved her phone back into her coat pocket. Alex motioned for her to guard the passenger door. She held her position.

"Mr. Samson, exit the vehicle, or I will remove you from it," Alex commanded him again.

The man continued to try to get the pickup to start. Genevieve could tell he'd flooded it with gas and it would be a while before it went anywhere. The man looked out the window at her and started to try to slide across the bench seat.

"No, that's not what I said," Alex barked.

Alex yanked the door open and pulled the man from the cab. Alex easily overpowered him and forced him to the ground. Genevieve hurried over around the front of the vehicle.

"George Samson?" Alex asked as he pulled the man to his feet. He clamped handcuffs onto the man's wrists.

"Ow. That hurts my wrists," the man complained.

"We have some questions for you. We can ask them here, inside your trailer, or you can ride in our cruiser back to the station. Your choice," Alex informed him.

"Which option makes the cuffs go away?" the man asked.

"Neither for now. You started running before you even knew who we were, but you didn't stop once we identified ourselves. What are you hiding, Mr. Samson?" Genevieve asked.

"Nothing. I never said I was Samson," the man argued.

"Why don't we go inside, Mr. Samson? It's warmer in there, right?" Genevieve suggested.

"Not really. I don't have money to run the heater every day," the man explained.

"You're really trying my patience, sir," Alex told him. "And I didn't have a lot of that to begin with."

"He's not lying," Genevieve agreed. "Shall we step inside?"

"You got a warrant to go inside?" the man asked. "I know my rights."

"Fine. We want to know about your relationship with Mr. Rutherford 'Jet' Jackson," Alex stated plainly.

"Why is everyone asking about Jet?" the man complained.

"So, you are Samson," Genevieve concluded.

Genevieve peered into the cab of the pickup again. The driver's door was still open. She could see the glove box was open as well. She walked around to the passenger door and opened it. The inside of the cab reeked of every bad smell she could imagine. She choked back a gag. Inside the open glove box was a sheet of paper that looked a lot like a car registration form. She leaned toward it.

"Hey, I didn't say you could get in my truck!" the man shouted.

"I'm just looking at things in plain sight," Genevieve called out. "You said this is your truck?"

"Yeah…" the man retorted and then paused. "I mean, I borrowed it from…uh, Samson."

"Nice try," Genevieve said under her breath.

She stepped back and closed the passenger door. She walked back over to her partner and the man she knew was George Samson. "Mr. Samson, this truck is registered to you. We've already looked at your driver's license. We know it's you. Stop lying and let's have a chat about your pal Jet."

Samson's shoulders slumped. "What do you want to know?"

"When did you last speak to Mr. Jackson?" Genevieve asked.

"Years ago. In high school. I dropped out and he finished. He's too good for me now," Samson told her.

"You didn't call him yesterday? Several times?" Genevieve pressed him.

His face reddened. "How does everyone know that? Did you subpoena my phone records already or something? I haven't done anything. That's an illegal search."

"Mr. Samson, I'm tired of the lies, and I'm tired of standing out here in the cold. We're going to the station. Since your hands are a little, um, out of commission, I'll grab your keys and get your truck and trailer locked up for you," Alex offered.

"Don't you dare go into my trailer!" Samson hissed.

Alex nodded to Genevieve. She climbed into the truck. The smell of body odor and rotten food almost made her gag again. The man was a slob. She yanked the keys out of the ignition and got out of the vehicle as quickly as she could. Hopefully, the smells hadn't stuck to her clothing or hair.

"Don't you want some socks and shoes? I can go grab them for you. Your feet must be freezing," Genevieve observed.

"Stay out of my trailer! You don't have my permission to enter it," Samson informed her.

"The door to your trailer is open, Mr. Samson. Whatever I can see from the doorway is fair game," Genevieve told him as she made her way up the steps.

As she'd told Samson, they couldn't search his trailer yet. They needed a warrant. However, if she saw anything illegal from the doorway, she could claim probable cause to enter the premises. She pulled her phone back out and turned on its flashlight. The light illuminated a desk covered in papers and the edge of a license plate. She really wanted to step inside and get a photo of the plate. Unfortunately, having a license plate in your home wasn't against the law, so she had to stay put. She couldn't make out any of the words on the papers either. Genevieve pursed her lips and sighed. She stepped back from the doorway and swung the door closed. Samson's keyring had several keys on it. She tried three before she found the one that locked the trailer.

"We'll be getting a warrant for the trailer, Mr. Samson. I promise you that," Genevieve told him. "Let's go to the cruiser."

* * * * *

Cari started her workday by reading through her notes from the day before. As far as she knew, they still didn't know who the dead man was or who owned the Corolla. Ollaman wanted her to clear his friend of any wrongdoing, but Jackson didn't want to cooperate with her or the police. She decided to give Jackson a call and confront him about Samson. She found his number and punched it into her desk phone.

"Jackson's Used Cars. How can we help you today?" a man's voice asked.

"This is Cari Turnlyle with the Beagle. I'm looking for Jet, please," she answered.

"Is Mr. Jackson expecting your call?" the man asked.

"Not exactly," Cari responded. "Can you connect me?"

"One moment."

An ad about buying the best used car of your dreams started to play in Cari's ear. She tapped her pencil on her notebook. She felt like he had zero appreciation for her help. He'd obviously called Ollaman to ask for assistance from the newspaper, so why couldn't he be more forthcoming? She wondered if Alex and Genevieve had tried to get Samson's phone records yet. They hadn't said how they connected him to the case. She suspected fingerprints on the car or something to that effect.

She looked at the little screen on her desk phone. She'd been on hold for over two minutes already. Jackson was really being a pain. The line finally clicked and made a ringing sound.

"This is Jet," Jackson said into the phone.

"Jet, thanks for taking my call. I had a question for you about a friend of yours: George Samson," Cari explained. She heard Jackson take a quick breath.

"George, uh, who?" Jackson asked.

"Samson. I believe you were in high school at the same time," Cari reminded him.

"Wow, George Samson. I haven't heard that name in years," Jackson said grandly.

"Really? I have reason to believe he called you yesterday," Cari pressed him.

"A lot of people call here. Did Samson say something about me…or where did you get his name?" Jackson stuttered through his sentences.

"Jet, my boss tasked me with clearing your name, but you won't be honest with me. It's hard for me to help you if you won't tell me anything," Cari explained.

"I…Samson isn't exactly someone you want to parade around to the newspaper as your friend," Jackson confessed. "I throw him some help every now and then. He's good with cars, but not good with money. I only pay him for the work he does, nothing more…but it's been quite a while since he came by looking for work."

"What kind of work does he do for you?" Cari asked.

"He's a very skilled mechanic. He can rebuild any engine and diagnose any problem a car is having. He can almost always fix it too," Jackson told her. "But like I said, he hasn't come by asking for work in a long time. Whoever told you he was calling me was misinformed."

Cari frowned. "I see. Well, thank you for your time. I'll be in touch if I think of any other questions."

"Goodbye, Ms. Turnlyle," Jackson said and ended the call.

Cari replaced the receiver in the cradle. Jackson wasn't willing to admit Samson called him the day before. Likewise, Samson had been adamant he hadn't talked to Jackson in years. Cari was certain they were hiding something and the Corolla was connected somehow. She knew the VIN was removed from the windshield. Anyone who'd ever watched a crime drama knew that meant the car was stolen. The question was, who stole it and why? Jackson wouldn't be able to sell a car without a VIN on it, but he might be able to use the parts from a stolen car in one of his used cars.

She wasn't sure how many places the VIN got etched besides the windshield. She logged into her computer and opened her internet browser. She typed in "where is the VIN on car parts" and clicked the search button. The AI robot told her it varied from vehicle to vehicle, but it was on the engine block for sure and another place called a firewall. It seemed like most of the parts weren't tagged with the VIN, so they could be moved from one vehicle to another.

Cari ran her fingers through her curls as she rolled her thoughts through her mind. If the car was stolen, it must have been stolen within hours of the man entering the trunk. Otherwise, whoever stole it would have smelled the dead body and changed their mind. Was it possible that Jackson was taking advantage of Samson's thievery and maybe using parts from stolen cars to repair any broken-down cars on his lot? He'd need to be careful with this method; too many stolen cars and the authorities would get suspicious. She had no idea how many cars were stolen each year or what warranted extra scrutiny. When she'd asked Genevieve and Alex for numbers, Alex had directed her to call the station. She wondered if she could find the numbers on the internet.

A quick internet search informed Cari almost thirty-three thousand cars were stolen every year in the state of New York, which meant an average of just under three thousand a month. The internet couldn't break it down for her by city or county, so she called the information desk at the police station for some more specific stats.

"Brenington PD, how may I direct your call?" a man's voice asked. He sounded young to Cari.

"Hi, this is Cari Turnlyle. I'm trying to find out how many vehicles are stolen in our county every month. Do you have access to that information?" she asked him.

She could hear him typing on a keyboard. "It will take an information request to get the breakdown by month, but we've already had thirty-eight stolen this year. We're five weeks in," the man reported. "Occasionally, the cars are found and returned, but most frequently, we suspect they're sent to chop shops and used for parts."

"How does that number compare to years past?" Cari asked.

"Uh, without looking, I'd say it's par for the course. Let me run a query. Just a moment," he said and resumed typing. "Last year at this point, only twenty-five cars had been stolen, but we finished the year at an all-time high. The year before, we were at forty-two already at this point, and the year before that, it was thirty-two. What else can I help you with today?"

"That's all I need for now. Thanks for the help," Cari said and ended the call.

She wasn't sure what to expect, but thirty-eight seemed like a lot. She'd never had a car stolen and she wasn't sure she knew anyone who had either. Her thoughts drifted back to Samson. Their conversation hadn't divulged a lot of information. Alex was just starting to be open to collaborating with her and she didn't want to jeopardize that rocky relationship. She knew the two detectives were either already at Samson's home to speak with him or they might have decided to bring him in for questioning. She didn't want to get in their way, but she did want to know more about Samson's habits. It couldn't hurt to interview his neighbors.

She pushed back from her desk and picked up her coat from her chair. It had been frigid outside earlier; she hoped the sunshine was warming things up a bit. After fastening her coat, she grabbed her messenger bag and checked it for her phone and digital recorder. Satisfied she had everything she needed, she locked her computer and walked to the elevators.

"Turnlyle! Did you get a new lead?" Ollaman hollered at her from his office doorway.

She turned around and walked toward his office instead. "Possibly. I thought I might learn some more about Samson if I spoke with his neighbors."

"Good idea. Keep me posted," he said and went back into his office.

"I always do," she muttered under her breath on her way back to the elevators.

She knew Ollaman was sensitive about this story as it involved his friend, but when had she ever kept him out of the loop? She sighed and rolled her eyes as she waited for the elevator to arrive. The doors opened and she stepped into the car.

Her hand went to her bag to get her phone out. She hesitated. She wanted to call Bob and ask what CSU had found regarding the car. They'd decided now they were married, it was better for her not to call him at work *about work* unless she couldn't avoid it. She knew that put him in an awkward position. Old Cari would have plowed ahead and called. She smiled. Maybe they could chat about the case after work.

Cari got into her car and quickly turned it on. The walls of the parking garage blocked some of the wind, but it was still very cold in the garage. She put her bag in the passenger seat and backed out of her space.

The trailer park was about fifteen minutes away. It was almost eleven o'clock, so the traffic was light. She drove across Brenington and thought about the investigation. Samson had a lot of experience with cars. Jackson owned a used car lot and had been a friend of Samson's at one time. Both men had made an effort to conceal that connection from her: Samson flat out said he didn't associate with Jackson anymore; Jackson tried to hide the incoming phone calls and then gave her the run around on the phone. Neither man was a good liar. Samson didn't strike Cari as a killer. It seemed like he was connected to the used car lot in some way, and if Jackson didn't want people to know about it, maybe it was related to the dead body in the trunk. If Samson was on Genevieve's radar, then it seemed likely evidence of the man was found at the used car lot.

Were you on the surveillance video or did you leave something behind, George?

Cari reached the entrance to the trailer park and pulled her car up to the curb. She fished around in her bag until she found her digital recorder. She switched it on and put it in the outer pocket of the bag. It wouldn't pick up everything, but it would help. She walked up the dirt road toward the rows of trailers. The access road went across the front row of trailers and down the side to additional rows. She put her hand up to shield her eyes from the sun and tried to count how many rows of trailers were in the park: four. Samson's was the third trailer on the front row, which meant the people most familiar with him would be in the first two trailers on his row and maybe the fourth one just past his. She saw vehicles parked in front of the first three trailers, but nothing in front of the fourth one. She walked up to the first trailer and knocked. A grey minivan that might have been older than her sat in front of it. She heard the floorboards creaking inside as someone approached the door. The footsteps were uneven as though the person walked with a limp.

"Who's there?"

Cari couldn't tell if the person was male or female. The voice was scratchy and low.

She raised her voice so she could be heard through the closed door. "It's Cari Turnlyle. I'm with the Brenington Beagle. Do you have time to talk?"

"About what?"

"This might be easier if you opened the door," Cari requested.

The door stayed closed.

She frowned. "How well do you know your neighbor, Mr. Samson?"

"The guy with the green truck?"

Cari looked to her left. A green pickup was parked in front of the third trailer. "Yes, that's the one."

The door opened a crack. "What did he do?"

Cari rolled her eyes in frustration. She took a deep breath and exhaled before she responded. "I'm not sure if he *did* anything. His name came up while I was doing some research for a story," Cari explained.

The door opened a little further. Cari wanted to lean to her left to try to see the face of the person she was talking to, but didn't want to spook them.

"The police were here before. They took him away. I don't know why," the person told her.

"Does Mr. Samson ever have any visitors?" Cari asked.

"Sometimes. I think it's a cousin who comes over or maybe a friend."

The door opened halfway. An old woman with tanned, leathery skin and deep-set eyes looked at Cari. When she opened her mouth to speak, Cari noticed she was missing at least three teeth.

"I don't want my name in no paper," the woman told her.

"That's perfectly fine," Cari agreed. "What else can you tell me about Samson?"

"I don't trust him. He comes and goes at odd hours. He used to have a girlfriend, but he broke up with her when she got pregnant," the woman said and turned toward the green pickup with a glare.

"Did you meet his girlfriend?" Cari asked hopefully.

"No. I heard him yelling at her sometimes. She usually drove a black station wagon with a big dent on the back right fender," the woman said with a frown. "Her name was…let me think…Christine? No. Kirsten. That was it: Kirsten. He'd curse at her if she parked too close to his truck. She'd curse back at him. I nicknamed her. Cursin' Kirsten."

Cari tried not to laugh. "How long ago did he break it off with Kirsten?"

"A week or two ago. I'd noticed she was putting on weight. She'd started wearing bigger clothes instead of the tight stuff all the time. I thought she just got tired of him ogling her constantly, but then I heard him calling her all sorts of names. He threw a bunch of stuff out the door and said she better not try to pin that baby on him." The woman shook her finger at Cari as though she were Samson and Cari was the girlfriend.

"Any chance you know her last name?" Cari asked.

The woman shook her head. "No, sorry. They were together a long time though. The longest he's ever had the same woman. She's better off without him. He was way too old for her."

Cari hoped Kirsten had used Samson's address at some point. She might be able to find her last name that way.

"Why did the police take him in?" the woman asked.

"I'm not sure, ma'am," Cari answered. "You said he comes and goes at odd hours. What times specifically?"

She scratched her head. "Real late at night. I know it's him because his p-o-s truck never starts on the first try. He sits there and grinds away at the starter over and over. It usually backfires once after he gets it going. Scared me to death the first time I heard it. I thought someone had fired a gun."

"Late as in after midnight?" Cari asked for clarification.

"Way later. He wakes me up at two or three in the morning most of the time. I've heard him come back home at five or six in the morning too. I don't know what he's up to. He ain't got a job," she told Cari.

"You know he's unemployed?" Cari asked her.

"Course I know. When he had a job, he was gone all day. Regular hours. Never left in the middle of the night. He's been out of a job for a few years now," she told Cari.

Cari pulled out her cell phone and quickly found an image of Jet Jackson from his website. "You mentioned a cousin or a friend sometimes visits Mr. Samson. Is this the person?"

The woman squinted at Cari's phone screen. "I'm not sure. Can you zoom in some?"

Cari enlarged the image and turned the screen back to the woman.

She rubbed her chin and leaned closer to the phone. "That might be the man. This photo makes him look thinner than he is in real life, though."

"How often does he visit?" Cari asked.

The woman scrunched up her face. "I don't know. Maybe once a week? Maybe a little less. He parks out where you did."

This sparked Cari's interest. "What does he drive?"

"A black Mercedes. Bold. Driving that nice car out here," the woman remarked.

"A sedan or something bigger?" Cari asked for clarification.

"Just a car," she responded.

Cari needed to look up what kind of car Jackson drove. This could definitely help link the two men. She already knew they were lying, but this would be stronger evidence of their association.

"When the police were here, did they go into his trailer?" Cari asked.

"I don't think so. They wanted to go inside to talk to him, but he must have had something in there he didn't want them to see. Probably drugs," the woman conjectured.

Cari's eyebrows shot up. "Was Samson known to do drugs?"

"Seems like everybody is into something," the woman responded with a shrug.

Cari heard a creak and looked to her left. The door to the second trailer was slowly opening. Cari didn't want to get caught staring, so she looked away.

"Don't worry about him. He's just going to his afternoon shift," the woman explained and jerked her head to Cari's left. "He's a burger flipper at one of the fast-food places in town. He goes on at one, gets off at nine, I think. He's out a little early today though."

Cari looked back at the man. His hair was on the longer side and stuck out from the black beanie on his head. He looked thin, though it was hard to tell from the grey puffy coat he was wearing. She checked her watch. It was a few minutes past noon. The man walked past the car in front of his trailer and toward Samson's trailer.

"Maybe he's going to feed Samson's dumb dog," the woman proposed.

"There's a dog in the trailer?" Cari asked in a surprised tone.

"Samson's got a small mutt. He feeds it too much. Probably going to shorten its life by several years. Poor dumb dog," the woman remarked.

"Is he friends with Samson?"

The woman shrugged again. "I guess. They don't really hang out. They just do neighbor stuff for each other, I think."

Cari wanted to talk to the man too, but didn't want to stop her interview with the old woman. "What else can you tell me about Samson?"

"That's about it. He's not that interesting," the woman replied.

"Do you have a phone by any chance?" Cari asked and hoped she didn't offend the old woman.

"Why?" she asked.

"I want to give you my card in case you think of something else to tell me about Samson," Cari said as she pulled her business card from her bag.

"I don't know much else. You're not going to put my name in your story, right?" she asked again.

"You have my word," Cari assured her and handed her the card. *You never said your name, so pretty easy not to mention it.*

"Nice talking to you," the old woman said. "You better get inside and warm up. It's cold out here."

"I will soon," Cari promised. *We could have been warmer if you'd invited me inside!*

She walked down the steps and headed toward the next trailer. She didn't think it would take long to get the dog on a leash and walk it or whatever the man planned to do. Cari passed the second trailer just as Samson's door opened. A small dog led the way out of the trailer on a leash. Its round belly waddled back and forth with each step. It tumbled down the steps and almost tugged the leash out of the neighbor's right hand. Cari looked up and saw the man hurriedly pushing two license plates inside his coat from the top. She only sort of saw the last two letters: QL or possibly QI. She gave him a quizzical look.

He returned a goofy grin. "These are my plates for my car. I went mudding the other day and they were…really messy, so…uh…I asked George to clean them up for me."

Cari wondered if a worse liar existed anywhere in the world.

"That was nice of him," she remarked.

"Well, I need to walk his dog before I go to work," the man told her. The dog was already sitting and didn't look like it was going to do any more walking.

"Are you friends with Samson?" Cari asked.

The man furrowed his brow. "Why?"

"I'm trying to learn more about him for a story I'm working on. I haven't found many people who know him well," Cari explained.

"I'm just a neighbor," the man said and started to tug the dog up onto its feet.

Cari had an epiphany. "Do you know his girlfriend?"

"Kirsten? They broke up," the man told her.

"Kirsten. Right. What's her last name?" Cari asked.

"Dunleavy," the man replied. "Don't ask me how it's spelled. She introduced herself to me once. I'm a name guy. I don't forget a name. Or a face. I have a good memory is what I'm trying to say."

"That's great, Mr....uh, I didn't catch your name," Cari said as though just realizing it.

"My name is Stu. S-T-U. Stu Olivert," Olivert told her. "I really need to get going."

"I understand," Cari said. "Here's my card. Please give me a call if you think of anything you can tell me about Mr. Samson."

The man looked at her card, but couldn't take it. He still had one hand clutching his jacket to keep the license plates from falling out. The other was gripping the dog leash.

"I'll stick it in your door jam," Cari offered.

"Perfect," Stu replied. "See you around or whatever."

He tugged the dog to its feet and walked down the dirt road away from his trailer. Cari watched him for a few steps and then turned back the other way. She climbed the steps to his front door and slid her card into the jam. She looked at his white Chevy Malibu as she descended the stairs. It wasn't muddy in the slightest. It also already had a license plate. She looked his way before pulling out her phone. He was too close for her to snap a photo of his car without him noticing. She walked past his car and continued on the dirt road until it bent back toward the city street. She followed it about fifteen feet and then cut over to get a view of the back of Olivert's vehicle. It had a back plate too. She snapped a photo with her phone. She hurried to her car before the man got back with the little dog.

Once she was locked inside her vehicle, she pulled up Bob's name in her contact list and hit the phone button.

"Cari! How is my beautiful wife?" Bob asked in a happy tone.

"Bob! I need you to get someone over to the trailer park!" Cari said quickly.

"What? Why are you…?" he trailed off.

"I came over here to interview Samson's neighbors. Don't worry about how I found his name. Just get some officers over here. I'm certain his neighbor just removed evidence from his trailer!" Cari tried to keep from raising her voice.

She kept her eyes glued to the dirt road for signs of Olivert exiting the trailer park.

"Let me call you right back," Bob said. "Love you, Cari."

"Love you too," she said and lowered the phone.

She'd thought about calling Genevieve, but knew her friend wouldn't answer if she was still with Samson. Bob was employed by the city too, and worked in the same building. He could get officers over here just as quickly. Her phone vibrated. She swiped her thumb across the screen to answer it.

"Did you call it in?" Cari asked him.

"I talked to dispatch. They said they need evidence a theft occurred," Bob informed her.

"What if he destroys it?" Cari asked. She knew Olivert would be on his way out soon.

"I think you should come here and give a statement. Turn your car on and connect to the Bluetooth. Then tell me what happened," Bob suggested.

Cari hit the start button and put her messenger bag into the passenger seat again. She set her phone into one of the cup holders.

"Okay, I'm driving away now," Cari told him. "I came over to talk to Samson's neighbors. I thought they might be able to tell me if he was friends with Jackson or if they'd seen Jackson around."

"That's a good idea," Bob agreed.

"I talked to an old woman first. She seemed to know quite a bit about Samson and the neighbor in between," Cari explained and then told Bob what she saw him do with the license plates.

"You took a photo of his car?" Bob asked.

"Yeah. It has a license plate on the front and back," Cari told him again. "I'll send you the photo."

"Send it to Genevieve too. I'm going to go get you some tacos from the truck. We can eat lunch while the detectives finish with Samson," Bob said.

"I still think they should send someone over here to watch Samson's trailer. What if the neighbor goes back in and destroys more evidence?" Cari asked uncertainly.

"You don't know that he destroyed any evidence or that he intends to destroy evidence," Bob cautioned her. "I'm going to go get those tacos. Stay safe. I'll try to meet you at the front entrance to the station. Love you, Cari."

"Love you too," she replied and hit the end call button.

She really wanted to drive back to her office and figure out who Kirsten Dunleavy was. She'd told Bob about the girlfriend, but wasn't going to include it in her statement unless they asked her. She wanted to talk to the woman first. Part of her wondered if Samson had figured out who had gotten his girlfriend pregnant. Maybe the baby daddy was the man in the trunk.

Chapter 5

The drive back to the station had been anything but quiet. They'd read Samson his rights, which typically made people clam up. Not Samson though. He had complained and whined incessantly. Genevieve could see the muscle in Alex's jaw working overtime as he drove down the road.

"You don't have any reason to bring me in! I've done nothing wrong!" Samson shouted from the backseat. "This is a violation of my rights!"

"Mr. Samson, is there a lawyer you'd like us to call for you?" Genevieve asked calmly.

"I don't need a lawyer. I didn't do anything," he hissed at her. "These cuffs are too tight. They're hurting my wrists."

"We're almost to the station. When we get you in an interview room, then we can unfasten one cuff and hook it to the table instead," Genevieve told him.

"That's not better," he grumbled.

Alex pulled into the parking lot and Genevieve breathed a sigh of relief. They'd made it back to the station. Samson was muttering something under his breath.

"I didn't catch that. Could you repeat it?" Alex asked after he turned off the car.

"I said, 'the ogre cop better not lay hands on me again' and I meant it," Samson snarled.

"You'd prefer Detective Viacorte help you out of the cruiser?" Alex asked.

"Is that the lady cop?" Samson asked.

"She's a detective," Alex reminded him.

"She can't get me out of this car," Samson sneered. "She probably doesn't even weigh a hundred pounds. She's like a midget. And I can't get out with these cuffs on. There's no space back here for someone my size. Bring someone else out. Someone average-sized."

Genevieve marched around to the other side of the cruiser. She opened the back door and grabbed Samson's left forearm with her left hand. She reached around his large body to grip him under his armpit and then tugged him out of the car. She almost lost her balance when she pulled him free, but managed to stay upright. Alex climbed out of the driver's seat and closed the door.

"You were saying?" Alex asked with a smirk.

"That was police brutality. She pinched my armpit!" Samson complained.

"Right this way, Mr. Samson," Genevieve instructed him. "We'll get you settled in interview room two and then put our coats away."

"These stupid shoes you gave me don't fit. They hurt my feet. They're too small," Samson whined.

"We offered to go get your shoes from your home and you refused," Alex reminded him. "This was the best we could do."

"You were trying to plant evidence in my trailer is what you were trying to do," Samson claimed. "I know how you cops work."

"Let's go inside," Genevieve suggested. "It's cold out here."

"I haven't had anything to eat," Samson said as he shuffled his feet along the sidewalk. "You got any snacks inside there? I bet you've got donuts."

"We don't have any donuts. I can bring you some crackers and a soda," Genevieve told him.

"I don't like crackers," Samson replied. "And I want a Diet Coke."

"Perfect," Alex remarked. "Crackers it is."

They escorted Samson to interview room two and secured his handcuffs to the table. Genevieve got him a soda and crackers from the break room while Alex went to Grusky's office to give him an update. His office door was still open when she got there, so she stepped inside instead of knocking.

"How's Samson enjoying the crackers?" Alex asked her after she sat down.

"He tore into them despite his disdain for the snack," she replied.

Grusky cleared his throat. "Alex said you brought him in after he ran. What else do we know about him?"

"I saw some license plates peeking out from under a pile of papers on his desk," Genevieve reported. "My guess is they came from the mystery car at the used car lot."

"You think Samson removed the plates before he dumped the car at the lot?" Grusky asked.

"That's my theory," Genevieve replied. "We need to get a warrant to search his trailer."

Grusky nodded in agreement. "I'll get it going while you talk to Samson."

"Don't forget, he removed the VIN," Alex added.

"Right. You said it was removed from the windshield and the driver's door?" Grusky asked for confirmation.

"I'm sure it's still on the engine block and elsewhere. We just have to wait for the state lab to find it for us," Alex lamented.

"That might take a while," Grusky acknowledged and handed them a file. "They're always backed up. Go talk to Samson. See how he explains his fingerprints on the car and the gate."

"You got it, boss," Alex said and stood up.

Genevieve led the way back to the interview room. Samson's head snapped up off the table when she opened the door.

"I want another soda and more crackers," Samson demanded. "I'm starving."

"We'll get that in a minute," Alex said and leaned against the opposite wall.

Samson opened his mouth to protest as Genevieve sat down in front of him. She stared at his round face and angry eyes. His mouth clamped shut.

She opened the file from Grusky. It had images of Samson's prints on the door handle, steering wheel, and back gate. She took the sheets of paper from the file and spread them in front of him.

"We found your prints on a vehicle at Jackson's Used Car Lot. We also found a nice palm print on the bar of the back gate," Genevieve said as she pointed at the various images.

"It's not a crime to touch a gate or a car," Samson argued.

"True," Genevieve agreed. "But the car you touched had a dead body in the trunk. Care to explain how it got there?"

"Dead body! That's a lie. You planted it," Samson claimed.

"You aren't disputing that you touched the car or the gate at the used car lot?" Genevieve asked.

"Stop looking at me like that. I'm not a monster," Samson deflected.

"You told us you hadn't talked to Mr. Jackson in years, yet you agree you've been to his place of business within the last two days?" Genevieve asked.

Samson frowned. "You can't prove when my palm print got on that gate."

"True, but prints don't stick around for *years*, sir," Genevieve informed him. "Who was the man in the trunk?"

"I told you. I don't know about any dead bodies. You can't pin that on me," Samson said and lifted his chin.

"Your fingerprints were found on a vehicle with a dead body in it," Alex said and enunciated each syllable precisely. "Care to explain?"

Samson's eyes dropped to the table. "I work on cars. I must have worked on that one," Samson responded.

"Did you etch off the VIN?" Alex asked.

Samson's eyes jerked toward Alex. "Etch off…? I don't even know what you're talking about, man."

"You know about cars. They're familiar to you. Did you etch the VIN off the windshield so we couldn't identify the real owner?" Alex asked.

"Maybe the guy who killed the dude in the trunk did that. How should I know?" Samson challenged him. "I work on cars to make them sell for more. Not the other way around."

"When did you work on it?" Genevieve asked. She lifted her pen to signify she was ready to notate his response.

"I didn't say I *did* work on it. I said I might have. Try listening," he said flippantly. "I'm done talking. I want a lawyer," Samson demanded.

Genevieve restacked the papers and closed the file. "Do you have someone in mind, or are we calling legal aid?"

He narrowed his eyes. "Just get me someone."

* * * * *

The Brenington police station parking lot was fuller than usual. After parking in one of the visitor spaces, Cari looked around for Bob. The taco truck was a block away. She wasn't sure if he'd be back with lunch yet or not. She didn't want to stand in the cold any longer, so she headed for the front entrance. She had just placed her hand on the door handle when she heard Bob call her name.

"Cari!" he shouted from the sidewalk.

She turned and waved. He hurried up the walkway to her.

"I got you two chicken tacos and some water," he told her.

"You're the best," she said and kissed him on the cheek.

"Married twelve days already. I still feel like the luckiest guy in the world," he said as he handed her the tacos.

"Did you get any for yourself?" she asked as she opened the door.

"Of course. Three beef fajita tacos for me," he said with a grin.

"Mr. Hursley," the receptionist greeted Bob as they entered. "And…Mrs. Hursley?"

Cari blushed. "Technically, I'm still Turnlyle."

"Oh, a modern couple. I get it. More power to you," she said with a grin.

"Thanks, Dana. We'll be in the break room if Detective Viacorte comes looking for us," Bob said as he pushed the next door open.

"Got it," Dana responded.

They walked through the precinct to the employee breakroom. Several heads popped up from their computer screens when they passed their desks.

"Bring your wife to work day, is it?" one of the men asked Bob with a grin.

"Something like that," Bob responded.

"Don't give her all the secret codes," the man called out and laughed.

Cari felt her face redden again. She knew journalists weren't typically looked upon favorably by law enforcement. At least no one said anything mean. They reached the break room and Bob swiped his badge at the key card reader by the door. The light turned green and he turned the handle to let them inside.

"I guess everyone else is eating at their desks today," Bob commented. "We have the place to ourselves."

Cari draped her messenger bag over the chair nearest her and sat down. She shrugged out of her coat. Bob put the bag of food and the bottles of water on the table. He folded his coat neatly over the back of an empty chair and then sat down next to her.

"Lunch is served," he said and removed three foil-wrapped tacos from the bag. "Bon appétit."

She laughed. "They smell delicious."

"Best tacos in town," Bob replied. "Ask anyone here."

"They're also the closest tacos in town to anyone here," she said and laughed.

"It's like the realtors say: 'location, location, location'," Bob reminded her.

She opened a bottle of water and took a drink. Then she peeled the foil off of one taco. She could see cilantro, tomatoes, and chicken peeking out of the flour tortilla. She hoped there was some cheese hiding in there too. She took a bite.

"Wow, they are really good tacos," she said after she swallowed.

"I told you," Bob said between bites.

Cari heard a beep and looked at the door. It swung open and revealed Genevieve and Alex.

"You've been busy today," Genevieve said from the doorway.

"Just tracking down leads," Cari replied.

"Grab your tacos. We need to record your statement," Alex instructed her.

Cari popped the last of the first taco in her mouth. She balled up the foil and tossed it toward the trash can. It bounced off the rim and landed a foot away from her feet.

"You should probably stick to running," Alex joked. He stepped over to the foil ball and tossed it into the trash can.

"I was close," Cari responded with a laugh.

She stood up from her seat and draped her coat over her left arm. She grabbed her messenger bag and pulled it over her head so the strap crossed her torso. Genevieve reached around her to grab her taco and water.

"Have everything?" Genevieve asked.

"I think so. See you after work, Bob," Cari said.

"No kissing in the breakroom," Alex said quickly and pointed at the wall. A laminated sign read "NO PDA at the BPD".

Cari reached over and squeezed Bob's hand. She looked him in the eye and winked. He returned the squeeze.

"Okay, where are we going?" she asked the detectives.

"Interview room one. Right this way," Alex said after opening the door for her.

Genevieve led the way down the hall. She swiped her ID at the first door on the right. The light turned green and she opened the door.

"Have a seat. We're going to record this so we can refer to it later, if need be," Genevieve explained.

Genevieve and Alex sat across the table from Cari. She took off her messenger bag and set it on the table. Genevieve had a notebook in front of her and a pencil in her hand.

"Tell us about your time at the trailer park today," Genevieve requested.

Cari nodded. "Sure. I went over there to interview some of George Samson's neighbors. As you know, he lives in the third trailer on the first row. I started with the first trailer in hopes whoever lives there knew some of his habits. The woman who lives there was home and told me a lot about Samson. She doesn't like him much."

"What was her name?" Genevieve asked.

"Uh, she wouldn't give it to me," Cari replied. She glanced at Alex and caught him mid-eyeroll.

"That's fine. We can look it up," Genevieve remarked. "What else?"

"We heard their mutual neighbor leave his trailer," Cari explained.

"You just heard it, or you saw him leave?" Alex asked.

"I was still outside and she was kind of half-in, half-out," Cari told him. "I saw the other neighbor leave and enter Mr. Samson's trailer."

"He had a key?" Genevieve asked.

Cari tilted her head and tried to remember. "I wasn't watching when he entered. He might have a key or he might know where Samson keeps one hidden."

"Got it," Genevieve said and wrote in her notebook.

"I finished my conversation with the woman and hurried over to Samson's trailer. I wanted to catch the other neighbor before he left for work," Cari told them. "When he came out of the trailer, he was shoving two license plates into his coat. I don't think he was expecting to see me and he didn't want me to see those plates for some reason. He claimed to be taking Samson's dog out for a walk."

"You saw part of the plate number, right?" Alex asked.

"Yes. The plate I could see ended with QL or maybe QI. His hand was covering the bottom portion of the last letter," Cari told him. "He claimed Samson cleaned the plates up for him after he'd taken his vehicle through some mud recently. It was a terrible lie, but I think he believes I bought it. We only spoke for a moment; I took a photo of his car on my way out of the trailer park. It had a front and back plate. So, either he owns two vehicles or he was lying about those plates."

"And did you get his name?" Alex asked.

"I did. Stu Olivert. Stu with a U."

Alex snorted. "Stu with a U, huh? Sounds like we need to pay Mr. Olivert a visit too."

"You may already know this, but Jet Jackson drives a black Mercedes. The neighbor told me she's seen his car over there," Cari added.

Genevieve made a note. "Good to know."

Cari took a breath. She wasn't sure how Alex would respond to what she had to say next. "I think Samson is a car thief."

Alex's face remained neutral. Cari looked at Genevieve. Her friend was staring at her intently.

"Say more," Genevieve requested.

"It's not that big of a leap, right? He's already been busted for two petty thefts. His name came up in your investigation, which means he was either spotted on surveillance video or he left his fingerprints somewhere of interest. Either way, he's connected to the car. He doesn't strike me as a killer, but I'd believe he steals cars in a heartbeat," Cari explained.

"Interesting theory," Alex remarked. "Anything else?"

Cari didn't hesitate. "That's pretty much it."

"Thanks, Cari. This is a big help," Genevieve said and stood up from the table. "Please keep us in the loop if you find anything else."

* * * * *

"We have to charge Samson with something in the next twenty-two hours or cut him loose," Genevieve said to Alex. "For now, he's just stuck in our holding cell."

"Oh, I'm aware. We can't really charge him with theft of the vehicle, as we don't know whose vehicle it is. We can't charge him with murder as we have no evidence he committed it," Alex lamented.

"I guess we could charge him with breaking and entering," Genevieve proposed. "He isn't an employee at Jackson's Used Cars, but he did enter their lot after hours."

"Was it locked though? Do we know he didn't have permission to be there? Jackson isn't giving us anything. He's still trying to find the title to the car. This case is a mess," Alex said with a sigh. "Maybe Bob and Chris will have an easier time looking for a car with QI or QL at the end of its license plate. It could be a pretty long list. Are we any closer to identifying the victim?"

Genevieve unlocked her computer. "I have a list of people who fit the height and weight of our victim who have been reported missing. Brown hair, brown eyes…neither of which is unique and did little to shrink the list. I wasn't sure how much to limit it geographically. He isn't necessarily from Brenington."

"Let's look and see if any of them have a dark blue Corolla registered in their name," Alex suggested.

"Good idea," Genevieve replied and pulled up the list. "Let me just get the car registration site pulled up."

She quickly opened their database. She resized the two windows so she could have them open on her screen side by side. Alex rolled his chair over and watched her work for a minute.

"I can do that," he remarked. "Let's split up the list. How many names are on your list?"

"There were over a thousand before I added his height and weight, but Green's report says his eyes are brown, so that should cut the list down some."

She made the adjustments and ran the search again. This time only seven names remained. She highlighted the names and copied them into an email.

"I just emailed you the list. You start at the bottom; I'll start at the top," she instructed Alex.

He rolled his chair back to his desk. She watched as he reached into his pocket and pulled out a smartphone.

"What in the world is happening today?!" she exclaimed. "Did you get a new phone?"

His cheeks reddened. "I've always said I wouldn't get one of these unless not having one made the job harder. Two weeks ago, when we were chasing down Follard and his fake lawyer friend, uh, Brensteiner, it would have been better if I'd had something like this. Sophia has been helping me learn how to use it."

"I'm impressed, Alex. I'm not sure I can call you a dinosaur anymore," she said and pretended to wipe a tear from her eye.

"Funny," he said and unlocked the screen with his face.

"You can even unlock it with your face?! My mind is blown," she said and laughed.

"Get to work, Viacorte," he grumbled.

"I'm getting there. This is…just…wow," she said as she typed the first name into the search box.

She scrolled through the person's DMV results. No Corolla of any color. She deleted the name from the search bar and typed in the next one. Same story.

"Last guy is a no," Alex told her. "On to number six."

She looked out of the corner of her eye and saw him punching in the letters of the next name with his two index fingers. At least that hadn't changed. She entered the third name on the list. The person had an address in Brooklyn and didn't even own a car. The process was starting to feel like a waste of time. She typed in the next name and clicked the search button again. Another New Yorker without a vehicle.

"And another no. Here we go, lucky number five," Alex called out.

She got up and walked over to his desk. He finished entering the name into the list and clicked search. The person owned a Honda Accord.

"Well, I guess our vic hasn't been declared missing yet," Genevieve said, stating the obvious.

Alex slid his new phone into his pocket. "We need to talk to the neighbor who ran off with the plates."

"Yeah, too bad we didn't have a warrant to search the trailer before we got there," she said with a frown. "Speaking of warrants, did Grusky hear back on the one for Jackson's finances yet?"

Alex looked toward the lieutenant's office. The door was closed. He grabbed the phone receiver and entered Grusky's extension.

"Runimoss, what do you need?" Grusky asked.

"Did you hear back on the warrant for Jackson's finances? I think we might need to talk to him again, but I'd like to have something more than the suspicious vehicle issue to throw at him," Alex explained.

"Let me check my email," Grusky paused. "No, nothing yet. I'll let you know as soon as I hear something."

The line clicked and Alex hung up the receiver.

"What did Turnlyle say the neighbor's name is?" Alex asked.

Genevieve flipped through her notebook. "Stu Olivert."

"Let's look him up. Maybe we can find him at work," he suggested. "I'm fairly certain he warned Samson we were coming. That's why he was running to his truck in his bare feet."

"One hundred percent that's what happened. I'll look him up. Maybe he has an outstanding warrant or something we can throw at him," Genevieve proposed. "Cari said he works at a fast-food place."

She walked back to her desk and jiggled her mouse to wake up her computer. She logged in and then enlarged the database tab.

"S-T-U, O-L-I-V-E-R-T," she recited as she typed the letters. "Here he is. Employed at the Burger King near the freeway. No outstanding warrants, but we can still go have a chat with him."

"I'm starving. I could go for a double-Whopper right about now. I got so caught up in this case, I forgot to eat lunch," Alex remarked. "I've still got the keys in my pocket. I'm driving."

Genevieve shrugged. She didn't really want to go back outside into the cold again, but they did need to talk to Samson's neighbor. She bundled into her winter gear and followed Alex out to the cruiser. They climbed in and Alex rested his finger on the start button, but didn't push it.

"I'm not trying to be a jerk, but do you think Turnlyle gave us everything?" Alex asked.

"No. I'm certain she didn't, but she did let us know about the plate and the neighbor. They're both good leads for us to track down. My guess is she saved something else for herself. She's probably chasing it down as we speak," Genevieve admitted. "Now turn on the car. It's cold in here!"

* * * * *

After kissing Bob goodbye, Cari returned to her office at the newspaper building. Ever since Ollaman had to trim down the staff due to budget cuts, the office was especially quiet. It used to always be buzzing with activity, but it felt deserted lately. It had only been a handful of months since Ollaman restructured their benefits packages and switched the interns from paid to unpaid. Cari was afraid to ask if it had helped right the financial ship.

She sat down at her desk and logged into the computer. LexisNexis was still open, so she cleared out the search results and entered Kirsten Dunleavy into the first and last name boxes. Olivert hadn't told Cari much else about the woman, but she felt it was safe to assume that Dunleavy was still in New York. She selected NY for the state and then hit enter. The first result was a Kirsten Maribelle Dunleavy in Brenington. Cari selected it and scanned the information.

"Ugh, she has her address listed as Samson's trailer still. Olivert didn't say she was living there; just that they broke up," Cari grumbled to herself.

She opened a new tab and navigated to a social media platform instead. She typed in Dunleavy's name again and searched for users. LexisNexis did have a recent photo of Dunleavy, so Cari scrolled through the results until she found the correct person. Dunleavy's profile photo for the social media platform was of her with a dark-haired man. She knew what Samson looked like and it definitely wasn't him. She clicked on the image and expanded the comments. One friend remarked, *"You and Wyatt make the cutest couple ever!"* Another friend named Wyatt Ushlinson had liked the comment. Cari clicked on his name.

Wyatt Ushlinson's profile photo was of just him standing in a doorway. He had on a cowboy hat, boots, jeans, and no shirt. She smirked. It looked like something someone would use on a dating site. He was leaning against a bright orange sports car. Cari couldn't see the emblem, but thought it might be a Ford Mustang. Wyatt had dark eyes and looked pretty tall. She scrolled down to see when he last posted. His most recent post was several days old. She felt the hair on her neck rise. Maybe Wyatt was the dead man in the trunk!

She switched tabs back to Dunleavy's LexisNexis results. The young woman was employed by a local florist. The Budding Artist. Cari entered the address into her maps app. It was a twenty-minute drive from the office. She checked her watch. It was just after three o'clock in the afternoon. The Budding Artist would take her past her and Bob's new apartment. She decided to shut down her computer and pack up for the day. She tossed her notebook and pen into her messenger bag along with her phone. After ensuring her computer was off, she pushed in her chair and walked over to Ollaman's office and knocked on his door.

"Come in!" he hollered.

She pushed the door open and stepped inside. Ollaman didn't look up. He was intently focused on something on his computer screen. Cari cleared her throat to get his attention. His eyes popped up and met hers.

"Turnlyle. What's the update?" he asked after clicking his mouse once. Cari wondered if he was closing a tab or minimizing it.

"I spoke with Samson on the phone," she said and gave him a recap of the conversation. "Earlier today, I drove over to the trailer park where he lives and spoke with a couple of his neighbors. That led me to his girlfriend, excuse me, ex-girlfriend, Kirsten Dunleavy. She works at a floral shop. It's still open, so I'm going to head over there and talk to her."

"Good work, Turnlyle. What do the police know so far?" Ollaman asked. "I know you're married to them in more ways than one."

Cari flinched. "Sir, um, I'm not sure…"

She struggled to find the words to tell her boss he was overstepping an obvious boundary.

"I'm just kidding, Turnlyle," Ollaman said. "I just like to see you squirm sometimes. But seriously, you're friends with the detective on the case, right? Have they cleared Jet?"

"I'm not sure, Mr. Ollaman. My feeling is they don't think he did it, but they do think he's hiding something. Honestly, I feel the same way," Cari admitted.

"Hiding something?! What would he be hiding?" Ollaman scoffed. "He's just a little weird, that's all. He isn't hiding anything."

"Well, after I go talk to Dunleavy, I'm going to work from the apartment the rest of the day. I'll see you tomorrow," Cari told him.

"Okay, I'm putting together a brief update for our social media page. Would you say the police don't consider Jet to be a person of interest?" Ollaman asked.

Cari hesitated. "How about you let me handle the updates for this story? I'll give Detective Viacorte a call later and ask for something we can put in writing."

Ollaman clasped his hands. "Perfect. I'll let Michelle know to watch for it."

"Thanks. See you tomorrow," Cari said and let herself out of his office.

She went back to her desk and put on her coat. She buttoned it up and then pulled her scarf and gloves out of her pockets. Her messenger bag had her laptop, phone, and keys in it, so she swung it over her shoulder and made her way to the elevator. The elevator arrived quickly and Cari rode it down to the parking garage. She felt a little warm in her coat until she stepped into the garage. The sun was no longer shining and the wind had picked up again. She hurried to her car and started it as soon as she got inside.

Cari realized she'd never asked Bob about going to visit Grandmother one weekend. She didn't want to bother him again while he was working so she decided to send him a text using voice to text. She waited until she was out of the garage to give it a try.

"Siri, text Bob," Cari commanded by talking to her watch.

"Okay. What text do you want to send?" the robot voice asked her. The words also appeared on the screen on her dashboard.

"Grandmother's this weekend question mark," Cari recited to her watch.

"I got 'Grandmother's chicken?'" came the reply. *"Do you want to send?"*

Cari laughed. "No. Don't send."

The screen cleared. She tried again with more enunciation. "Text Bob 'Grandmother's this weekend question mark."

"I got 'Grandmother's speaking?' Do you want to send this message?"

"No. Don't send."

A car honked and Cari looked up. She had drifted a bit too close to the neighboring lane. Enough voice to text for now. She'd send him a real text later. She hoped Bob would be up for a trip to visit Grandmother. Normally, they volunteered at the soup kitchen on Saturday mornings. She didn't really want to miss that, so they'd have to make it just a one-night trip. They could go again for the whole weekend another time. It was too late to cancel on the soup kitchen, but Cari really wanted to spend some time with her grandmother. She knew her health had declined significantly in the last few months and while she never expected her grandmother to live forever, she hadn't ever tried imagining a world without her in it.

Cari looked down and saw her right hand was wrapped around her locket. She released it and sighed. Hopefully, the medications the doctors put Grandmother on would help her manage for several years to come.

She followed the instructions from her maps app and made it across town to the floral shop. It was sandwiched between a bakery and what looked to be a therapist's office. She parked in front of The Budding Artist and turned off her car. A big neon green sign above the door shouted the store was open. Cari got out of her car and slung her messenger bag over her shoulder again.

The shop was filled with very creative arrangements of flowers. Cari had thought the business name was cutesy, but whoever designed these arrangements really was artistic. She didn't know many flower names, but was impressed by everything she saw. One arrangement had deep purple roses paired with some sort of orange flower in a swirling pattern. She bent down to look at the label. Azaleas. The small card listed a price for the arrangement with the vase and without the vase. A small note informed her the vase was designed and made by the shop owner, Willa Persephone. Cari wondered if the woman had changed her name to make it sound more artsy.

"Can I help you?"

A voice pulled Cari from her thoughts. She looked up and saw Kirsten Dunleavy standing next to her. The young woman looked to be several months pregnant. She was wearing a dark green apron with a small plastic nametag. Her dark hair was pulled back into a ponytail, which drew attention to her rosy cheeks. Her dark eyes looked tired, but friendly. Cari wondered how pregnant she was. The young woman had a cheerful smile with straight white teeth.

"Hi, Kirsten," Cari responded. "I'm actually here to talk to you, if you have a moment. My name is Cari Turnlyle. I work for the Brenington Beagle."

The smile faltered a bit. "Talk to me? About what?"

"Did you use to be with someone named George Samson?" Cari asked.

The smile disappeared altogether. "Not for a couple weeks now. He kicked me out when he learned I was pregnant. I mean, I was planning on leaving with my stuff anyway. I went over there to officially break it off."

"It's not his baby, I take it?" Cari asked gently.

"George is sterile. I didn't realize it, but I know now. I guess he had a pretty serious relationship, maybe even a common law marriage at one point a decade or more ago. They tried to have a baby. He was told he was sterile. Zero sperm," Kirsten explained. "I know I look like a terrible person for stepping out on him while he was putting me up. And yes, technically, I was his girlfriend. He's quite a bit older though. I really just needed some place to sleep. I'm not proud of it."

"Um, so it sounded like George was pretty angry when he figured out about the pregnancy," Cari commented.

"Who said that? Was it that hooch that lives in the first trailer? She needs to mind her own business. I don't even know her name.

She sure doesn't know mine and she better not be tossing it around like this," Kirsten said. Her cheeks were flushed.

"I got your name from the man in the trailer next door," Cari confessed even though it wasn't completely true.

"Stu. He's only out for himself," Kirsten remarked. "So, I guess George did something if you were over at the trailer park talking to his neighbors. What was it this time?"

Cari hesitated. "I'm not sure if George did anything. His name came up through the course of my investigation."

"What kind of investigation?" Kirsten asked with a frown.

"How angry was George when you left his home the last time?" Cari asked, ignoring Kirsten's question.

"Pretty angry. I haven't heard from him since," Kirsten told her. "I'm not sure if he was angrier that I was pregnant or that I was breaking up with him."

"Does he know the baby's father?" Cari asked.

Kirsten pursed her lips. "I don't think he does. Why?"

"Have you talked to your new boyfriend recently?" Cari asked.

Kirsten's face darkened. "Why?"

Cari didn't want to alarm the young woman. "I'm just curious. When did you last speak with him?"

"I moved in with him. It was a lot quicker than I'd normally shack up with a guy, but with me being pregnant, he was happy to invite me. He's thrilled he's going to be a dad. I saw him before I left for work this morning," Kirsten insisted. "Why?"

Cari felt her apprehension fade away along with her lead. "A man was found in the trunk of a car yesterday morning. He'd been dead since the night before."

"Oh my gosh. Did you think it was Wyatt?" Kirsten asked, her face a mix of shock and anger.

"I did wonder, but I'm so glad it wasn't him," Cari said earnestly.

"George isn't a saint, but he'd never murder anyone," Kirsten assured her.

"What do you mean?" Cari asked.

"George is a thief."

Cari felt a surge of adrenaline as Kirsten seemed to be confirming her theory. "I've seen his record. Petty theft."

Kirsten's eyes danced like she was about to give away a big secret. She opened her mouth and then immediately clamped it closed. "Yeah, like I said, a thief."

"Wait. Are you telling me he's moved on from petty theft to something bigger?"

Kirsten kept her mouth shut and shook her head no.

Cari felt like Kirsten reeled herself back for some reason. She decided to try a different tactic. "Does the name Jet Jackson ring a bell?"

"The used car guy?" Kirsten asked.

Cari nodded.

Kirsten looked back toward the checkout counter. "I really need to get back to work. Do you have a card or something? I might be able to call you later."

Cari resisted the urge to let her shoulders slump. She rummaged through her messenger bag and pulled out a business card. "My cell is on there as well as my office phone. Are you telling me you are familiar with Jet Jackson? As in, you've seen him with George recently?"

Kirsten pulled her lips into her mouth and didn't speak for several seconds. "I'm sorry. I need to go. I'll call you if anything else comes to mind."

"Thank you for your time," Cari said as the young woman walked away.

She took one last look around the shop. She kind of wished she'd known about it before she got married. The practical side of her knew she couldn't afford any of the arrangements, so she was probably better off living in ignorance. She pushed the door open and got back in her car. Kirsten knew more than she was willing to say. Cari felt an adrenaline rush; she couldn't prove it, but her gut said George Samson had started dabbling in grand theft auto. It seemed like George might have stolen a car with a dead body in it. Whether he knew it or not remained to be seen.

Chapter 6

The Burger King was relatively empty by the time Genevieve and Alex arrived. They walked up to the counter to place their order. Genevieve stood a step behind Alex so he could order first. She could see Stu Olivert bent over the griddle in the back. His hair looked greasy and stringy under the hairnet. A middle-aged woman stepped up to the register and smiled.

"What can I get started for you today?" she asked the detectives.

"I'll get a double-Whopper and a Coke," Alex requested.

"Is this together or separate?" the woman asked after keying in Alex's request.

"Separate," Genevieve replied.

"Fries with your order?"

Alex nodded. "Yes, please."

"Tap or scan your card on the reader," she instructed him. "You're number 208."

"Thanks," Alex responded after tapping his credit card to the little machine.

"I'm surprised you have a card with a chip," Genevieve teased as she stepped up to the register.

"It's not by choice," he grumbled.

"I'll get a Whopper with cheese all the way and a bottle of water to drink. No fries for me," Genevieve said.

"Got it. Tap or scan on the reader, please," the woman said again.

Genevieve got out her credit card and tapped it against the reader. It gave her a green check mark in approval.

"Here's your receipt," the woman said. "You're number 209. It will just be a few minutes."

Genevieve joined Alex a few feet back from the counter. He was fiddling with his receipt and watching Olivert. She looked toward the burger flipper.

"Do you want to eat first or interview first?" she asked Alex.

"Eat. I'm right on the edge of hangry here," he said with a pained expression.

"Works for me," Genevieve responded.

She felt her bag vibrating and fished out her cell phone. Special Agent Dureski was calling her. She shook the phone at Alex and walked to the back of the eating area to sit at a table while she talked to him.

"This is Detective Viacorte," she said into her phone.

"Viacorte. Thanks for answering. We need you and Runimoss for some depositions on Friday. It would be a helluva lot easier if you came to us," Dureski told her.

"Depositions for the Follard case?" Genevieve asked.

"Yes, I mean, we've got him dead to rights. He basically confessed in front of Runimoss and me at the hospital. He's trying to get that vacated. We'd already read him his rights and his wife has filed for divorce. She is not going to invoke spousal privilege, but if we have two law enforcement people as witnesses to his words, it will go a lot further," Dureski explained.

"You said I need to give a deposition too?" she asked him.

"Yeah, the case only reopened because of your legwork. We need you to go on record officially with everything you did," he said matter-of-factly.

"You mean our interview with Stenoway that resulted in his death at the hands of Brensteiner?" Genevieve asked.

"That and tracking down Shelly Palladium as well as the interviews with Brensteiner's sister," Dureski added.

Genevieve felt a bead of sweat drip down her back. She hadn't exactly followed police procedure to track down Shelly.

"Palladium didn't seem too keen about testifying, sir," Genevieve said reluctantly.

"Well, try and talk her into it. We can keep her back if we have to, but if the lawyers think the case is too weak, we're going to have to bring her in as well," Dureski replied.

Alex arrived with two trays of food. He set them both on the table while watching Genevieve take notes. She mouthed 'Dureski' to him. He raised his eyebrows.

"I understand. What time on Friday for Alex and me?" she asked.

Alex crinkled his nose at the mention of his name.

"How about ten o'clock? You can avoid some of the traffic that way," Dureski offered.

"We'll be there," Genevieve responded.

"Great," Dureski said and ended the call.

Alex started to unwrap his double-Whopper. "What did you just sign me up for?"

"We have to give depositions for the Follard case. He's not ready to plead guilty yet," Genevieve explained. "Tomorrow at 10 in the city."

"Ugh, the city. I hate the city," Alex grumbled. "We're going to have to cut Samson loose before we go tomorrow. Or sign off on it or whatever."

"He's not going anywhere. Everything I've read about him says he's born and raised in the area and never left," Genevieve told him.

He lifted his burger to his mouth and took a bite. His brow furrowed and he peeled back the bun from the meat. "Ugh, I forgot to say with cheese! This is so disappointing."

Genevieve smirked. "Choke it down. You said you were starving."

They ate in silence for a few minutes. Both of them kept their eyes trained on Olivert in the kitchen. If it looked like he was going to go on break, Genevieve was ready to intercept him. She took a drink from the bottle of water. Alex had already finished his burger and was halfway through his fries. She didn't know how he could eat so fast and not get heartburn. He was close to fifty years old. She slowly chewed another bite. Alex took a drink of his soda and then quickly put it on the table.

"Olivert just untied his apron. I'll go grab him," Alex said and stood up from the table.

Genevieve took a final bite of her burger and wadded up the wrapper. She assumed Alex was finished eating too and piled all the trash onto one tray. She slid the wrappers into the garbage and placed the two trays on the ledge above the opening.

"Stu Olivert?" she heard Alex ask.

She hurried over to join them. Alex had his detective shield out for Olivert to see. The lanky man's eyes were wide with apprehension.

"Don't run. We just need to talk about your neighbor. You aren't in any trouble," Alex said with a hand raised in protest.

Olivert relaxed and hung his apron on a hook. "Can we do this away from my co-workers?"

"Come join us at the back table," Alex suggested. "This is my partner, Detective Viacorte."

Olivert took off his gloves and tossed them in the trash. Alex's soda was still sitting on the table. Genevieve picked it up and handed it back to him before she sat down.

"Have a seat, Mr. Olivert. Like I said, you're not in trouble. We just need to ask you a few questions about your neighbor, George Samson," Alex told him.

Olivert sat across from Genevieve at the table. Alex sat down one table over. Genevieve figured he was trying to be less confrontational. The eating area was deserted, so no one would overhear their conversation.

"I don't know Samson very well," Olivert remarked.

Genevieve watched the man closely. He was turned toward Alex more than her and was picking at his cuticles. His knee was bobbing up and down too.

"You seem nervous. I promise you, we just need some information about your neighbor," Genevieve told him.

"I saw you arrest him earlier today. What did he do?" Olivert asked.

"We can't discuss an active investigation," Alex said quickly. "Samson is a person of interest right now. Does Samson ever have any visitors?"

"Visitors? Do you mean, does he have any friends?" Olivert asked in a confused tone.

"Friends, guests, family. Who comes to see Samson?" Alex asked.

"His girlfriend used to, but he threw her out the week before last. That used car salesman comes by pretty often. I think they went to high school together," Olivert remarked.

"The used car salesman…do you know his name?" Genevieve asked.

"Uh, that guy on all the ads with the huge billboard…Jackson?" Olivert asked more than stated.

Genevieve pulled up Jackson's website on her phone. "This guy?"

"Yeah, he drives a Mercedes. He comes about once a week," Olivert replied with a nod.

"Okay. You mentioned an ex-girlfriend. What's her name?" Genevieve asked.

Olivert turned and looked at Genevieve directly. "Everyone wants to know her name today. Kirsten Dunleavy. She was giving me the eye, if you know what I mean, so I tried to talk her up the day he kicked her out. She wouldn't give me the time of day. She's stuck up and rude, so I'll tell her name to anyone who asks."

Genevieve felt a bit disgusted by Olivert's words. "What does Samson do for work?"

Olivert looked away from Genevieve and toward the exit. "I'm not sure. It's never come up when I talk to him. We're mostly just neighbors. I walk his dog for him if he can't get home in time or whatever."

Olivert gestured toward Genevieve and Alex when he said "or whatever" as though Samson getting arrested wasn't new.

"Does he work from home or go to an office or worksite?" Alex asked.

"I think…uh…I think he must do a little of both," Olivert responded vaguely.

"Just one more question, then we'll let you get back to work," Genevieve told him. "Why did you warn Samson we were headed toward his trailer this morning?"

Olivert's face turned red. He stood up from his seat and took a step away from the table. "How do you…I didn't…what are you talking about?"

"I'm just curious why you felt the need to sound the alarm when you saw us walking down the access road today," Genevieve explained.

"I didn't call him. He must have seen you himself," Olivert mumbled. "I need to get back to work."

"Here's my card. If you think of anything else you'd like to share with us, please don't hesitate to call," Genevieve said and presented Olivert with her card.

He waved it off. "I'm not taking that. I told you everything I know about the man."

Olivert stomped back to the kitchen. Genevieve watched him pull on a new pair of gloves and put on his apron before returning to his position in front of the griddle.

"Well, we got the girlfriend's name," Alex remarked. "Ex-girlfriend. Hey, did you throw out my fries?"

She gave him a sheepish grin. "I thought you were finished. It's after three o'clock. Let's head back to the station and see what we can find out about the girlfriend. I bet that's the piece Cari left out of her statement earlier."

"We didn't get anything new to throw at Samson. We could take another run at Jackson. Maybe he can tell us about his dealings with Samson," Alex suggested.

"The dealership is between here and the station. Should we call ahead or just show up?" Genevieve asked.

"Let's just show up with some follow-up questions. Maybe he'll have had time to come up with a car title for us," Alex said with a smirk. "Plus, we need to let him know about the person breaking in through the back gate."

"I'd really like to know which car those plates came from. Do you think Olivert put them in his trailer or his car?" Genevieve asked.

"Hard to say. The chances of us getting a warrant to search his property are pretty slim. We only have Turnlyle's word that he took the plates and no concrete evidence to say where they came from," Alex replied.

"Cari said he drives a Malibu…um, a white one," Genevieve said. "We could peek in the windows."

Alex shrugged. "Let's go see what we can see."

* * * * *

It took Cari longer than she expected to get home. She still wasn't used to driving to Bob's apartment complex instead of hers. It wasn't until she reached her old street that she realized she'd driven *home* on autopilot. She turned around at the entrance to the complex and pointed her car toward the correct location.

Everyone she'd talked to about Samson seemed to have the same sentiment: he wasn't trustworthy. The old woman from the trailer park definitely didn't like him. His ex-girlfriend still had a soft spot for the man for some reason. Maybe she felt guilty about giving up his secrets because he'd provided a home for her for a time. Whatever it was, Kirsten Dunleavy didn't want to be the one to squeal on Samson, at least not all the way.

Cari parked in one of their two assigned spaces and turned off her car. She had only interviewed the people from the first two trailers so far. She wondered if the neighbor in the fourth trailer knew any more about Samson. She didn't feel like driving back over there now, so she grabbed her messenger bag and got out of the car.

She set her messenger bag down on the sofa and went to the bedroom to change her clothes. Her eyes landed on her stack of boxes near the closet. She cringed. She'd been promising Bob she'd get the boxes unpacked since last weekend. The stack was a little off-kilter and partially blocked the doorway to the closet. She kicked off her dress shoes by the bed. She grabbed the first box and set it on the bed. It had a few of her tops spilling out of it already. She needed hangers for all of them. She wasn't sure where those were. Bob had a few extra hangers, but not enough for all of her clothing. She went back to the boxes and lifted the top one off the stack. It had a towel hanging over one edge. Genevieve had written "bathroom" on the box when she'd helped Cari pack it. Cari thought there was a chance the box had some random hangers in it. She pulled the towel out and tossed it on the bed. Two more bath towels were underneath it as well as a hand towel and some washcloths. She tossed those on the bed too. Her travel shower caddy was at the bottom. No hangers. Cari grabbed the shower caddy and went to the bathroom. She opened the cabinet under the sink and stuffed it on top of some of Bob's things. She went back and got the towels and refolded them. The bathroom had a linen closet, so she stacked the towels and washcloths on one of the shelves. *One box down.*

The next box wasn't labeled, so Cari knew it had been packed by her and her alone. She pulled open the flaps and looked inside. Socks and underwear. She grabbed several pairs of socks and somehow managed to open her dresser drawer without dropping them. She dumped them inside and then moved the partially emptied box out of the way. Some of her tops were a bit wrinkled from their extended time in the box, but she didn't want to iron them now. She just needed to get them hung up and then the wrinkles would probably fall out on their own. She tore into the last box and smiled. The hangers, as well as a few candles and notepads, were inside. She grabbed the hangers and pushed the box aside.

As she inserted the hangers into her shirts and dresses, she thought about Samson some more. Dunleavy had been adamant that he wasn't a killer. Cari felt the same way; he didn't strike her as honest, but he also didn't seem violent. To be fair, she'd only talked to him on the phone. The older neighbor seemed to find him suspicious and maybe lazy, while the next-door neighbor at least liked him enough to walk his dog from time to time…and hide evidence of some sort. She thought about the license plates again.

The last two letters weren't a lot to go off of, but they were better than nothing. She grabbed her stack of clothing by the hanger heads and quickly hung the items in the closet. She'd emptied three boxes in less than thirty minutes. She started to walk past the fourth box and paused mid-step.

"Cari Turnlyle, do not be such a slob!" she commanded herself and then laughed.

She grabbed the rest of her clothing from the box and put it all away in the correct drawers. She closed the bedroom door behind her and sat down on the sofa. Her laptop still had plenty of battery left, so she opened it and logged in without plugging it into an outlet. Unfortunately, she couldn't search the Department of Motor Vehicles for a license plate. She knew Genevieve and Alex could as well as any of the CSU staff, including Bob. There had to be another way to figure out the victim's identity.

She lightly drummed her fingertips on the keys. Something fishy was going on at the used car dealership. Jackson wasn't going to talk to her about it, but one of his employees might. She opened LexisNexis to find a list of the business's employees. The lot employed salespeople, mechanics, and a couple of receptionists. Cari wasn't sure which person would be the most willing to speak with her. At the bottom of the list was a link for former employees. Cari clicked on it. The used car lot had more former employees than current employees. She scrolled through the list to look for the employment period for each former employee.

"There's my guy: Antonio Mancino," Cari said aloud.

Mancino had worked as a mechanic for about six weeks, but had quit less than a month ago. It seemed like a rather short time to be employed somewhere. Mancino was still local, so he hadn't stopped working because he'd relocated. He seemed like a prime candidate to squeal on his old place of employment. Cari clicked on his name and scanned the entry for his contact information. She entered his phone number into her cell phone and hit the talk button. The call rang four times and went to his voicemail.

"Hello, spam caller. You've reached Tony! If you're not a scammer, leave a message. Otherwise, get lost."

Cari snorted at the recording. "Hi, Tony. No scammer here. It's Cari Turnlyle with the Brenington Beagle. I'm doing some research on used car lots and thought you might be able to fill me in on some things. Call me back when you get a chance."

She stared at her phone screen and wondered if she should have sent a text instead. She really preferred talking to people. Their hesitations and vocal emphasis really helped her read between the lines of their words. She pressed the messaging icon. She hadn't added Mancino as a contact yet, so she had to reenter his number. She'd barely entered the area code when her screen lit up with an incoming call.

"Tony! Thanks so much for calling me back," Cari said when she answered the call.

"You said you're a reporter?" Tony's rich baritone sounded as Italian as his name.

"I'm a journalist, yes," Cari confirmed. "Do you have a few minutes to talk?"

"I don't want to talk on the phone, but I'd meet you for coffee tomorrow. It has to be early. My shift starts at 7:30 in the morning," Tony told her.

"I can do that. Which coffee shop?" Cari asked him.

"The Starbucks over on Meridian Avenue. It's next to where I work. I can park at work and walk over," he explained.

"Seven o'clock?" Cari asked.

"I'll be there. You're buying," Tony responded and then ended the call.

Cari quickly added it to her calendar and then set an alarm for six in the morning. It was too cold to run outside these days, but she could go to the eight o'clock yoga class after meeting with

Tony for some exercise. She heard a key slide out of the lock to the front door and looked over. Bob stepped inside with two sets of keys in his right hand.

"Missing something?" he asked with a grin.

"Whoops," Cari said sheepishly. "My bad."

"How was your day?" Bob asked. He sat down next to her on the sofa and kissed her cheek.

"It was busy, but I feel like I made some headway. Plus, I got to eat lunch with this really hot guy…" she teased and kissed him on the mouth.

"Oh, really? Anyone I know?" Bob asked with a grin.

"I think you've met him once or twice," she said and laughed. "How was your day?"

"Slow. We're waiting on a lot of warrants. Green at least finished the autopsy, but we can't identify the guy. Everything feels like it's taking forever," Bob said with a sigh.

"Did you have any luck with the license plate?" she asked.

"Not yet. There are a lot of cars with a Q in the second to last spot on their license plate in New York," Bob explained.

Cari nodded. "I know. I just can't believe we still don't know who the victim is. It's been almost two days since he died."

"We'll figure out who he is. Someone will report him missing before too long," Bob said encouragingly.

Cari looked down and saw her hand on her locket. She released it and made eye contact with Bob. "What would you say if I proposed going to see Grandmother this weekend? We could leave on Saturday after we finish at the soup kitchen?"

Bob squeezed her hand. "If Grandmother is up for it, it sounds like a plan to me."

Cari smiled. "Awesome! I'll give her a call and let her know we'd like to visit."

Bob stood up. "I'm just going to change my clothes and then we can start on dinner. What should we have tonight?"

"Tacos? I mean, we had those for lunch, but they sound kind of good," Cari suggested. "By the way, I found one of Jackson's former employees. I'm meeting him for coffee early tomorrow. He only worked at the used car lot for a few weeks before quitting."

"You're hoping he's a disgruntled employee and he'll tell you all the secrets?" Bob asked as he walked toward the bedroom.

"One hundred percent. Something isn't on the up-and-up there. I want to know what it is," Cari responded.

Bob stepped into the primary bedroom. Cari heard him take a quick breath. "Oh, you unpacked your boxes…"

"I did. I'm sorry it took me so long. I finally just sat down and made myself do it," Cari confessed.

"You know, we can flatten these cardboard things so they take up less space. They'll even fit in the recycle bin for the apartment complex that way," Bob teased.

"I hear your sarcasm, Hursley," Cari said with a laugh. "I'll get the beef out for the tacos while you take care of the boxes."

"Deal," he called out from the other room. "Hey, have you seen my suit?"

Cari's eyes bulged. "Oh no! Bob! I'm so sorry. I took it to the cleaner's yesterday. I was supposed to pick it up today. Ugh. They're already closed for the day too."

Bob came out of the bedroom. "No big deal. I'll just swing by and pick it up on the way to court tomorrow. It's not a problem. They open before I need to be at the courthouse."

"I'm really sorry. It completely slipped my mind," Cari apologized again.

"Seriously. It's not a big deal. Thanks for taking it to get cleaned for me. I appreciate it," he said and pulled her in for a kiss.

* * * * *

"All I see are fast-food wrappers," Genevieve said to Alex. "He must have hidden the plates somewhere else."

"Worth a shot," Alex commented. "Let's go talk to Jet again. Maybe he found the car title."

Genevieve smirked. "You don't believe that any more than I do."

They got back in the cruiser. Jackson's Used Car Lot was only about a five-minute drive from the Burger King. Genevieve drummed her fingers on her thighs. Dureski's conversation replayed in her mind. He wanted her to contact Shelly Palladium again. Genevieve hated the idea of bothering the woman another time. She decided to wait and see how things played out. There was no reason to bring up old hurts if they didn't actually need her to testify.

"What's on your mind?" Alex asked.

"I was just thinking about the depositions," Genevieve admitted. "Dureski asked me to talk to Palladium and get her to agree to testify. I don't think she's going to want to do that. I think she'd rather leave all of it in the rearview mirror."

"I can understand that. Does he really think they need her testimony?" Alex wondered.

"He said there was an outside chance. I think I'm going to leave her out of it unless they force my hand," Genevieve told him.

"We're going to lose the whole day tomorrow with those depositions. I hope we can get something from Jackson now that helps us charge Samson today. Otherwise, he's gone in the morning," Alex reminded her.

"I hope so too, but it feels like a long shot," Genevieve remarked. "Jackson hasn't been very cooperative. He acts like he wants to cooperate, then obfuscates and offers half-truths. It's getting old."

She felt her phone vibrating and pulled it out of her pocket. Cari was calling.

"Cari, did you find something new?" Genevieve asked her.

"Sort of. I went to see Samson's ex-girlfriend…I'm sorry I didn't mention her before, but I thought she would talk to me before she would talk to the police. Anyway. I did a little research on her before I went to see her. I knew she had a new boyfriend and he sort of fit the description of the guy in the trunk," Cari told her.

"You identified the body?!" Genevieve exclaimed.

"No. I eliminated a potential match, though," Cari informed her. "The new boyfriend is Wyatt Ushlinson. He's alive and well. She saw him this morning."

"Good to know, I guess. Thanks, Cari," Genevieve ended the call.

"I got the name of the baby daddy. He sounds like a dead end. We can interview him, but I think he's just tangentially connected because he got involved with Samson's girlfriend," she told Alex. "Let's hope we can get something from Jackson."

"Well, we're here. Let's see if we can make him talk," Alex said confidently as he put the cruiser in park.

The wind was howling again. Genevieve tugged her beanie further down over her ears. She knew it was messing up her hair, but she'd rather be warm than cute. They hurried to the entrance. Alex pulled the door open and Genevieve ducked under his arm. She savored the warm air for a moment before she looked around the large room for Jackson.

"Good afternoon. How can I help you…oh, hello again, officers, I mean, detectives," Dave stuttered. "Are you looking for Jet?"

"We are. Where can we find him?" Genevieve asked.

"He's in his office. Do you need me to help you find it again?" Dave asked.

"We're good," Alex replied. "Thanks anyway."

Jackson's office door was closed, so Alex knocked on it firmly. Genevieve could hear him talking to someone. She peered into the glass window and waved. Jackson was on the phone. His eyes widened when he saw her. He put up a finger and his mouth started moving quickly. She turned her head to try to hear what he was saying, but he'd lowered his voice when he saw her in the window.

"He's on the phone," she told Alex.

He rolled his eyes. "We don't have all day."

She put a hand on his arm. "More flies with honey and all that."

His eyes narrowed, but he didn't barge into Jackson's office. Moments later the knob turned, and Jackson swung the door open.

"Detectives!" he said cheerfully. "Come inside. How can I help you today?"

"Did you find the car title, Mr. Jackson?" Genevieve asked as she took a seat.

His cheeks reddened. "I haven't quite put my hands on it yet, but I know it's here somewhere."

"Mr. Jackson, you know we watched the security video. I'm guessing you've watched it too. The car arrived on your lot in the middle of the night. Why won't you admit that someone smuggled it in?" Alex asked.

Jackson leaned back in his cushioned office chair. "Smuggled? People bring cars to the lot at all hours. It's neither here nor there."

"Kind of like the car title," Alex muttered under his breath.

"I'm sorry?" Jackson asked Alex.

"You were expecting a dark blue Corolla to arrive in the early hours of Wednesday morning?" Genevieve asked him.

"Things are not so precise around here," Jackson said and put his hands up. "It's a fluid business."

"We were able to lift fingerprints from the car. The same person's prints were on your back gate. That person doesn't work here," Alex pointed out.

"Oh, I bet it was George Samson's prints. He's someone I knew in high school. He's really good with cars and will occasionally do some work for me. Nothing nefarious at all," Jackson said and crossed his legs.

"You've seen Samson recently?" Genevieve asked.

"Um…it's been a while. I can't really say when I saw him last," Jackson responded.

"You've talked to him?" Alex pressed him.

Jackson frowned. "Uh, maybe? I can't remember. He pops up from time to time in need of work or with a car he thinks I could sell."

"Is Samson a friend of yours?" Genevieve asked. "We have at least one witness who has seen you parked outside Samson's residence."

"A friend? No, I would say an acquaintance," Jackson explained. "I've been to his…home…if you want to call it that. It's been a while, like I said. I have to bring him a paycheck if he does any work for me. Since he's not officially on our payroll as an employee. You know, he's more of a contractor."

"You sure have a laissez-faire arrangement with him. It seems like something you'd do for a friend…for someone you really trust," Genevieve commented.

"I'm a trusting sort of person," Jackson said nervously. "But I've got a lot of work to do…"

"Like finding the car title?" Alex asked.

Jackson's eyebrows jumped up. "Uh, yeah. The title. Right."

"Our instructions to not go out of town still hold, Mr. Jackson," Alex told him. "We'll be in touch."

Jackson nodded his understanding and got up to open the door for them. "My door is always open, detectives."

Genevieve looked him in the eyes for a moment as she exited his office. He acted like he was being cooperative, but she wanted him to know she could see right through the charade. Jackson followed them to the front entrance of the building and waved goodbye as they stepped outside.

"We've got to figure out what he's hiding," Alex remarked once they were out of earshot.

"We know he has a connection to Samson. He didn't really give us anything to charge Samson with. I feel like we're going to lose him in the morning," Genevieve lamented.

"Same, but he's lived here forever. We can always pick him up again," Alex told her. "Are we going to take the subway into the city for the depositions tomorrow?"

"That's my plan. I don't want to drive in the city if I don't have to," Genevieve responded.

They reached the cruiser and Alex unlocked it. The sun was low in the sky and the temperature was dropping quickly. Genevieve got inside and slammed the door closed. The season of winter lasted far too long in her opinion.

"Let's start sifting through license plates when we get back. That's going to take forever," Genevieve noted.

"You're telling me," Alex agreed. "I'm not looking forward to it, but we don't really have any other leads."

"We have Samson's ex-girlfriend," Genevieve reminded him. "We could look her up too."

"She might want to squeal on him if she knows anything," Alex said hopefully as he steered the cruiser back toward the station. "Jilted lover and all that."

"Let me see if I can find out where she works from my phone. I'll log in to the database and look her up," she told him.

She unlocked her phone and opened a browser window. She navigated to the database and entered her information to access it remotely.

"Olivert didn't tell us how to spell her name. Do you think it's just phonetic?" she asked Alex.

"How should I know?" he said and shrugged.

She typed "Kirsten Dunleavy" into the name fields and added Brenington for the city. She crossed her fingers she would only get one result and touched the search button. Sure enough, a single Kirsten Dunleavy showed up on the screen. She touched the name and waited for the information to load.

"Her address is still listed as Samson's trailer, but we know that's wrong," Genevieve told Alex. "Oh, but she works at a floral shop in town. I'll call and see if she's there today."

She looked up the number for the florist's and hit the call button. The line rang once before someone answered.

"The Budding Artist. How can we help you today?" the woman's voice said.

"Hi, this is Detective Viacorte with BPD. I'm looking for one of your employees: Kirsten Dunleavy. Is she working today?" Genevieve asked.

The woman was silent for a moment. "Uh, she was here earlier, but she had some sort of personal emergency and had to leave. I can give her a message if you'd like."

"When is her next shift?" Genevieve asked.

"Not until Sunday," the woman told her.

"Do you have a number where I could reach her before then?" Genevieve requested.

"Um, don't you need a warrant or something like that? I don't think I can give out employees' phone numbers," the woman explained.

Genevieve rolled her eyes. "Thanks for your help."

She ended the call and looked at Alex. "She was there earlier, but had to leave because of a personal emergency. She isn't working again until Sunday. I could go over and chat with her."

"Gen, boundaries. You aren't on-call on Sunday. It's your day off. You should take advantage of it," Alex instructed her.

"This is a murder investigation, Alex! We don't even know who the victim is. I can't take a day off," Genevieve admonished him.

"You know, Gen, I started out like you. Gung-ho to work myself to the bone on every case. I worked extra hours for free constantly," Alex told her.

"I know, I know—"

Alex cut her off. "It cost me a lot more than money."

Genevieve was about to snap off a retort, but his words caught her off guard. "What do you mean?"

"I got married young. Right out of high school," Alex explained.

"I thought you and Sophia just celebrated twelve years together or something," Genevieve said.

"We did," Alex confirmed. "Sophia is my second wife, Gen."

Gen's jaw dropped. She closed her mouth and opened it to respond, then closed it again. She couldn't come up with the right words.

"My first wife, Kelly, was really patient at first. She knew what being a cop's wife was like. She had an uncle who was a patrolman and later a detective," Alex said as he turned into the parking lot. "But once I made detective, I kept working longer and longer days. I was constantly chasing down leads. It was my duty, my *calling* to find the bad guys and put them away. We grew further and further apart. She begged me to spend more time at home; to leave work at work. I didn't listen…and…I lost her. We divorced about six months after I made detective. She moved out of state, got remarried, went to college…she has a good life now. I'm happy for her. I'll always be thankful for what she taught me."

"Alex…I had no idea. I'm sorry you had to go through that," Gen told him as she undid her seatbelt.

"It's my own fault. I made my choices. When I met Sophia, I promised her I'd do better," Alex said emphatically.

"Thanks for telling me about your past," she replied. "I appreciate that…"

"But…" he prompted.

"I'm not married, Alex. I'm not even dating anyone. All I have is free time and work," she explained. "And I want to find the guy who did this and put him behind bars."

Alex stared at her for a moment, but remained silent. She could see in his eyes he pitied her. She grabbed the door handle and pushed her door open.

"Let's go dig through the license plate records, shall we?" she asked before she closed the door. She marched inside without waiting for an answer.

Chapter 7

The parking lot at Starbucks was packed when Cari arrived. At least nine cars were in the drive-thru line. She managed to snag the last space in the lot. The cold air fogged up her sunglasses when she stepped out of the car. She pushed them up on her head as she walked to the entrance. She pulled open the glass door and looked around for Tony. A man in coveralls was sitting at a table near the windows. He looked like the man from the LexisNexis profile. His dark hair was cut a little shorter than it was in the digital image, but the square jawline and sharp cheekbones were unmistakable. She walked over to introduce herself.

"Tony?" she asked when she reached him.

He stood up and put out his hand. "That's me. I've only got about ten minutes. What did you want to know about the used car business?"

Cari smiled. "Where do used car lots get most of their vehicles?"

"A lot are trade-ins from buyers," Tony answered. "I've only worked as a mechanic at a used car lot, though. I've never owned one, so I don't know a lot of the business side of the operation."

"Oh, which used car lots have you worked at?" she asked casually.

"Only one: Jackson's Used Cars here in Brenington. I wasn't there long," he added.

"I know that place. It sounds like there's more to that story," she encouraged him.

"You're not going to print my name with this or something, are you?" Tony asked cautiously. "I don't want to get blacklisted for airing their dirty laundry."

"Off the record. I'm just curious," she assured him.

"I'm a naturalized citizen," Tony explained. "My parents moved here from Italy when I was a baby. My dad had a job offer at some university and my mom was a housewife. My dad died before I was twelve. Heart attack. My mom and I got citizenship way before that, but I'm always cautious about following the laws. I have brown skin and it makes people nervous."

Cari swallowed. "I'm so sorry you lost your dad at such a young age. I'm sure that has made your life a lot more challenging."

"Yeah, it has. I barely finished high school because I was working so many hours to help my mom out. When I started working for Jackson, I was really excited. It's the biggest used car lot in the area. He paid me a lot more than I make at my current position, but I hadn't been there long when I started noticing some weird things," Tony told her. "Cars would show up out of nowhere. I asked Jet about one that was near the back gate one morning. It looked like it needed some bodywork. The back panel had some dents and scratches. He told me it was just there as a stop-over. It wasn't staying. I asked another mechanic about it and he told me to leave it alone. Jackson had a guy who stashed cars in our lot on occasion and then took them to a chop shop."

"Oh, wow. That's risky," Cari remarked.

"It felt really illegal and I didn't want to get caught up in it. I started looking for a new position that would pay me a reasonable amount and I quit," he said. "It was the most nerve-wracking few weeks of my life."

"I bet," Cari agreed.

Tony lit up his phone screen. "I'm sorry I couldn't help you too much with your article. I've got to get back to work, though. I could maybe meet again another day if you have more questions."

"Are you sure you don't want a coffee?" she asked him.

"No, I'm good thanks," he replied.

"I appreciate your time. Have a great day, Tony," Cari said.

She walked outside with him and waved goodbye when she turned toward her car. Tony hadn't given her Samson's name, but he'd confirmed her suspicions. Cari wished Kirsten hadn't gotten spooked when they chatted the day before. It seemed like the ex-girlfriend knew Samson was stealing cars and somehow funneling them through Jackson's lot. Cari started her car. The clock on the dashboard read 7:28. She could still make the yoga class if the traffic lights cooperated.

She put her car in gear and pulled out of the parking lot. She needed to update her grandmother and see if it was still okay for her and Bob to come for a quick visit, so she accessed her phone with the Bluetooth button.

"Call Grandmother," she commanded the computer.

"Calling Grandmother," it responded.

The ringing sound reverberated in the car. She heard a click followed by someone clearing their throat and then coughing.

"Grandmother?" Cari asked with concern.

"I'm here. Just choked myself a bit. How are you, my dear?" Grandmother asked.

"I'm a little cold, but doing well. I'm still trying to figure out who the dead guy in the trunk was," Cari told her. "How are you?"

"Right as rain. Have you made any progress?" she asked.

"Not really. No one is cooperating, especially the guy who asked my boss for our help," Cari explained and filled her in on what she knew. "The police are really struggling to identify the victim."

"That probably makes it doubly hard to find out who killed him," Grandmother remarked.

"It sure feels that way," Cari agreed. "So…I talked to Bob. How do you feel about us coming for a quick visit? We thought we'd drive up after we volunteer tomorrow. I think we could be to your house before lunch."

"That sounds wonderful. What do you want me to fix for dinner?" Grandmother asked in a cheerful voice.

"Why don't you let us cook for you? Well, Bob's the cook. I can make a pretty decent grilled cheese," Cari admitted.

"We can talk about it after you get here," Grandmother responded. "I'm very excited to see you!"

"Me too. I've gotta run. I'm going to yoga this morning. Love you, Grandmother," Cari said with a smile.

"I love you more."

Cari was almost to the yoga studio when a call came in over her Bluetooth from Michelle. She clicked the accept button.

"Hey, Michelle! What's up?" Cari asked.

"Ollaman asked me to remind you that you volunteered to write the updates to our social media pages regarding the dead body. He's really hoping you'll mention Jackson has been cleared," Michelle told her.

Cari cringed. "Oh, right. It slipped my mind…probably because I can't write that about Jackson, at least not yet. I'll do it soon. Thanks for the reminder."

"Good luck," Michelle replied and ended the call.

Cari felt like she was going to need a lot more than luck.

* * * * *

The subway wasn't too full when Genevieve and Alex took their seats.

"How long do you think this deposition is going to take?" Alex asked her.

"Dureski didn't say. I'm guessing an hour or more each. Haven't you done this before, old man?" she teased him.

"For the feds? No. I've only testified for the local DA in cases we work for the city," he told her. "Did you call Palladium?"

Genevieve pursed her lips. "No, I couldn't bring myself to do it. I really hope they don't need her testimony. If Follard was any sort of decent human being, he'd just plead guilty and waive his right to a trial."

"I don't see that happening," he remarked. "The guy is a complete narcissist. I'm disappointed you didn't get to see his wife smack him. That was funny."

"Kind of her to just lay it all out there for you and Dureski," she agreed. "And since there are two witnesses to what she said, Follard can't claim it didn't happen."

"Well, really there are three. She said she's waiving spousal privilege. I'm pretty sure she already filed for divorce," Alex reminded Genevieve.

"Oh, right. Even better," she agreed.

Alex unlocked his phone. "I thought you said these trains have Wi-Fi. My phone is just searching for a signal."

She leaned toward him to look at his screen. It had the cancel symbol instead of bars. She took her phone out and looked at it. It was connected to a Wi-Fi signal. "Go to your settings."

"Where are settings again? Oh, wait. I got it," Alex said and maneuvered to the correct screen.

"Now select that one," she said and pointed at TransitWirelessWiFi. "And just follow the prompts."

Alex poked his index finger at his phone for a minute. She watched him with an amused grin. Eventually, his phone connected.

"It says it isn't a trusted signal," he remarked.

"It's public Wi-Fi. We'd have to set up a VPN if you want something more secure. That costs you data and I don't think the department will reimburse you for it if you go over on your usage," Genevieve told him.

"Sophia told me we have unlimited talk and text," Alex said with a confused look.

"I think we've had enough technology lessons for today. Why do you need Wi-Fi right now anyway?" she asked.

"What if Grusky calls? I feel like we're wasting a day with the investigation by getting called out here," Alex lamented.

"Grusky knows where we are. I told him to cut Samson loose unless he decides to spontaneously confess," she said ruefully.

"Man, I really wish we could hold him longer. I don't think he killed the guy, but he's definitely up to something shady," he said with a frown.

"Cari is still out there chasing leads. Maybe she'll stir up something useful for us," Genevieve told him. "I'd like to know what Dunleavy told her."

"She didn't fill you in?" Alex asked.

"Not yet, but that doesn't mean she won't," Genevieve replied. "It bothers me that Dunleavy left work early yesterday. Something about that feels off."

"Turnlyle spooked her. Usually it's us that does it," Alex remarked. "We can catch her next week."

"I'm going to try on Sunday," Genevieve reminded him.

"You're too stubborn for your own good. You know that, right?" Alex asked her.

"I get things done," Genevieve said matter-of-factly.

Alex stayed silent for a moment. She knew it meant he was about to change the subject. "How's your long-term goal of working for the FBI going? Still on track?"

She pantomimed weighing things on a scale. "Maybe. Maybe not. Dureski is still talking to me, so that's a good sign. I'm hoping they'll do another training session like I went to last summer. The more I interface with them, the better my chances are of getting into their real training program at Quantico."

"And you want to be a profiler, right?" Alex asked.

"That's the goal. Dureski doesn't work in that group, but he knows people. If I stay on his good side, maybe he'll refer me," Genevieve replied.

"You're a great investigator, even if you work too hard," Alex encouraged her. "I'll vouch for that."

"Three more stops until we get off. Then we have a five to ten minute walk," Genevieve told him. "I'm hoping we can still work our case some this afternoon."

He nodded in agreement. Genevieve wished they could put the old case behind them and focus on the current one. She liked the opportunity to interact with the FBI again, but she couldn't help but wonder if it was costing them more than just time.

* * * * *

The yoga class left Cari feeling refreshed. She took a quick shower and twisted her curls into a bun of sorts. She wanted to get over to the floral shop again and see if Kirsten would talk to her one more time. Maybe if she explained she knew about Samson's arrangement with Jackson through someone else, the ex-girlfriend would be willing to corroborate the story.

She got dressed and hurried outside. The sub-freezing temps felt extra cold against her damp hair. She put a hand up to her head and felt frozen locks of hair. She patted down her pockets and found her beanie. She was about to tug it onto her head and then wondered if the wool would freeze to her hair. She stuffed it back into the pocket and jogged to her car instead. She jumped into her car and turned it on. The vents blew more cold air at her, but she knew the heater would kick in soon.

During the yoga class, she'd thought about what Tony shared with her. Was Jackson flipping cars like people flipped houses? Or was he a cover for some sort of chop shop? He seemed friendly and charming, but he was definitely hiding something. Cari navigated back to the floral shop. The lights were on and the open sign was lit up. She got out of her car and locked it.

The bell above the door rang to signal her entry into the business. She looked toward the checkout desk and saw a young man seated near the register. He waved as she approached the desk.

"How can I help you today?" he asked.

"I was hoping to talk to Kirsten. Is she in today?" Cari asked.

The man's face darkened. He glanced over his shoulder and then back to her. "I'm sorry. She was originally on shift today, but canceled it yesterday afternoon. That's why I'm here…" he paused. "On my Friday off. I could be skiing, but I'm working."

"Right," Cari remarked. "Do you know how I could reach her?"

The young man looked over his shoulder again. "I'm sure I'm not supposed to do this, but she owes me for working this shift for her. I'll give you her number. She's at her new sugar daddy's house, I'm sure."

Cari smiled in appreciation while the man pulled out his phone. She held up her phone and opened her contacts app. He recited Kirsten's number and then put his phone away. Cari quickly entered the number and hit save.

"Thanks," Cari said as she put her phone away.

"Can I help you with anything else?" he asked.

"That's all I need. Thanks again," Cari said and walked out.

She got back in her car and started it. She hadn't checked in with Ollaman yet for the day and needed to update him on her whereabouts. She found his number in her contacts and hit the call button.

"Ollaman," he answered.

"Hey, boss," Cari said quickly. "I'm trying to find Samson's ex-girlfriend this morning. She kind of clammed up on me yesterday when I spoke with her. I think she knows more about his interactions with Jackson than she was willing to tell me."

"And you think one night's sleep will have persuaded her to talk?" Ollaman asked in a doubtful tone.

"No, but I have some new information from another source. I think that might give her a little comfort in sharing what she knows," Cari replied and explained her discussion with Tony, the mechanic.

"Wait, are you saying Jet is doing something against the law at his business?" he asked her.

"I'm not sure, sir. That's why I want to talk to Samson's ex-girlfriend again. Jackson might not be part of whatever scheme Samson is running," she replied even though it seemed pretty obvious he had to know about it.

"Good work, Turnlyle," Ollaman affirmed her.

"Thanks. I should be in the office at least by the afternoon. I think I know where Ms. Dunleavy is. I'll keep you posted," Cari told him.

"I still haven't seen an update on our social media pages about the investigation. Can we just say Jackson isn't a person of interest?" he asked.

"I'm sorry, sir. He's involved somehow, maybe not with the murder, but he knows something about that car he isn't willing to share with anyone yet," Cari lamented.

"Please post an update by the end of the day. Be…respectful to Jackson," he instructed her.

She heard him grunt and then the call ended. She needed to look up Wyatt Ushlinson's address. She didn't want to try calling Kirsten until she was outside his place in case the woman tried to take off and hide somewhere else. It bothered Cari that the woman hadn't come into work today. She hadn't meant to spook her when they talked yesterday; she just wanted to know more about Samson's relationship with Jackson.

Cari found his address and put it into her GPS. It was twelve minutes away. She pulled away from the florist's and followed the turns to Ushlinson's house. She had sort of expected him to live in an apartment, but it appeared he owned a house. LexisNexis listed him as the homeowner of the three-bedroom, two-bathroom home. She hadn't read his whole profile and wasn't sure how he was employed, but apparently, he was ready to be a dad.

Unfortunately, even if Cari could get Kirsten to admit Samson had upgraded to stealing cars from petty theft, she still wouldn't know who the victim was. Samson would have to tell them where the car was when he stole it. She wondered if Samson had removed the VIN from the windshield at the used car lot. The sticker inside the driver's door was easier to peel off than getting the etched numbers on the windshield filed off. She wasn't even sure if *filed* was the right word for how it was removed. Maybe he needed acid or something, but it seemed like that might damage other parts of the car. She decided to call Bob since it was close to lunch time and he'd be on break. She could ask him about the removal process while she drove to the new boyfriend's home.

Bob answered on the first ring. "How did your meeting with the mechanic go?"

"He was helpful. I was right: he left Jackson's business because he felt like they were doing something illegal or at least unethical. He didn't want to get caught up in it, so he quit as soon as he found a different job," Cari explained. "How was court? Did you get your suit okay?"

"I was the best-dressed CSU guy there. Broke a few hearts when they saw my wedding band. This man is taken, ladies," Bob joked.

"Yeah, he is," Cari laughed. "Uh, I have a question about the VIN on the Corolla."

"We don't have it," Bob stated quickly. "We're still waiting for the state to process the car."

"Right, but how would someone remove the VIN from the windshield? Aren't those etched onto the glass now?" Cari asked him.

"I think that's typical. This vehicle had the VIN etched onto the glass," Bob told her.

"If someone gets a new windshield, do they transfer the VIN from the old one?" Cari asked.

"I believe so," Bob answered.

"I'm trying to decide if the car thief removed the VIN or if the murderer did it to conceal the identity of the victim for as long as possible," Cari said thoughtfully.

"Those are both good theories," Bob responded. "I've got to get back to work. Did you need anything else?"

"I'm good. Thanks for the help," Cari replied. "Love you."

"Love you too," he said and ended the call.

Cari pulled into Ushlinson's neighborhood. His house was on the second block after the entrance. All the houses were similar: some kind of siding painted beige or tan or grey, white or black shutters and trim, and wooden front doors. It looked like they were all one story too. She decided to park one house away and call Kirsten. She hit the call button and listened to the ringing sound. After four rings, her voicemail picked up.

"You've reached Kirsten, leave a message."

Cari ended the call without leaving a message. She tried texting her instead.

Kirsten, it's Cari Turnlyle. We talked at the floral shop yesterday. Can we meet?

Cari stared at the screen and willed it to tell her the message was read. She was glad she kept her car running. The dashboard told her it was still below freezing out. It was after nine-thirty now and her head was starting to hurt. She hadn't had any coffee yet and the lack of caffeine was not treating her well. She wished she'd grabbed a latte from Starbucks while she was there two hours ago, but she didn't think it would sit well with the yoga class. She touched the phone screen to keep it from going to sleep. The word 'read' finally showed up under her message. Cari wanted to text something else, but held back in case Kirsten responded first. The three little dots bounced and then disappeared. Cari touched the screen again and started entering a new text about grabbing coffee, then deleted it when the dots appeared again. She just needed to be patient.

"C'mon, c'mon, c'mon. Just give me another chance," Cari said to the phone screen. A text popped onto the screen.

I don't have anything else to say to you.

Cari frowned.

I'm not trying to get you into trouble. Please. Talk to me one more time.

Her message was immediately read and the dots appeared again.

I'm late for an appointment. Maybe later.

Cari sighed. She looked at the boyfriend's house and watched to see if Kirsten came out the front door. There wasn't a car in the driveway, so Cari wondered if the woman had called a rideshare for the appointment. Maybe she was lying about the appointment. She wasn't even sure the woman was at her boyfriend's house. She decided to try one more time.

Do you need a ride?

The message was quickly marked as read again. Cari clenched and unclenched her left hand. Her right foot was hopping with nervous and hopeful energy. She pumped her left fist in the air when another text came through.

How soon can you get to my boyfriend's? He lives on the east side.

Cari smiled.

I'll be there in less than a minute.

She put her phone into her messenger bag and then tossed the whole thing onto the backseat. She put her car back into drive and pulled forward to Ushlinson's house. Kirsten stepped onto the porch and shielded her eyes from the sun. Cari rolled down the passenger window and blinked when the cold air hit her face. The woman walked down the steps and leaned into the window.

"Were you following me or something?" she asked with a glare.

Cari shook her head. "No. I found your new boyfriend's address and took a gamble you might be here this morning. It paid off."

"I have a prenatal appointment at ten at Brenington West," Kirsten said as she opened the door. "Wyatt was supposed to come back and pick me up, but he has too much going on at work to get away today. I texted some of my girlfriends, but they're all at work this morning too."

The streets were too narrow for her to flip a U, so she pulled into the driveway instead. Cari noticed her messenger bag on the seat when she looked into her rearview mirror. She mentally berated herself for not turning on her digital recorder before tossing it back there. She backed out of the driveway and pointed the car toward the neighborhood exit.

"I thought you owned a black station wagon," Cari said as she drove down the street.

Kirsten's head swung toward her. "How do you know that?"

Cari forgot she'd learned that from the neighbor. "The neighbors mentioned it. The flower shop isn't close. How do you get to your shifts?"

"I do own a station wagon, but it needed an oil change. Wyatt helped me drop it off there last night. We'll pick it up later today," Kirsten explained.

"Weren't you supposed to be at work today?" Cari asked.

"Yes, but I called in sick. I left early yesterday too," she confessed.

"Something we talked about scared you. I promise, I haven't told anyone about you or given your name to anyone," Cari told her. "Why are you scared?"

"Someone gave the police my name! My boss called and told me they had called to look for me near the end of business hours yesterday," Kirsten said, her voice rising with panic. "Thankfully, I left early."

"Kirsten, dating a thief doesn't make you a criminal," Cari told her. "Withholding evidence might get you in trouble though."

The woman's eyes filled with tears. "I haven't done anything illegal, but…I did know George was stealing and not just from retail stores like before."

"You knew he was stealing cars," Cari filled in the blanks for her.

Kirsten's eyes widened and more tears fell down her cheeks. "I never helped him steal a car. I just knew…he'd go out late at night and sometimes I'd see a different vehicle parked in front of the trailer. I never asked about them. I didn't want to know."

"How long ago did this start?" Cari asked.

Kirsten rubbed her forehead. "About a year or so ago. I'm not sure exactly. George lost his temper at work a lot and got fired for it. He was constantly bouncing from one job to another. I guess he thought working for himself would be easier."

Cari nodded. "How long were you two together?"

Kirsten took a deep breath. "Oh, geez. A long time. Almost three years, I think. I probably should have moved out way before I did. I mean, before he found out about Wyatt and threw me out."

Cari wasn't sure what to say. The woman's life was so different from her own.

"You must think I'm such a horrible person," Kirsten blurted out.

"No, of course not," Cari said and meant it. "I appreciate you telling me all of this. You said you knew he was stealing cars. How can you be so sure?"

"He would bring in the license plates. One time I watched him use some kind of solution on a car's windshield. It frosted the glass, but not in a decorative way," she told Cari. "Anyway, the license plates were in the trailer on his desk. He'd eventually destroy them or have the guy next door pick them up and take care of them."

"Stu?" Cari asked.

"Yeah, that creep," Kirsten confirmed. "Sometimes, he'd have the keys for the cars. He used to laugh that people were so dumb to leave them under the visor in the car or in the console. He didn't even have to pick the lock on those. Just easy in and out."

"He bragged to you about it?" Cari asked her.

Kirsten nodded. "He thought he was tough stuff for what he was doing."

"Did Jet Jackson ever come to the trailer to meet with George?" Cari asked. She hoped she wasn't pushing Kirsten too hard; she wanted her to keep talking.

Kirsten rubbed a hand over her face. "I saw him once. It was early in the morning. I woke up to them arguing outside. Jackson was mad at George. I couldn't hear everything they said, but I got the idea that Jackson felt like George was bringing stolen vehicles to his lot too frequently. It was putting his business at risk."

"Does George know you overheard part of that conversation?" Cari asked.

"I don't think so. He didn't come back inside. Jackson left and I heard George start his stupid truck," Kirsten replied. "And it's not like it was always bad with George…we had a lot of fun together the first two years or so…back when he was still employed. I met him at a bar in the city and found out he lived in Brenington. I'd been kind of couch surfing from friend to friend at the time. My apartment building was condemned and I couldn't afford another place unless I wanted to move much further away. George invited me back to his place…and I never left," she paused. "Well, until just recently, that is."

"You said George has a temper. Was he ever violent with you?" Cari asked gently.

"No. He's just a yeller. He yells at you and tells you how dumb you are, but he'd never hit anyone," her eyes widened. "Are you asking because…because you think George killed the man in the trunk?"

Cari chewed the inside of her cheek. "It's something I've considered. It seems pretty obvious he stole a car. The car has a dead body in the trunk. It's hard to imagine he doesn't know how it got there."

"No. George is no killer. I don't believe it," Kirsten insisted. "He's all bark."

"Maybe he'll realize he's in over his head and tell the police where he got the car," Cari replied. "Otherwise, they're going to think he killed that man."

"They'll be wrong," Kirsten insisted. "I know George. I hate him right now, but I'd never believe he's a murderer. Let's talk about something else."

Cari saw her cross her arms across her chest and knew she wasn't going to say any more about George or his thieving ways. She changed the subject.

"If you don't mind me asking, when is your baby due?" Cari asked.

"I have fourteen weeks left. I guess that's a little over three months," Kirsten told her. "I've been trying to work extra shifts to save up. Babies are expensive. I'm not sure how long Wyatt and me will work out. I mean, he's a really nice guy and all. He even has a real house. I just don't know if we're meant to be…forever, you know?"

"It sounds like you're planning ahead. That's smart," Cari replied as she turned into the hospital parking lot. "I'm not sure which entrance you're wanting…?"

"Oh, the front is just fine," Kirsten said and pointed to the left.

Cari drove through the parking lot around to the front of the hospital. She looked at the clock on the dashboard. It was just a couple minutes past ten o'clock.

"Was your appointment at ten?" Cari asked.

Kirsten nodded. "I'm here within fifteen minutes of it, so I should be okay. Thanks for the ride."

Cari reached into her console and fished out an old business card. "This has my cell on it. Please call me if you need anything."

"Thanks. I will," Kirsten promised.

Kirsten got out of the car and started to close the door when she turned back to Cari. "Um, if you talk to George, can you keep what I said between us? Like I said, he has a temper and…I'd just rather not anger him again."

"No problem," Cari said with a nod. "Best of luck with everything."

Kirsten smiled and hurried into the building. Cari clapped her hands together. She needed to call Gen and tell her she knew Samson was a car thief. She put her car back in drive and hit the Bluetooth button.

"Call Genevieve," she requested.

"Calling Genevieve."

The call immediately went to Gen's voicemail. Cari frowned. She wasn't sure why her friend's phone would be off. She didn't want to leave a message, so she hoped Genevieve would see the missed call and call her back later. She'd passed a coffee shop a few blocks back and was more than ready for a large latte. As she drove, she mentally pieced together the social media update Ollaman was begging her to do. She spoke aloud to get a feel for the wording.

"Let's see…the investigation into the identity of the dead body discovered earlier this week continues. BPD is exploring all angles, but hasn't named a suspect or the victim, for that matter. Stay tuned for updates from your favorite newspaper!" she exclaimed. "Maybe the ending is a bit too cheesy."

She reached the coffee shop and put her car in park. Then she opened her email account and thumbed in her update. She sent it to Michelle and hoped it would keep Ollaman off her back for a few hours.

* * * * *

The depositions were taking forever. Dureski's office staff had arrived late because of some sort of last-minute administration meeting. Genevieve and Alex weren't allowed to have their phones with them during the depositions in case they interfered with the recording equipment. They had to turn them over to Dureski's secretary, who promptly turned both phones off. Genevieve wished she could have kept hers while she waited her turn. She could have been mining through the list of license plates to find one for a dark blue Corolla with a QI or QL at the end instead of stuck reading magazines in the conference room. The door finally opened and Alex stepped out with Dureski and the US attorney.

"Detective Viacorte, why don't we grab some lunch before we record your depo?" Dureski suggested. "I'm starving."

"Me too," Alex agreed.

"Why not?" Genevieve said. "Can we at least take our phones to lunch?"

"I thought we'd just order in," Dureski explained. "Don't worry. Yours won't take as long as your partner's did. We have your interview with Stenoway already recorded. We just need to go through how you tracked down Brensteiner and the photo you got from the fraternity president to connect him to Follard. You didn't witness the car crash, so we don't have to walk through all that again."

"Got it. So, what's for lunch?" she asked him.

"Chinese? They're pretty fast," Dureski added.

"Kung pao chicken for me. White rice," Genevieve requested.

"Do they have beef and broccoli?" Alex asked.

Dureski raised his eyebrows. "I would have taken you for more of a sweet and sour pork guy."

"I'll get some wontons too," Alex added.

"Consider it done," Dureski said and left the room with the US attorney.

"You were in there for over an hour," Genevieve remarked.

"Tell me about it," Alex said and sat down next to her. "It was a lot. The questions just kept coming."

"Do you think the case will really go to trial?" Genevieve asked. "We have so much evidence against him."

"A lot of it was Brensteiner though, right? He killed Stenoway," Alex reminded her.

"They were both in it together," she argued. "Neither acted without the other's knowledge. And Follard tried to help Brensteiner run the Rialtos off the road."

"You didn't witness that," he pointed out.

"Right, but several other people did. Plus, they have his wife's statement and all the financial records," Genevieve replied. "Maybe they'll hire a forensic accountant to go through all of that."

"Through all of what?" Dureski asked from behind her.

"The accounts. All the financials between Follard and Brensteiner and Stenoway," Genevieve explained.

"Right. You did a great job linking all of that, but you're also correct in saying a forensic accountant is more reliable and trusted to present that sort of information to a jury," Dureski told them. "The food should be here in ten minutes or less."

"So, you think this is going to go to trial?" Genevieve asked.

"Follard seems hell-bent on having his day in court," Dureski said and shrugged. "He's responsible for several deaths…seven, maybe? I can't offer him anything less than life in prison without parole. He seems to think he can convince a jury it was all Brensteiner."

"Will Robby have to testify?" Genevieve asked.

"I've already recorded his deposition," Dureski confirmed. "He's a vital part of our case."

"I'm still hopeful his lawyer will get him to change his mind," another voice said.

The US attorney had rejoined them. Dureski had introduced them earlier, but she couldn't remember his name. She stuck out her hand.

"Apologies, I can't remember your name," Genevieve said sheepishly.

"US Attorney Marvin Taber," he said and shook her hand. "Viacorte, right?"

She nodded. "Yes, sir."

"As I was saying, our team meets with Follard and his lawyer every few weeks. The lawyer knows what he's up against. Follard is basically out of money. He's got a little savings left that his wife didn't know about. She cleared out the rest of their accounts and put all the money into an account in her name only. We explained to her that some of it is evidence and will have to be returned. She's working with us on that," Taber told the group.

"If he runs out of money, what happens?" Alex asked. "Doesn't the lawyer have to stick with the case?"

Taber nodded. "Ethically, he is obligated. However, he wasn't assigned to the case by the judge, so he can request to be released because of lack of payment. Then Follard will have to get the next-in-line on the public defender's list."

"Money talks," Alex remarked.

"Let's hope Follard's listening," Genevieve replied.

Chapter 8

Genevieve climbed into her Ford Expedition at the park-n-ride as Alex slid into the passenger seat. Her deposition had taken almost as long as Alex's, despite Dureski's earlier assurances. They wanted to get all of her legwork on record for the presentation to the grand jury in a few weeks. She started the car and pulled out her phone again.

"I couldn't get a good enough signal on the subway to call Cari back. Care if I ring her up now?" she asked Alex.

"Go for it. Maybe she has new information for us," he replied.

She pulled out of the lot and then pressed the Bluetooth button. "Call Cari Turnlyle," she commanded.

The dialing sound played in their ears twice before Cari answered.

"Gen! I tried to call earlier. Where have you been?" her friend asked.

"We had to go into the city for depositions with the feds," Genevieve told her. "Why did you call?"

"I talked to people today: a former employee of Jackson's and Samson's ex-girlfriend," Cari said.

"By the way, Alex is with me," Genevieve interrupted.

"Hi, Alex," Cari said sweetly.

"Turnlyle," Alex grunted her name more than spoke it.

"Anyway, the former mechanic told me he saw some suspicious things happen at the used car lot. He didn't work there long. He said unknown cars would occasionally show up at the lot. They usually needed body work, but he was told not to ask about them. They'd be there for a day or so and then disappear without being purchased. He didn't want to get caught up in something that felt illegal, so he found a new job and quit," Cari told them.

"And the ex-girlfriend?" Genevieve asked.

"She told me yesterday she knew Samson was a thief, but when I asked what he stole, she clammed up. I'd already asked her about her new boyfriend slash baby-daddy in relation to the dead body in the trunk—"

"You what?!" Alex exclaimed.

"Shh. Just listen," Genevieve ordered him.

"Right, didn't we already talk about that? I thought her new boyfriend might be the dead guy. He's the right height and build for it, but he's fine," Cari assured Alex. "She put two and two together and realized Samson might have been involved in something worse than car theft."

"That's why she left work early. You spooked her," Alex remarked. "That's usually our job."

"Well, I got her to talk to me today. She knows he's been stealing cars," Cari told them.

Alex made two fists and pressed them against his forehead. "Ugh, we let him go this morning."

"We'll pick him back up. Where is he going to go?" Genevieve asked. "Call Grusky. Tell him to put out an APB on Samson."

"He played us," Alex said. "I really didn't read him as a killer, though."

Genevieve had to agree. "Same. He's a criminal and a liar, but I thought he was just covering for a friend by saying he didn't know anything about the body in the trunk."

"One more thing," Cari's voice broke into her train of thought. "Kirsten, the ex-girlfriend, insisted George wasn't a murderer. She said he was all bark, but he'd never hurt someone physically."

"We still have to pick him back up," Genevieve told her. "Killer or not. He can help us identify that body. Thanks for the help, Cari. I'll check in with you later."

She ended the call and looked at Alex. He already had his phone in his hand.

"I'm calling Grusky now. Hopefully, we can catch up with Samson again quickly," Alex told her. "I'll put the call on speaker."

"We should have suggested he have some officers keep tabs on him. I know he's never lived outside of the area, but I feel like he's going to be harder to find the second time around," Genevieve said as they waited for Grusky to pick up.

The line clicked and Grusky's voice filled the SUV.

"Runimoss, what is it?" Grusky asked.

"Hey, LT. I've got you on speaker. We just learned Samson has been stealing cars and funneling them through Jackson's lot. How long ago did you let him go?" Alex asked.

"Let me think. It's been a few hours now," Grusky answered. "I'll send some patrol officers over to his trailer."

"We'll meet them there. We're about fifteen minutes away," Genevieve informed him. "Let them know he tried to run the first time we went to see him."

"Roger that," Grusky said and ended the call.

Genevieve saw Alex staring at his phone screen after Grusky hung up. "Did you want to ask him something else?"

"Yeah, did we get any of the warrants yet? It feels like those are taking forever for some reason," Alex complained.

"It does seem slow. I'm sure he'd tell us if he got them though," Genevieve said.

"Samson flat-out lied to us. He stole that car. I'm on the fence as to whether or not he knows who was in the trunk, but I am certain he stole the vehicle," Alex said confidently.

"Me too. He had believable explanations for our questions. We didn't have enough to charge him. What else could we do?" she asked him.

"Nothing. Ugh," he groaned. "This sucks."

"We can have another chat with Jackson. It seems obvious he knows what Samson has been up to," Genevieve added.

"Agreed. Let's get Samson back first. We can worry about Jackson after that," Alex suggested.

A gust of wind rocked the Expedition toward the shoulder. Genevieve held the steering wheel tighter to keep it from swerving into the guardrail. She could see the exit for Brenington up ahead and was ready to be off the highway.

"Supposed to get some snow this weekend," Alex said from the passenger seat.

She looked at him through the corner of her eye. He was looking at his cell phone. "You have a weather app too?!"

"It came with the phone. Standard," he told her.

She smirked as she took the exit. "Next, you're going to start giving me sports updates."

"Nah. I'm not that guy," he assured her. "Grusky's calling. Just a sec…Runimoss…you're kidding me! Ugh! I guess we'll come talk to the neighbors. What's that?"

Genevieve wished he'd put the call on speaker so she could hear what Grusky was saying too.

"At least we can search his trailer now that we have a warrant. We'll look at Jackson's finances when we get back," Alex said. "Later, LT. Thanks."

"Samson isn't home?" Genevieve asked after the call ended.

"No. His truck is gone. I think he split," Alex told her. "Let's go see what we can find. We have a warrant to search his trailer.

143

Grusky sent it via email. I'll get it downloaded in a sec. He got us the warrant for his finances too."

"Cari said the woman in the first trailer is like the neighborhood watch if there is such a thing at the trailer park. She had all sorts of things to say about Samson. Hopefully, she knows something about where he went," Genevieve said as she pulled up to the curb behind the police cruiser.

They walked up the dirt road toward the trailers. Before they reached the first one, the door to it opened and an older woman stuck her head out.

"Are you back here for George Samson?" she shouted.

"Have you seen Mr. Samson, ma'am?" Alex hollered back.

The woman put her hand up to her ear to indicate she didn't hear him. Alex started to shout back and Genevieve put a hand on his arm.

"Just wait. She'll hear you better when we get to her trailer," she reminded him.

Genevieve took out her badge and held it up for the old woman to see. "Detectives Viacorte and Runimoss, ma'am. Have you seen your neighbor George Samson today?"

The woman squinted at them and then nodded. "He got dropped off earlier today by you guys, by the police, that is. Within an hour, he had loaded up that piece of junk he calls a pickup and tore out of here like the place was on fire. I thought the truck might break an axle when he jumped the curb instead of following the road like you're supposed to. For someone who works on cars for a living, he sure doesn't treat them very well. It's a miracle he even got that clunker to start."

"Do you know where he might have gone?" Genevieve asked her.

"I have no idea. He had a girlfriend, but he kicked her out. I don't know if he has family in the area or not. I haven't seen anyone that seems to be a mother to him around ever, but maybe he's been disowned. Wouldn't surprise me none," she said flippantly.

Genevieve opened her messenger bag and pulled out one of her cards. "Here's my card, ma'am. My cell phone number is on the back. If you see Samson, would you give me a call?"

The woman looked her in the eyes. "In a heartbeat."

They nodded their thanks and walked the rest of the way to Samson's trailer. Two patrolmen were standing near the trailer's porch. It seemed like they were trying to use it as a shield against the wind.

"Officers," Alex said in greeting. "We have a warrant to search the trailer. If one of you wants to join us while the other keeps an eye out for Samson—"

"I'll help search," the taller officer said. "It has to be warmer inside."

"Wimp," the other one muttered under his breath.

Genevieve remembered Cari mentioning Olivert was able to get into the trailer with a key. She lifted the doormat, but nothing was underneath it. A pot with dirt and a dead plant sat to her left. She lifted the pot from its spot and smiled when she saw the key below it.

"Here we go. Now we don't need to kick the door in," she told the other two.

She stuck the key in the lock and turned it. The door popped open. A regretfully familiar smell wafted out of the trailer.

"Smells like the cab of his truck in here," she said and scrunched up her nose. "Gross."

They stepped inside the trailer. If she didn't know any better, she'd think he had been robbed. The dresser drawers hung open with a few stray pieces of clothing hanging out of them. The mattress was askew on the bed frame. A lamp was overturned near the sofa. The desk was completely cleaned off except for an overturned router. She saw an Ethernet cable dangling free from the back of it. The previous morning, the desk had been covered in papers, amongst other things. Genevieve pulled on a pair of gloves and walked up to the desk. All of the drawers except one were open. The one closed drawer had a keyhole in the drawer face. She tugged on the handle. Locked.

"We need to get into this drawer. He obviously didn't feel like he had time to empty it," Genevieve told the officer.

"I'll see what I can do," he offered.

Alex was on the bedroom side of the trailer. He bent down to lift the mattress off the frame. Genevieve hurried over to help him.

"I got it," he argued.

"No need to throw your back out. Mattresses are heavier than they look," she told him.

They picked up the mattress and leaned it against the wall. Several loose sheets of paper were scattered under the frame. Genevieve took a photo and then bent down to pick them up. One was an old utility bill. The back of it had notes scrawled on it. She couldn't read the handwriting. She flipped through the other pages. More bills with chicken-scratch writing on them.

"Maybe someone can interpret the messages on here for us. Let's get these in evidence bags. Do we need to call in CSU?" she asked Alex.

Alex ran a hand through his dark hair. "Probably. I hate to do it to them this late in the day."

"Chris is back on today. He's out of his free Fridays," Genevieve told him.

"Maybe Judith is still in too. Hopefully, they can bring the whole team out," Alex remarked. "I'll call Grusky back and update him. He can get CSU out here."

He pulled out his phone and unlocked it. Genevieve watched him for a moment; she still couldn't believe he actually got rid of his old flip phone.

"I see you watching me, Viacorte. I know I'm nice to look at, but no need to stare," he said with a grin. The smile faded as he swiped his finger across the screen. "Where is the phone feature again? The part that makes this an actual phone?!"

It was her turn to smirk. "There's my favorite dinosaur. It's right there. It's always in the same place," she said and pointed at the screen.

"There are too many extra features. I'm going to delete most of them. I'm just not sure which ones I absolutely have to have to keep the phone working," he grumbled as he hit the call button next to Grusky's name.

"Put it on speaker?" she requested.

He hit the speaker icon and the ringing sound filled the trailer. "Runimoss, did you get Samson?"

"No, he seems to have moved out," Alex informed him. "We need CSU to come out. We've found some cryptic notes on old bills. The place is a mess. It's like he ransacked his own home."

"I think he had a laptop or something connected to the internet in here. There's a loose Ethernet cable attached to a router or modem," Genevieve added.

"I'll get a team out there. I think a few of our CSU members are still here. What else?" Grusky asked.

"We need to put out a BOLO for his pickup. It's an old green Ford Ranger," Genevieve said and pulled out her notebook to get the details. "A 1997 green Ford Ranger."

"Do you know the plate number?" Grusky asked.

She read it to him from her notes. "His neighbor said the pickup barely runs. Maybe it will break down before he gets too far away."

"If he's really a car thief, that won't slow him down a bit," Grusky pointed out.

"We're going to bring in Jackson. He's been lying to us from the moment we arrived at his business. Maybe he's heard from

Samson again today," Alex said. "Did we get his phone records yet?"

"They're in your inboxes. I'm going to call down to CSU now. Let me know when you get Jackson to the precinct. I want to watch the interview," Grusky told them.

The call ended. Genevieve looked around the trailer again and then took out her phone. She wanted to search Jackson's phone records and see if they could identify Samson's phone number. She knew the approximate time he'd called Jackson. Hopefully, they could track the thief down quickly.

* * * * *

A knock on the side of Cari's cubicle wall startled her. She looked up and saw Ollaman peering down at her.

"Turnlyle, I need an update. I missed a call from Jet just now. He left a voicemail and sounded panicked," Ollaman said. "I want to be able to reassure him when I call him back. Where are you in your research?"

Cari looked at her screen. She'd been assembling her notes from interviewing the ex-girlfriend, the neighbors, and Samson. She still didn't see Samson as a killer, or Jet for that matter.

"I haven't made a lot of progress, sir. Samson's ex admitted she knew he was stealing cars. I've gathered the police know he was at Jackson's used car lot. I think he left his fingerprints on the car or somewhere else. I know Jackson called Samson the morning the car was discovered in the lot, but neither of them would admit to it," Cari told her boss. "He doesn't want me to know Samson is a friend or acquaintance of his for some reason. Jackson is hiding something. In fact, he promised to send me the video surveillance of the lot from Tuesday night and Wednesday morning, but he never did it."

Ollaman frowned. "I've known Jet for years. I bought both of my kids' cars from him. He's an honest man. He's not a killer."

"That's the vibe I get from him and Samson, too. They're up to something together, though. It makes them both look guilty," Cari explained. "I wouldn't be surprised if the detectives pick Jackson up and bring him in."

Ollaman's face reddened. "But Jet's not a criminal! He's just a salesman. Can't you talk to the police? Tell them he's a good person?"

Cari swallowed. "I don't think my input would sway them one way or another, sir. I'm sorry. The detectives are following the evidence. Whatever he's hiding, he needs to be honest about it. The longer he tries to cover it up, the worse it will be."

A loud ringing sound came from Ollaman's office. He looked over his shoulder with a frantic expression. Cari felt bad for him.

"I need to go see who's calling. Keep trying to clear his name!" Ollaman barked as he hurried back to his office.

Cari winced when the office door slammed closed. She looked at her computer screen again. No one had come out and said it yet, but Kirsten had basically confirmed Samson was somehow funneling cars through Jackson's lot. It sounded like he removed the VIN from the vehicle before he stashed the cars there, so Jackson wasn't selling stolen cars. He was just a stopping point along the way to the chop shop. If Kirsten was to be believed, then Samson wasn't a killer. It seemed like he must have been so focused on stealing the Corolla, he didn't realize someone had stashed a dead body in the trunk. If that was the case, Cari doubted the car would ever be reported stolen. They needed to hope Samson would tell them where the car was when he stole it, or they were going to continue to struggle to identify the victim from the trunk.

Ollaman's door opened and then slammed closed again, making Cari jump. She turned her head just in time to see him almost jogging toward the elevators. She wasn't sure she'd ever seen her boss do anything remotely close to running. He pressed and repressed the down button to call the elevator to their floor. She saw him swing his head toward the stairwell and wondered if he was considering hoofing it down the stairs instead of waiting half a minute for the elevator to arrive. He took a step toward the stairwell just as the bell sounded to indicate a car had arrived. He slipped inside without speaking to anyone. His urgency suggested Jackson had called with an update. Cari could only assume Genevieve and Alex had picked up the used car dealer.

"What was that all about?" Bryson's voice made her jump again.

"I'm not certain. I think it might have to do with the story he has me chasing right now," Cari responded vaguely.

"Which is…?" Bryson prompted.

"Sticky," Cari replied after a moment.

It wasn't that she didn't trust her coworker; she just didn't want to offend their boss by airing his friend's dirty laundry. Bryson raised his eyebrows in response.

"I'm sorry. It's kind of complicated. It's the story I mentioned to you the other day with the dead body in the trunk," Cari explained. "I can't really tell you more than that."

Mostly because I don't really know any more than that.

"Ollaman's involved somehow?" Bryson pressed her.

Cari waved her hands. "Oh no. Nothing like that."

"You're more tight-lipped than the police department. I thought journalists were supposed to be gossip-hounds," he ribbed her.

Cari opened her mouth in protest and he put a hand up.

"I'm just kidding. It does have me intrigued though. I'm out of here. We're going skiing this weekend and the boys are about to get home from school. Gotta get an early start. See you Monday," he said and walked away.

Cari looked at her watch. It was almost four o'clock. She was out of leads and needed to get a few things packed for their trip to Grandmother's tomorrow. The words on her screen stared back at her. No matter how hard she looked at them, she wasn't going to find the victim's name unless Samson confessed to stealing the car and told someone where he got it. Unfortunately, if he was guilty of killing the man too, Cari had zero confidence he would ever admit to the theft.

* * * * *

"Am I under arrest or what?" Jet Jackson asked from the backseat of Genevieve's Expedition. "Aren't you supposed to pick me up in a city ride? Isn't this your personal vehicle? Isn't that violating policy?"

Jackson continued to pepper them with questions as they drove to the station. Genevieve could almost hear Alex's teeth grinding together as he forced himself to stay quiet. She looked in the rearview mirror. Panic and fear stared back at her through Jackson's eyes.

"Mr. Jackson, as we've already explained, you are a person of interest in our investigation. A dead body turned up at your place of business. You haven't been honest with us and we need answers. Someone was killed. It's our job to find out who did it and why," she told him plainly.

"So, I am under arrest?" Jackson asked again. "You read me that Miranda warning. That means you arrested me, right? Should I call a lawyer?"

"Person. Of. Interest," Alex spat from the passenger seat. "We're almost there. You can tell us everything you know once we get inside. Or you can call your lawyer. Up to you."

Jackson glared at Alex's back. Genevieve swallowed a laugh. She wasn't sure who was more annoyed with whom: Jackson or

Alex. She turned into the parking lot and parked in her usual spot. Alex hopped out of the car and hurried around to the back to help Jackson get out.

"I am capable of getting myself out of the car," Jackson grumbled. "Cars are my livelihood. I do *not* need your assistance."

Alex shrugged, but stayed close to Jackson. They knew he wouldn't try running. The pudgy man wouldn't make it more than a block before he collapsed.

"Right this way, Jet," Alex said in mock sweetness.

Genevieve locked her vehicle and walked in just behind Jackson and Alex. She heard tires screeching and whipped her head around to see what the commotion was. Alex yanked Jackson into the precinct. A Lincoln Town Car swerved into the parking lot. Genevieve squinted to see who was driving. It looked a lot like Cari's boss. She shrugged and went inside.

Alex and Jackson were already in the interview hallway. She unbuttoned her coat and pulled off her hat as she hurried after them. She felt the static in her hair cling to the knitted beanie. She quickly removed her gloves and ran a hand over her hair to smooth it out. Between the wind and taking her hat off repeatedly, she was certain her hair was a mess. She shoved her gloves and the beanie into her coat pockets.

She slowed down when she saw Alex open the door to interview one and direct Jackson inside. He leaned into the room and then stepped back into the hallway. She joined him as he closed the door.

"Let's go update Grusky, then we can have a chat with our talkative friend," Alex suggested.

They turned to walk back to Grusky's office. Genevieve started to tell him about seeing Cari's boss in the parking lot when he quickened his pace and ran toward the entrance to the detective bay. She jogged after him. Alex pushed the door open and she heard Dana speaking sternly to someone on the other side.

"You cannot go in there without an escort. Who are you here to see, Mr. Ollaman?" Dana asked.

The bald man's entire head was beet red. He had both hands palm down on the counter and was leaning toward Dana. Alex held the door for Genevieve and then took another step toward the man.

"Is there a problem, Dana?" Alex asked.

Dana smiled at him. "No problem, Detective. Mr. Ollaman is just taking a moment to learn how to conduct himself at our precinct, aren't you, Mr. Ollaman?"

Ollaman peeled his hands off the counter and clenched them into fists at his sides. "My friend has been unlawfully detained. I demand to know why."

"Could I get his name?" Dana asked.

"Jet, uh, Rutherford Jackson. He was just arrested," Ollaman growled.

"I assure you, he was not arrested," Genevieve remarked. "Are you his legal counsel?"

Ollaman's face returned to a more normal color. "I, uh, I…I'm not a lawyer."

Genevieve turned to Alex. "I can get Mr. Ollaman settled. I'll meet you in Grusky's office shortly."

They nodded and left her alone with Dana and Ollaman.

Genevieve looked at Ollaman. "I'm afraid you can't see your friend. You are welcome to wait for him in our family room if you'd like. I can take you there now."

"Why did you bring him here?" Ollaman demanded as they walked toward the family room.

"I'm sorry, sir. I cannot talk about an active investigation. All I can tell you is he is not under arrest," Genevieve repeated her earlier statement.

"He's innocent. He's done nothing wrong!" Ollaman exclaimed.

"And as I said, he is *not* under arrest. Please have a seat. We'll be in touch," Genevieve said after she opened the door to the family room.

"When?" Ollaman asked.

"As soon as we can," she replied and let the door close.

Alex was waiting for her outside Grusky's office. He knocked lightly. "He wanted to catch up on some paperwork while you dealt with the newspaper guy," he explained.

"Come in!" Grusky hollered from inside.

Alex opened the door and they sat down across from Grusky. She hadn't noticed it before, but his suit was rumpled and one flap of his shirt was untucked. Genevieve wondered if he'd had to drive to the courthouse to beg for the warrants. Regardless, he looked worn out.

"What's the update?" he asked without looking up from his computer screen. "Did you have a chance to review Jackson's phone records on your way here?"

"No. The man wouldn't shut up. It was too distracting to look at the records with him yammering on about being innocent from the back seat. We have him in interview one," Alex told him. "He's a little panicked. The newspaper editor just showed up to try to bail him out. We explained he wasn't under arrest."

"Is he going to be under arrest?" Grusky asked.

"Undecided. If he cooperates, we have no reason to hold him," Alex replied.

"Unless his cooperation implicates him in a crime," Genevieve added.

"Of course," Alex said quickly.

"CSU is still at Samson's?" Grusky asked.

Genevieve nodded. "Yes, they're collecting evidence. It seems like we might have a bit of a paper trail to follow, but I think it might be unrelated to the murder."

"What do you mean?" Grusky asked.

"I think Samson steals cars and sells them for parts. I don't have proof, but I think Jackson could get us there if he's willing to talk," Genevieve said.

"Well, here's hoping," Grusky replied and gestured toward the door.

They exited his office. Genevieve motioned to their desks. "I want to print out his phone records. The ones from his office. I also want to print out the name associated with one of the callers from those records. Then we can go talk to him."

Alex nodded. He sat down at his desk while she logged into her computer. She pulled up her email and found the attachment from Grusky with the phone records. She keyed in the print request and scanned her email. Her eyes lit on the recent email from Grusky with Jackson's finances.

"Hey, can you pull up his finances while I print the other thing?" she asked Alex.

"Good idea," Alex said and started poking at his keyboard to log in.

She located the phone number from Jackson's records and highlighted it. She copied it and pasted it into the database to search for the owner. George Samson.

"Got the phone calls from Samson to Jackson and vice versa on Wednesday that Cari told us about," Genevieve told Alex.

"Good. I'm seeing cash deposits of five hundred dollars about every other week on here. I'll print it. We can ask him about that too," Alex said. "Can you grab all the printouts?"

She was already on her feet. "We're literally going to walk past the printer on our way to the interview room. Join me."

He smirked and got up from his desk. She grabbed the papers from the printer and handed the financial statement to Alex. "Should we lead with Samson being a car thief?"

Alex nodded. "Float the idea. See how he responds."

She turned the knob and pulled the door open. Alex followed her inside.

"Good afternoon, Jet. Do you need anything? Water? Soda?" she asked him.

He shook his head no.

Genevieve sat down across from the sad-looking salesman while Alex leaned against the wall in the corner.

"You said if I cooperate, you'll keep me out of all of this, right?" Jackson asked. "I didn't murder anyone."

"Good to know. As we told you, you are just a person of interest right now. You don't have to talk to us. You can call a lawyer," Alex reminded him.

"I'm just…you read me that, uh, Miranda warning. I thought you only read that to people who were under arrest," Jackson asked.

"At this time, you are not under arrest. We have obtained evidence that leads us to believe you know more about how the Corolla showed up at your business this week. We're hoping you'll cooperate and tell us what we need to know. A man was killed. Our best chance of identifying the killer is figuring out who the victim is. To do that, we need to know more about that car," Genevieve explained.

"Okay, well…what do you want to know?" Jackson asked uncertainly.

"We've talked to you about an acquaintance of yours at least once already. George Samson. Car thief," Genevieve said pointedly.

Jackson lifted his shoulders and shook his head. "I told you. We went to high school together. I throw him work on occasion."

"Are you sure about that, Jet?" Genevieve asked.

Jackson's eyes flicked toward Alex and then back to Genevieve. "I wouldn't know anything about how George Samson spends his time."

Genevieve picked up the papers in front of her and restacked them. "Wrong answer, Jet. Do you know what I have here?"

She picked up the first page and turned it toward him. "These are the phone records from your office phone line. On Wednesday, you received three calls from the same number within minutes of each other. You didn't answer the calls. Then several minutes later, you called that number from your office line."

Jackson shrank back from the table. "Nothing wrong with making a phone call."

"Very true. The person you called? George Samson. You keep telling us he's just an acquaintance. Someone you toss work to from time to time. Why do you talk to him so often?" she asked and pointed out the number on page after page of his phone records. "It looks like you talk to him every week, Jet."

"He's struggling. He needs work," Jackson said uncomfortably.

"He's a car thief," Genevieve said matter-of-factly.

Jackson's face paled. "G-G-George? No way."

Alex stepped up to the table. "I really don't like being lied to, Jet. Tell me, what are these cash deposits? You seem to deposit five hundred dollars in cash about once a week. What's the deal with that?"

Jackson looked up at Alex. "Some people pay for their cars in cash."

"But that would go in your *business* account, right, Jet? Not your personal account. There are pretty strict rules about that kind of thing," Alex reminded him.

"Oh, sorry. Of course. I thought you had my business account there. I see now it's my personal account," Jackson squirmed in his seat.

"And?" Genevieve asked. "What are the deposits?"

Jackson looked from Alex to Genevieve and back. "It's…the money…uh…it's not a big deal."

"Perfect. Where did the cash come from?" Genevieve asked.

He scrunched up his face. "It…it's a payment. I…" he sighed and tilted his head back. "Fine. It's from George. He pays me five hundred dollars any time he stashes a car at the lot overnight. I pretend not to notice it and he usually picks it up the next night."

"How did you have the keys to the Corolla then?" Genevieve asked.

Jackson ran a hand over his head and down his face. "Unbelievable. George makes copies. All the cars have fobs these days, right? If you know the VIN, you can easily make a copy. He leaves a copy for me in the drop box. It's the same box my mechanics return keys with…if I'm not in the office, they drop the keys in there. They all have a tag for each car. George's don't. One of the tags fell off the other day in the box. That's how I ended up with the wrong ones."

"You're telling us Mr. Samson stole the Corolla and made a copy of the key fob," Genevieve repeated.

"Yeah, but he didn't know about the body. He just stole the wrong damn car," Jackson said.

"Where is Samson now?" Genevieve asked.

Jackson shook his head. "I have no idea. I haven't talked to him."

Genevieve pointed at the phone records again. "I see a three-minute call here just after noon today. That sounds like a real conversation, not a missed call, Jet."

"He just told me he got cut loose and he was going to lay low for a while. I swear, I don't know where he is!" Jackson exclaimed.

"Where did he get the Corolla?" Alex asked.

Jackson shrugged. "I don't know where the stolen cars come from. He just finds cars he thinks are ideal for his chop shop operation. Usually, they're on the older side with some body damage. He thinks people are less likely to leave those locked or something."

"Where is his chop shop?" Genevieve asked.

Jackson put his hands up. "I have no idea. He just stashes the cars at my lot for a day or so. He can't steal the car and get it to the chop shop on the same night. Maybe it's far away. I haven't asked because I don't want to know."

"We appreciate you being candid with us, Mr. Jackson," Alex said. "Unfortunately, we are going to have to arrest you."

"What?! You said if I was honest and cooperated—"

"We will tell the district attorney how helpful you've been. You are under arrest for aiding and abetting," Alex explained. "Another unfortunate circumstance: it's after five o'clock, so you can't be arraigned until Monday. We're just going to have to hold you here over the weekend."

"You can't do that!" Jackson yelled.

"We can and we will," Alex assured him. "On your feet."

Chapter 9

As Bob drove toward Cari's grandmother's home, she realized he hadn't been to her house before. They'd met her halfway for dinner several times, but this would be his first time staying with her. It was also their first trip since getting married.

"What's on your mind?" Bob asked.

"I was just thinking. This is our first official trip as a married couple," Cari said with a smile and patted his leg.

"That's right. What's the bed like at your grandma's? Does she have decent pillows?" Bob asked and grinned.

She grimaced. "Oh, rats! I completely forgot about that. She has the worst pillows. Seriously, I think they were manufactured in the nineteen-twenties and run over by several trucks to get them extra flat. I can't believe I didn't grab our pillows. It could be rough."

"Are you for real?" Bob asked, concern written all over his face.

"They're really bad. Should we stop somewhere and buy a couple new ones?" Cari asked.

"I mean, will that hurt her feelings?" Bob wondered.

"I almost always bring my own pillow. I think she's come to expect that," she told him.

"Well, add it to our route. There has to be a Target or a Walmart somewhere along the way. We're getting close to her town, so maybe we'll pass one," he remarked.

Cari unlocked her phone and searched on the maps app for one of the businesses. "Looks like we're going to pass a Target in about two miles," she informed him. "I guess we should buy a couple pillowcases too."

"Those are going to stand out. They'll have creases from being folded in the packaging for months. Ha!" he laughed. "This is going to be quite the adventure in sleeping."

"I promise you, anything is better than what she has on her guest bed," she assured him. "Here's the exit for the Target."

Bob put on his blinker. "How much further to her house from here?"

Cari checked the GPS. "Seven miles or so."

"Do we get back on the highway?" he asked.

"It's faster. Otherwise, you have to stop at all the lights," she explained.

He pulled into the Target parking lot and picked a spot near a cart return. "In and out. We're just here for pillows and pillowcases."

She put her hand up like she was swearing an oath. "You have my word. No extras, except maybe a coffee."

He laughed. "Two pillows, two pillowcases, and two coffees."

"Oh! And we should get coffee for the apartment…we've been out for a few days," she reminded him.

"I'll allow it," he joked.

They got out of the car and walked inside. The overhead signs directed them to bedding in the middle of the store. There were multiple bins with pillows in both standard and king sizes. Cari picked one up and pressed her hand into it.

"This one seems pretty firm. It's not going to pancake under my head," she told Bob.

He reached out and picked up one like it. "Agreed. I can sleep on this. Where are the pillowcases?"

"Next aisle," she responded.

They walked over to the adjacent aisle. It had shelves and shelves of bedding in every color and design you could imagine. Their bedding at the apartment was blue and white. Cari picked up a set of pillowcases with light blue and white stripes.

"These could be backup pillowcases for our bed at home," she suggested.

"Works for me. Plus, since they're striped, the creases and folds will be harder to see," he said and grinned.

"I promise you, she won't care," Cari laughed. "Coffee?"

Bob nodded. They walked toward the checkout aisles. About halfway there, Cari saw a fake plant in a cute wicker basket.

"Maybe we should get Grandmother a little gift for having us?" she asked.

"That's not on the list," Bob reminded her.

"Look how cute it is!" she said and pointed at the basket. "Plus, it can't be killed."

"You're killing me. We have a four-item list. Plants are not on it," he said and laughed.

"Fine. No plant. It probably wouldn't fit in the car with the suitcase anyway. It's pretty tall," she admitted.

"Exactly. No room. Let's check out and get our coffees," he proposed.

"Deal," Cari agreed.

They went through the self-checkout line and then walked over to the Starbucks near the exit.

"What can I get for you today?" the barista asked.

"One tall black coffee and one tall latte, please," Bob requested and picked up a bag of ground coffee. "Plus a bag of coffee."

"Coming right up," she responded and scanned the bag.

"Have you always drunk your coffee black?" Cari asked while they waited.

Bob nodded slowly. "Yeah, it was bitter, but necessary in college. Late nights studying. I had to stay awake, but I'm not a huge fan of milk and didn't want to be downing a ton of sugar either."

The barista set his coffee on the counter and went back to making Cari's latte.

"I only started drinking it because everyone was always taking coffee breaks. Now, I'm fully addicted to the caffeine," she laughed. "I don't think I could take it black though. It's just too bitter."

"It's an acquired taste," he agreed.

"One tall latte," the barista said and handed Cari a sleeved cup.

"Thank you," she said and took a sip.

"Back to the car with our new pillows," Bob instructed.

"Onward," she replied.

They stuffed the pillows into the backseat and returned their shopping cart. Cari was excited to see Grandmother. It had only been two weeks, but she always enjoyed spending time with her. She buckled her seatbelt and settled into the passenger seat again. Her thoughts drifted to Grandmother's health. Cari hadn't had time to read about congestive heart failure much.

"Are you worried about your grandmother?" Bob asked as he pulled out of the parking lot. "You're rubbing your locket."

Cari looked down and released the necklace. "I am. I mean, I never thought she'd live forever, but heart failure seems bad. How long can someone live in heart failure?"

"Everyone is different. There is no cure, though. Only treatments," Bob explained. "Maybe she'll be more open to talking with you about it this weekend. I know she kept it under wraps during the wedding weekend. She probably didn't want people fussing over her when they were supposed to be celebrating you."

"Celebrating *us*," Cari corrected. "Mr. and Mrs. Hursley."

"That's my parents," Bob asserted. "You're still Turnlyle."

"That I am," she paused. "Is that okay? We never really talked about it."

"I'm happy with whatever name you choose. I'm just glad you're my wife," Bob said and grabbed her hand.

She squeezed his hand and released it. "Me too. It just feels easier not to change it. I'm kind of known as Cari Turnlyle."

"Then Turnlyle you shall remain," he said in an official-sounding voice.

"I love you, Bob Hursley," she said and smiled. "Oh, take this exit!"

Bob quickly turned on the blinker and steered the car down the exit ramp. "I'd prefer a little more warning, if possible."

"My bad," she apologized. "Turn right at the light. She lives about three blocks from here."

Cari's phone rang as Bob made the turn. Genevieve was calling. She decided to take the call and keep it short.

"Gen, what's up?" Cari asked.

"Hey, I'm trying to go through all the license plates that end in QI or QL that the rest of the team didn't get to yet. Want to join me? Grusky won't mind, but I can't pay you," she joked.

"Oh, bummer! I'd love to help, but Bob and I drove up to see Grandmother. Just a quick trip. We'll head back tomorrow after lunch," Cari explained.

"No worries. Alex told me I should take the weekend off too. I feel like I'm spinning my wheels. We really need to figure out who our victim is," Gen said and sighed.

"Someone will report him missing sooner or later," Cari said. "I've gotta go. We're just pulling up to her house now."

"Have fun with your grandma. I'll talk to you later," Gen replied and ended the call.

Cari directed Bob to her grandmother's house. He pulled into the driveway and turned off the car. Grandmother was watching from the window and came outside to greet them. They climbed out of the car.

"Wow! I didn't realize it was so cold out here. Hurry inside," she said and rubbed her arms. "Well, give me a hug first."

Cari hugged Grandmother and then opened the back door to get the new pillows. They were still covered in plastic wrap. Grandmother glanced at them, then looked away. Cari stifled a giggle.

"I'll get the suitcase," Bob offered. "Or do you need help with the pillows?"

"I can carry one pillow," Grandmother told him. "Let's get inside before we all freeze to death out here."

Cari led the way and held the door for her grandmother to get inside. It smelled like cinnamon and cloves inside, as though it was still Christmastime. Bob followed Cari into the house and closed the door behind them.

"The guest room is right over here," Cari said and pointed to the hallway.

"I put your new pillow on the bed. Do you want me to open up your new pillowcases and wash them for you?" Grandmother called out from the guest room.

Bob's face reddened. Cari kissed him on the cheek. "She's just teasing. I promise."

"We don't need to wash them. Thanks, Grandmother," Cari told her when she reached the room. "Have you eaten lunch yet?"

"I was waiting for my two lovebirds," Grandmother replied. "I didn't realize how cold it is outside. Maybe we should stay here and have a sandwich instead of going somewhere."

Grandmother barely got the words out before she started coughing. She put her hand up to say she was fine. Cari went to the kitchen and filled a glass with water. She rushed back to the guest room with it.

"Have a drink. Let's take a seat on the couch and discuss our lunch plans," Cari suggested.

"I'm fine. No need to coddle me," Grandmother insisted.

"How would you feel if I made some BLTs for lunch?" Bob offered. "I've got a pretty good recipe. Even Cari likes it…probably because I don't use lettuce."

"That's good. I'm all out of lettuce," Grandmother laughed and then started coughing again.

Cari looked at Bob with concern.

"I see that face, sweetheart. I'm just fine. People get old. I'm old. Let's go sit down while this boy of yours cooks us some lunch. You can tell me all about your latest story," Grandmother encouraged her.

They retreated from the guest room and Bob continued into the kitchen. Cari sat down next to Grandmother on the couch. She heard Bob opening and closing cabinets.

"Do you need help finding anything?" Cari asked over her shoulder.

"I found a frying pan for the bacon and a cutting board for the avocado…I think I've got it," he responded.

Grandmother patted Cari's knee. "So, tell me all about the story you're chasing right now."

"It's sort of stuck," Cari told her. "No one can figure out who the victim is."

"Not even Genevieve?" Grandmother asked with her eyebrows raised.

"She's working on it this weekend, but I don't think she's made much headway," Cari said.

"Both of you work too hard. I don't know if she ever takes time off. When was her last vacation?" Grandmother asked.

Cari thought about it for a moment. "I can't remember her ever going on vacation. You're right. She is always working. She really wants to get into the FBI, so I think she tries to be seen as reliable and dedicated."

"She's both of those things and more. She needs more balance," Grandmother remarked.

"Probably true for everyone," Cari agreed. She paused and grabbed Grandmother's hand. "I've been worried about you. How are you really?"

Grandmother patted Cari's hands with her free one. "I'm not dying today, sweetheart."

"What about your cough? Isn't there something you can take for that?" Cari asked.

"It's not really an infection. My heart is tired, so it isn't pumping enough blood anymore. That makes fluid start to build up in my lungs. I take a diuretic to try to clear that out, but then I get dehydrated, so I have to drink more water. If I eat too much salt, I retain more fluid. It's a lot to stay on top of," Grandmother told her. "I'm doing my best."

"Is there a…prognosis?" Cari asked uncertainly.

"The doctors say I'm at stage C, which is the third level of diagnosis," Grandmother informed her. "I've been taking medication for high blood pressure since I was in my mid-thirties and I guess that's a mark against me."

"How many stages are there?" Cari asked.

"Four," Grandmother responded.

Cari tried to blink back tears, but a couple slipped down her cheeks. "What does that mean?"

"It doesn't mean anything right now. I'm still here. I'm just a little out of breath and I'm no longer going to be a contender for the gold medal in the marathon," she said with a smile. "Enough about my health. I'm not going to live forever, but I'm going to keep enjoying life for as long as I can."

"Who is ready for lunch?" Bob called out from the kitchen.

Grandmother raised her hand. "It smells delicious. I have to warn you. I'm a little skeptical of a sandwich without lettuce."

"Don't be. Lettuce is the absolute worst," Cari said.

"I know you've always hated it," Grandmother said as she pushed herself up from the couch.

They sat down at the kitchen table and Bob placed a sandwich in front of both women. He had already filled three glasses with ice water and set them on the table too.

Grandmother took a bite. "I'm impressed. This is delicious!"

"Thanks. This is my new go-to sandwich if I have bacon on hand," Bob told her.

"Who doesn't have bacon on hand?" Grandmother asked with a grin. "I want to talk to you about a plan I've been cooking up since your wedding weekend. We had such a great time together and I want to do that more often. What would you think about going on a family trip to Hawaii? My treat."

Cari's eyes grew wide. "Hawaii?! Really?"

Grandmother's smile widened. "Yes! I've always wanted to go. I'd love to experience it for the first time with the people I love the most. I haven't mentioned it to anyone else yet, but I can't imagine anyone will say no to Hawaii."

"I'm in. When are we going?" Bob asked.

"I think Bea's children have spring break in April. She would probably prefer it if they didn't miss school," Grandmother replied.

"Count us in, Grandmother. I'm so excited!" Cari exclaimed. "Thank you."

"My pleasure," Grandmother responded.

* * * * *

The list of license plates felt endless. Genevieve had at first tried to narrow down the list by limiting it to men around six feet tall with brown hair and brown eyes. She quickly realized the vehicle could belong to the dead guy's significant other or friend, so that wasn't going to get her anywhere. It felt like a pointless task, but she didn't know what else to do. She decided to run a new search and ignore the possibly stolen plates for now. It was possible those plates weren't from the stolen Corolla. She opened the database and filled in the information she knew about the Corolla: dark blue, Toyota Corolla, 2017. She paused at the blank for county of registration. She decided to skip it for now. If the list was too long, she could go back and add their county. She clicked the search button and the results scrolled onto her screen. She sighed. New York had thousands of 2017 blue Corollas registered. She added the local county and tried again. The list decreased to twenty-seven.

"That's a little more manageable," she told herself.

Her cell phone rang and she looked at the screen to see who was calling: her brother. He never called. To be fair, she never called him either. She started to silence it and then thought better of it.

"Hey, Eric. What's up?" she asked her little brother.

"Not much. I wasn't sure you would answer," he replied. "Took you a bit to pick up."

"Sorry. I'm working on something," she explained.

"You work too much. Or that's what mom says. She told me she hardly hears from you anymore," he said.

"Is that why you called? To accuse me of neglecting our parents?" she asked. "The phone works both ways, you know."

"Chill. No. I have some news. Zoe and I got engaged," he said cheerfully.

Zoe? Genevieve didn't think she'd even met Eric's girlfriend, scratch that, fiancé.

"Wow! Congrats, Eric. I, um, I wasn't expecting that announcement," she confessed.

"You're so easy sometimes, Gen. I didn't get engaged. I'm not dating anyone. Not that you'd know. I got hired to be a chef at a restaurant near you. The Yellow Duckling. Have you heard of it? It's pretty upscale," Eric bragged.

Genevieve felt like she had virtual whiplash. "Wait, what? You're moving here?"

"Don't sound so excited," he grumbled. "Yeah, I'm the new sous chef at The Yellow Duckling. I start next week. Do you think I could stay with you until I get my own place? I can sleep on the couch. They're expecting a busy week around Valentine's Day and want me up to speed by then."

"Uh, sure, I guess. When are you arriving?" she asked.

"I'll be there by lunch tomorrow," he responded.

She blinked. "You're already on your way?"

"Well, yeah. I start on Monday, remember?"

"Right. I may or may not be home. Just call me when you're getting close," she requested.

"Are you working tomorrow too? I thought you might be able to show me some good apartments," he whined.

"I'm always working, Eric. It's part of the job," she reminded him.

"Well, give me a few hours. I've got a moving truck I need to park somewhere until I get my own place," he added. "Is it easy to get apartments in Brenington?"

Genevieve rolled her eyes. She wanted to get back to the license plates. "I don't know. I haven't gone apartment shopping in over seven years. I'm sure you can search online."

"Not while I'm driving," he reminded her.

"I'll try to see what I can find between now and then. I need to get back to work for now," she told him.

"Thanks. Guess I'll see you tomorrow," he said and ended the call.

She stared at her phone for a moment before setting it back down. Eric sounded kind of disappointed at the end. Maybe she should have shown more enthusiasm about him moving closer to her. She shrugged it off and went back to her list.

She wasn't sure how close to zero the chances were someone would report their vehicle stolen if they'd also hidden a dead body in it. It seemed like most people wouldn't want the extra attention. She felt pretty certain Samson had stolen the Corolla. She couldn't say if someone had directed him to the car to make it disappear or if he was just unlucky and stole a car with a dead body in it.

Genevieve saved the list of registered dark blue Corollas. She opened a new tab and ran a search for stolen dark blue 2017 Corollas in the area. The search returned six results. She'd been hoping for more, but she could work with this. She enlarged the first list and pressed control plus F to run a search within the list. She swapped over to the second list and highlighted the first name. She pasted the name into the Find window on the first list and hit return. Her computer highlighted the name on the list. She selected the entry and changed the text color to red. She repeated the process for the other five names on the stolen car list. She was down to twenty-one vehicles. Now she just needed to contact the owners.

She went back to her original search and clicked on the first name to get the owner's information. The computer opened a new window. She entered the number into her cell phone and hit talk. The call rang to the person's voicemail.

"Hi, Mr. Windham. This is Detective Viacorte with Brenington PD. I'm calling about your 2017 Toyota Corolla. If you could return my call, I would appreciate it," she said and recited her phone number for him.

She ended the call and went back to the search results. Part of her wanted to drive around and see if the cars were at the owners' homes. If the list had been shorter, she might have considered it. She clicked on the next name and repeated the process.

By the time she got to the eighth name on the list, she felt like she was beating her head against a wall. No one answered her calls and no one had called back yet either. She entered the next number and hit talk. The call connected and she took a breath as she got ready to recite her spiel to the voicemail service again.

"Hello?" a man's voice answered.

"Mr. Montgomery?" she asked.

"You got me," he responded. "Who's calling?"

"This is Detective Viacorte with the Brenington police department. I'm trying to track down the owner of a dark blue Toyota Corolla. Do you still own one?"

"I sure do. Very reliable car. You'd never guess it was ten years old," he replied.

Her shoulders drooped. "And you've driven the car in the last three days?"

"Of course. Was there a hit and run or something?" he asked with concern.

"No, nothing like that. I can't really get into the details. Thank you for your time. I'll cross your name off my list," she told him and ended the call.

Thirteen names to go. She pushed back from the table and went to the kitchen to refill her water bottle. She wished she could talk Alex into helping her. If she could knock the list down to five or six names, she could conceivably drive by those addresses to check if the cars were there or not. So far, she'd only eliminated one name. She wondered if anyone listened to voicemail messages anymore. If not, she was going to have to go visit each of the owners who didn't answer. If the state lab would take two minutes to find the VIN on the engine block, they could have the owner's name by now. She sat down at the table and punched in the next number.

An hour later, she'd only gotten through to three people. All of them assured her their cars were still in their possession. She didn't want to drive to eighteen addresses the next day, especially since she had committed to helping Eric look for an apartment. She needed a new approach while she waited for the Corolla owners to call her back.

She picked up her cell phone and called the station.

"Brenington PD. How can I direct your call?"

"Kurt?" Genevieve asked.

"At your service, Detective Viacorte," he replied.

"Any new missing person reports in the last day or two?" she asked.

"Let me see," he said. She heard him typing. "I've got a woman in her eighties. They did a silver alert for her…oh, wait. They found her. That's everything in the last forty-eight hours."

"Is that just for Brenington?" she asked.

"Let me expand the search," he offered. "Okay…what are you looking for?"

"Our vic is male, six feet tall, about one-eighty-five, dark hair, dark eyes," she told him.

"Males…in a fifty-mile radius…I've got sixteen for you in the last forty-eight hours," Kurt told her.

"Can you email the list to me?" she requested.

"Consider it done. Anything else?" he asked.

"That's all for now. Thanks, Kurt," she replied and ended the call.

Her laptop dinged with a new email. She clicked on the message from Kurt and opened the attachment. It would take some time to go through the list. She still had the seven names from before that they'd cross-referenced with DMV records for a Corolla. She frowned. It was a faulty assumption to eliminate names just because they didn't own a blue Corolla. They needed to compare the victim's fingerprints or DNA with the missing persons list.

She leaned her head back and groaned. She felt like her search was worse than one step forward, three steps back. She wasn't making any progress on identifying their victim. Even if some of the people on the missing persons list had their prints in the system, she would need someone from CSU to help her compare their prints with the victim's prints. The CSU team had people on call, but not to do grunt work like this. She'd get in trouble if she called any of them to help her sift through the prints. She closed her laptop. They needed to catch a break in this case, or they were never going to find the killer.

She picked up her phone again and called Alex, even though she knew he'd berate her for working on the weekend. He answered after three rings.

"I thought you were going to send me to your voicemail for a second there," she told him.

"I thought about it," he confessed. "What are you working on today?"

"I started to go through license plates. I narrowed the results down to twenty-one owners who haven't reported their blue Corolla stolen," she told him. "I called each of them, but only three answered. I left a voicemail with the others. Hopefully, they'll return the call soon. In the meantime, I called the station to get an updated missing persons list."

"What are you going to do with that?" he asked.

"Nothing. I need CSU to help me and I can't call them in for that," she grumbled.

"So, you're just venting?" Alex asked in an amused tone.

"No, I had another idea. I think I know how we can lure Samson into a trap," she replied.

"This weekend?" he asked.

"No, we'll do it on Monday morning, but I might call around to get it set up this weekend," she remarked. "I'm planning on stopping by the floral shop tomorrow so I can talk to the ex-girlfriend. I thought I might be able to talk her into contacting Samson for us."

"Why would she do that?" Alex asked.

"She's a concerned citizen. I don't know. I thought she could call him and say she found something of his in her belongings. Something of value like a thumb drive or credit card…" she trailed off as she brainstormed.

"What if she refuses?" Alex sounded doubtful.

"We can get Olivert to reach out to Samson and say he got something important delivered to his trailer," Genevieve answered.

"Like what?" Alex asked, sounding interested.

"What about back wages or something? Like a check from his most recent employer. He can say he opened it because it looked important. Then he can suggest they meet somewhere so Olivert can deliver it to him. We'll meet him instead," Genevieve explained.

"That could work. Do you think Olivert will do it?" Alex asked.

"He will. I'll tell him we know he took the license plates and he'll get charged as an accessory if he doesn't help us out," she told him.

"Keep me posted…scratch that. Just call me if something doesn't work out. Not until Monday, right?" Alex asked.

"Yeah, we can wait until Monday," she assured him. "Thanks, Alex."

"Take a break. Enjoy the weekend! Watch the Pro Bowl or something," he responded and ended the call.

* * * * *

Normally, Genevieve was irritated when she woke up before her alarm went off. She had a long list of things to do before her brother arrived with his moving truck. She still didn't know where to stash that. Maybe they'd luck out and find an apartment he could move into immediately.

She picked up her phone and turned her alarm off. No missed calls while she was asleep. Two people had returned her call before she went to bed the night before. Both of them assured her their Corollas were parked in their driveways. That left sixteen house calls. She checked her weather app. It was too cold to run outside. She thought about skipping a treadmill run, but it was too early to knock on people's doors. She quickly changed into her running gear and grabbed her water bottle. She decided to climb the stairs to warm up rather than take the elevator. It didn't matter how good of shape she was in, climbing stairs always left her winded. She swiped her resident card at the gym entrance and went inside. The place was deserted, which was just how she liked it. She hopped on a treadmill and gradually increased the speed.

The gym televisions were all set to ESPN. The talking heads were discussing the Pro Bowl, which was set to kick off later that day. The sound was off on the TVs, but the closed captioning was on. She watched the words scroll across the screen as she pumped her arms and legs. Everyone seemed excited about some of the first-time Pro Bowl players. She wondered if Alex was watching. She figured he valued his sleep more than football stats. Her phone rang when she reached 3.5 miles. She answered it while slowing the pace to a walk.

"Detective Viacorte," she answered.

"Oh good. I was worried I might wake you up. I'm returning your call about the Corolla," the woman's voice said. "Uh, this is Paula Atwood."

Genevieve decreased the speed to zero so she could focus on the woman's words. "You're still in possession of the 2017 Corolla?"

"Uh, yeah. It's a very reliable car," Paula responded.

Genevieve put the call on speaker for a moment so she could make a note to cross the Atwoods off her list. "Sounds good. Thanks for returning the call."

It was almost 7:30, so she slowed the treadmill to a stop and stepped off of it. By the time she showered and got dressed, it should be late enough to knock on the Corolla owners' doors. She took a drink of water and left the gym. She took the stairs again as she hated riding in the elevator when she was sweaty, especially if someone else got on with her. She unlocked her apartment and set her water bottle and phone on the table. Just as she reached the bathroom, her intercom sounded. She hurried over to the door and pressed the button to respond.

"204?"

"Gen!" Eric practically shouted into the microphone. "I drove all night. My moving truck is parked outside your complex along the curb. I didn't think it would fit in one of the spots here and I was right. Buzz me up?"

"You...drove...all...night?" she repeated in a confused tone. "Right, uh, yeah. Come on up. I need to take a shower. I just finished running."

She hit the button to let him into the building and waited by her door. Less than a minute later, she heard his footsteps. She looked through the peephole to confirm it was him and then opened the door before he could knock and bother her neighbors. He was six years younger than her, but a foot taller. His chin-length dark hair was tucked behind his ears. He took off his coat, revealing several new tattoos on his arms. She tried not to stare.

"Wow, you do need to shower," he said and scrunched up his nose. "Do you not wear deodorant when you exercise? Gross."

"Good to see you too," she said and locked the door behind him. "Make yourself at home. I'm going to shower."

"Got any eggs?" he asked. "I could make us some omelets."

"Knock yourself out. I'll be fast," she told him.

She grabbed a change of clothes from her bedroom and went to the bathroom. Eric had managed to completely disrupt her day. She frowned. She should feel happy he wanted her help. Instead, she was annoyed she had to pause her investigation.

Chapter 10

After spending the majority of the day helping Eric find a place to live, Genevieve was more than ready for work Monday morning. Eric was still asleep on her sofa when she woke up. She left him a note with a spare key and reminded him to lock the door on his way out. She stepped outside and discovered it was snowing. From the looks of it, it had been snowing for a while; there was at least an inch or two on the ground. She looked at her footwear: dress shoes were not going to work today. She snuck back into her apartment, and saw Eric sitting up on the sofa, rubbing his eyes. This was sure to delay her by several minutes.

"Back so soon?" he asked groggily.

"It snowed. I need to change my shoes," she explained. "I left you a spare key. Are you going to visit more apartments this morning?"

He pressed the home key on his phone. "How early do most offices open? I have to report to the restaurant at ten."

She stifled a groan. At this rate, he was never going to find a place to live. "I'm not sure. Maybe call around. Or maybe some of the other restaurant staff will have suggestions. Wait. Isn't The Yellow Duckling closed on Mondays?"

He nodded. "They aren't open for food service, but they do prep for the following day. I have to sign some papers and stuff. Meet some people. You know."

"Okay. Well, I'm going to change shoes and be on my way. Good luck with everything," she said and retreated to her bedroom.

She kicked off the dress shoes and pulled on her fleece-lined boots. She put her dress shoes on her shoe rack and closed the closet door. Eric was staring at his phone screen.

"Cool, this place opens at 8:30. Maybe they have an apartment I can afford," he said cheerfully. "Also, I found the letter from the restaurant owner showing I've been hired and my salary. That should help grease the wheels a little today."

"Oh, good. I'm sorry to desert you, but I'm right in the middle of this investigation. Hopefully, the snow won't slow us down much. We're probably going to have to track down the owner of the stolen car by driving to their homes or workplaces. I'd rather not do it in a blizzard," she said as she reached for the doorknob.

Eric held up his phone. "My weather app says it will be sunny and windy in just a few hours."

She smiled. "Good. Thanks. See you later. Let me know what your plans are for dinner."

He gave her a thumbs-up as she exited the apartment. She couldn't help herself and locked the door with her key.

"I'm not a child you know," he called out from inside.

"Love you too," she said and stomped off to the stairs.

The roads were still clear, which felt like a good sign. It was just after seven o'clock, so she figured she had close to an hour to organize everything before Alex arrived. Her jaw dropped when she entered the parking lot and saw his truck already parked there. She parked next to him and hurried inside. The sky was dropping huge wet snowflakes on her. She hoped Eric's weather prediction would prove to be true.

Alex was at his desk when she reached the detective bay. He had a mug of coffee up to his mouth and was looking at his computer screen. She waited until he set the mug down to speak.

"You're here early," she remarked.

"Couldn't sleep knowing you'd spent the entire weekend working to get ahead," he said with a smirk.

"Very funny. For your information, I spent nearly the entire day with my little brother yesterday," she said smugly.

"You have a brother?" he said with genuine surprise.

"Yeah, he's a chef. Just when I think he doesn't have room on his arms for another tattoo, he goes and proves me wrong," she said with a laugh.

"Sounds like you two couldn't be more different," he replied. "So, you didn't make it to the floral shop to talk to Dunleavy?"

She shook her head. "I didn't get to track down all the Corollas either. I crossed a handful off the list. I keep rolling it around in my head. Did someone whack this guy on the head and stuff him in his own trunk? Did someone whack the guy and stuff him in their trunk? Then Samson stole the vehicle? Did someone pay Samson to steal the vehicle? I feel like I'm going around in circles."

Alex held up a sticky note. "Well, this might help."

She stepped closer and took it from him. "Reginald Black? The name isn't familiar to me at all."

"He was *just* reported missing, so he's probably not on any of your lists yet," Alex suggested. "Regardless, Mr. Black was reported missing by his employer this morning. He also happens to drive a dark blue 2017 Corolla."

Genevieve felt goosebumps rise on her arms. "Let's go see if he's playing hooky. I assume the address is his?"

"One and the same," Alex responded. "Let's take my truck. It has four-wheel drive and it's newer than your clunky Expo. I don't want to drive one of the cruisers in snow. Accident waiting to happen."

"Deal," she said. "Can I get a cup of coffee first?"

"On your desk," he said and grinned.

She looked at her desk and saw a mug. "You even remembered the milk!"

"And the honey. I'm a good partner," Alex reminded her.

"I'll keep you around. Especially now that you can use Google," she said and picked up the mug. "But seriously, thanks for getting me a coffee. Let's go see if we can find Mr. Black."

"By the way, I put in the paperwork for Jackson's charges when I got here too," he informed her. "I think he'll be arraigned later today. Hard to say."

"I wonder if Samson has realized we scooped up his friend," Genevieve remarked.

"Who knows? Let's go see if Mr. Black is at home. Then we can worry about finding Samson. Maybe Black's our guy and we can get on with the murder case and let someone else take over on the car theft," he said as they exited the detective bay.

They got outside and she was relieved to see the snowflakes weren't quite as large as they had been fifteen minutes earlier. Maybe the weather would let up. Alex unlocked his truck and they climbed inside.

"Do you need a step stool to get in? I might have one in the back," he teased.

"Hilarious. Glad you still have a few short jokes rolling around up there," she said and rolled her eyes.

"I'm here to entertain," he replied. "Pull up the directions?"

"Sure," she said and took out her phone.

She entered the address into her maps app while Alex backed out of the spot. "Left out of the parking lot. The house is over on the west side of town."

"Got it," he said and turned left.

"Tell me about the missing person report. When was he last seen?" she asked. "Right on the next street…at the light."

"He hasn't been at work since last Tuesday, so that fits with our timeline," Alex told her.

"They're just trying to find him today?" Genevieve asked in surprise. "Why hasn't anyone else noticed he's missing?"

"They said something about him taking some vacation time, but there was some confusion about that. Dispatch took the information and called your work phone since you've been bugging them about missing people. I picked it up since I was there. I called the employer to get more of the backstory," Alex explained. "They said he'd requested time off, but it had been for Thursday and Friday, not Wednesday. When he didn't show up on Wednesday, they gave him the benefit of the doubt. Maybe he had his dates messed up and didn't realize he blocked off the wrong ones or something. He was supposed to be at work at seven o'clock this morning. They tried to call him and it went straight to voicemail."

"What time did they call? 7:01?" she asked with a sneer on her face.

"More like 7:10," Alex responded.

"I mean, I get that he's late, but good grief. Is there no grace period? Where does he work?" she asked.

"He's a paralegal. They said he has been taking classes to get his law degree. He wants to move up within the firm, but couldn't afford law school straight out of college," Alex remarked.

"What about his emergency contact?" Genevieve asked. "Make a left at the stop sign."

"That went to a disconnected number. They said he sometimes made mistakes with numbers, so it might have been a simple error on his part," Alex told her.

"Sounds fishy," Genevieve said. "Has he ever skipped out on work like this before?"

"Never. They said he's one of their most reliable employees," Alex said.

"Turn left on the next street. His house is the second one on the right," Genevieve told him.

Alex pulled up to the curb in front of a one-story house. It had tan siding and a turquoise door with a wreath on it. They got out of the truck and walked up the sidewalk. Genevieve rang the bell and knocked.

"Brenington PD. We're here for a well-check for Mr. Reginald Black," she said loudly.

They heard footsteps and a deadbolt disengage. The door opened slowly. A young woman with sand-colored hair and big brown eyes stood before them. She was about the same size as Genevieve, but wore more makeup than she'd seen on anyone since the nineties.

"Mrs. Black?" Alex asked.

The woman blinked. "Is everything okay?"

"Is your husband home?" Genevieve asked. "His office reported him missing."

"He's out skiing. He was supposed to be back last night. I figured he got snowed in," she replied. "Did you want to come inside?"

She stepped back from the door. They walked into the small house, which was furnished with well-worn furniture. The love seat had a few snags in its fabric along the base, and the two upright chairs were frayed where the fabric connected to the wooden legs. Genevieve stood next to the love seat while Alex moved further into the room and stood by the fireplace. A tabby cat slinked into the room and scratched at one of the chairs.

The woman scolded the cat. "Jasper! Stop it!"

The cat looked back at her and then returned to scraping its claws along the chair leg. She hurried over and scooped him up. The cat squirmed, but she held him tightly.

"Have you heard from your husband, Mrs. Black?" Alex asked with his hands in his coat pockets.

She shook her head. "He is a cross-country skier and he likes to go up into the boonies where there isn't any cell reception. I usually don't hear from him the whole time he's gone."

"And when did he leave on the ski trip? His office was under the impression he wasn't taking off until Thursday, but they said he missed work on Wednesday too," Genevieve explained.

The woman nodded her head slowly. "He must have forgotten to call and add the extra day. He ended up leaving Tuesday night instead of Wednesday after work. He was worried he might miss the big snow if he didn't leave a day early."

"We understand you own a dark blue 2017 Toyota Corolla. Did he take that vehicle skiing?" Genevieve asked.

"Sort of. He drives it to a parking lot and then gets picked up by the ski resort shuttle. It's in Vermont. He stays in one of their cabins," she responded.

"There's no Wi-Fi calling from the cabin?" Alex asked in a surprised tone.

"Beats me. I've never gone with him. There isn't much to do up there if you don't ski. That's what he tells me anyway," she explained.

"Can you give us the address of where he parks the Corolla?" Genevieve asked.

The woman nodded slowly. "I think I can find it. Just one moment."

She pulled her cell phone from her back pocket and unlocked it. Her thumbs tapped on the screen a few times. She held up her phone. "Here it is."

Genevieve took out her phone and snapped a photo of the address displayed on the screen. "Thanks. By the way, uh, your husband's employer tried to reach out to you, but he has the wrong number entered on his employee records for his emergency contact. You might want to have him update it. Saves everybody a trip."

"He has a tendency to mess up numbers sometimes. I'll call later and give them the correct number," she promised.

"Can we get the name of the resort?" Alex requested.

"Uh, sure. It's…right on the tip of my tongue," she said and scrunched up her face. "If you hadn't asked, I could have told you. It's not far from Burlington. Like I said, I've never been before. How many ski resorts could there be in Vermont?"

Genevieve blinked. "I couldn't say really. I don't ski."

The woman stared at them for a few moments. "Sorry, I can't think of the name…it's just…I realized you said you're detectives. Why did they send detectives out for a well-check?"

Genevieve took a breath and let it out before responding. "I'm not sure if you've heard, but a body was found in a trunk at a local used car lot. We're trying to identify the victim. I'm not saying it's Mr. Black, but if we could get something of his, like a hairbrush to compare with the DNA of the victim…"

The woman dropped the cat and it yowled in protest. "Dead…body? You think Reggie was killed?"

"No, we don't really know, Mrs. Black. We're trying to narrow it down. It sounds like your husband just got caught in the snowstorm. We just need to eliminate him from our list of possible victims," Alex explained.

"Of course. Let me see what I can find," she said. Her voice sounded distant, like she was thinking about something else as she spoke. "I'll be right back."

She left the room and they heard a drawer squeak open in the bathroom. It squeaked closed a few seconds later. The woman reappeared in the hallway with a toothbrush in her hand.

"Will this work or does the fluoride damage the DNA?" she asked.

Genevieve nodded. "That should do the trick. You can put it in here."

She held out an evidence bag and the woman slipped the toothbrush inside.

"You'll let me know when you get the results?" the woman asked.

Genevieve sealed the bag. "Yes, one of us will give you a call or come by to let you know."

The woman nodded. "Anything else?"

Genevieve pulled out one of her cards. "This is my number. Please give me a call when you hear from your husband or if you remember the name of the ski resort."

"Of course," she replied.

Alex opened the front door and they walked down the sidewalk back to his truck. Genevieve turned and looked back at the house before she climbed into the vehicle. She saw the curtains flutter and wondered if the woman had been watching them walk away.

"What?" Alex asked once they were in the cab.

"There was something familiar about that woman," Genevieve said. "I can't put my finger on it."

"Probably her height. Was it weird finally meeting someone over the age of twelve who isn't taller than you?" Alex teased.

"Wow. Two short jokes in one morning," she joked. "And, no, it wasn't her height. Something about what she said or how she said it…? I just can't place her."

"In all seriousness, it seems odd she wasn't worried about him not being home yet," Alex remarked.

"Right? That whole conversation felt off to me," Genevieve agreed.

"Should we confirm the Corolla is in the lot?" he asked.

Genevieve looked up the address. "It's sixty miles away and on the edge of the city. I'd rather not sit in rush hour traffic. Let's request the traffic cam footage. We can confirm he arrived when she said and that the vehicle is still there."

"Good call," Alex replied.

"I'd like to see if we can get Dunleavy to coax Samson out of his hiding spot before we head back to the station," she said as she took out her phone to put in the request.

"Do you think she's working today?" Alex asked.

"I'd rather not call ahead and scare her off. She probably can't miss too many shifts and still have a job. Let's just show up and hope for the best," she responded. "We're already out anyway."

"Flower shopping it is," he replied. "Maybe I'll get an arrangement for Sophia."

"Don't commit to that yet. When I looked them up, I saw their price range. Not at all cheap. The owner clearly views her work as art," Genevieve cautioned. "We should get a unit to come get the DNA sample. Green can start running it to see if it's a match while we try to connect with Dunleavy."

"Tell them to meet us at the flower place. We'll be there shortly," Alex suggested.

Genevieve pulled up the lieutenant's number and hit the call button. "Hey, LT. I have a couple requests if you have a minute."

"Go ahead," he replied.

"We need a unit to meet us at The Budding Artist to collect some evidence for a DNA sample," she said and explained where it came from. "We also need some traffic cam footage from a park 'n ride near the city. I'll text you the address. We need it for last Tuesday evening through today, if possible."

"Will do. Any update?" he asked.

"We visited the spouse of the missing person. She thinks he's snowed in at a ski resort in Vermont, but can't be certain as the reception there is poor. We're still trying to locate Samson. His ex works at this flower shop, so we're hoping she might be able to tell us where he's hiding," Genevieve told him.

"Good luck. Let me know if you need anything else from me," Grusky said and ended the call.

She texted him the address as Alex drove down the street toward The Budding Artist. The snow still wasn't sticking to the road. Genevieve watched the flakes kiss the windshield and get smeared across the glass when the wipers swept by them. If it was snowing in Brenington, she figured it was probably snowing more in the mountains. Maybe Reggie Black *was* just unable to get home until the storm cleared. She wished they could have laid eyes on him, but his wife wasn't worried until they mentioned the dead body, so maybe it was a regular weekend at the Black house.

* * * * *

Morning came too early for Cari. They'd gotten home a little later than they planned from Grandmother's. Cari had been reluctant to leave; her grandmother seemed more lonely and frail than she had in the past. She silenced her alarm and rolled toward Bob to say good morning. He was already out of bed.

"Bob?" she called out.

"Mmrshing feef," came the response from the bathroom.

"Brushing your teeth?" she laughed.

She got out of bed and joined him in the bathroom. He was dressed in his usual button-up shirt and khaki pants with loafers. It had been a few weeks since he'd gotten a haircut and she could see some of his normally close-cut hair starting to curl. She reached up and patted his head.

"Starting to grow some curls there, Hursley," she commented.

"I made an early appointment for today to take care of that," he said after rinsing his mouth. "That's why I'm up so early."

Cari yawned. "I'm tired. I think I need to start going to bed earlier or something."

"Don't forget, you promised Bea you'd pick Hilary up from the dance team tryouts this afternoon," Bob reminded her. "4:30 at her middle school."

"Right. Thanks. I'm pretty sure I put it in my calendar, but it's always good to have it on my radar too," Cari replied. "Hopefully, Bea will get released to drive again soon."

"It could be a few more weeks. She's dislocated her shoulder so many times, the ligaments are getting pretty loose. She really needs to let it heal before she takes off the sling," he pointed out.

"It must be such a pain for her not to be able to drive herself places," she said. "I think my mom almost decided to stay another week after the wedding to help out."

"Your dad couldn't take any more of the winter weather though. Ha! I think it's over seventy down in Florida today. Meanwhile, it's snowing here," Bob told her.

"Snowing?! Really?" she asked.

"It hasn't accumulated much, but it's coming down," he assured her.

"Maybe they have a snow day and I'll be off the hook from my pick-up duties," she said hopefully.

"No way. We don't live in the south. This is nothing," Bob laughed.

Cari kissed him on the cheek and went to the kitchen to look out the window. Sure enough, big white flakes were falling from the sky. She strained to see the ground below, but it was blocked by their balcony. She thought about stepping outside for a better look, but her feet were bare and she was still in her pajamas. She poured herself a cup of coffee and added milk to it. When she opened the pantry to get out the honey, she remembered she'd used all of it the last time. Bob joined her and poured himself a cup too.

"Darn. We're out of honey. I'll add it to the grocery list. Guess I have to sweeten this with sugar today," she told him.

"Hard times for sure," he teased. "What are you up to today?"

She thought about it. "I'm trying to find a new lead to chase down. As far as I know, they haven't identified the body yet."

"I haven't seen anything," he told her. "Someone will eventually realize he's missing and call it in."

"Until then, I'm sort of spinning my wheels. I'm thinking about reaching out to Samson's ex-girlfriend again. She might know where he goes when he's trying to lay low," Cari remarked.

"Not a bad idea. Well, I've got to get to my haircut. I'll talk to you later," he said and tipped his head down to kiss her. "Love you, Cari."

"Love you too," she replied after they kissed.

"Don't forget Hilary," he said over his shoulder.

"Right. Hilary. I won't," she promised.

Cari didn't feel like trying to make it to the yoga class, so she took another drink of coffee and returned to the bathroom. She was about to turn on the shower when she heard her phone vibrating with an incoming call.

"Kirsten? Is everything okay?" Cari asked.

"I'm sorry to call so early, but I thought you should know this," she paused. "George texted me last night. He told me not to talk to the police. He insisted they were trying to frame him for murder."

Cari raised her eyebrows. "Have you spoken with the police?"

"No, I've been avoiding the flower shop since they tried to talk to me there last week," Kirsten explained.

"Kirsten, do you know where George hides when he's trying to stay out of trouble?" Cari asked her.

"I don't think George is ever trying to stay out of trouble," Kirsten responded. "But he has some guys who will let him crash on their sofas if he needs to."

"Do you know their names?" Cari pressed her.

"I just know they're friends of his…guys he used to work with before he got fired, or just people he knows," Kirsten said. "I'm not sure what to do, though. I need to go to work, or I'll lose my job. What if the police try to find me there again?"

"The detectives are honest people, Kirsten. They aren't going to frame anyone," Cari assured her. "You said George wasn't a violent person, but it sounds like you're afraid of crossing him. Why is that?"

Kirsten was silent for a few moments. "George was good to me. He gave me a place to live and food to eat. I don't want to betray him."

"I get that. Do you think he would watch the flower store to see who talks to you?" Cari asked.

"That feels too risky for him," Kirsten responded. "I'm sure he realizes they'll talk to me…that's why he texted me."

"Kirsten, you said you didn't want to betray George, but you still called me to tell me he'd contacted you. That doesn't quite track for me," Cari told her.

"Ugh," she groaned. "I know. I just…I don't want him to get hurt. If the police think he's violent or capable of murder, they might use more force to bring him in."

"Are you telling me you know where he's hiding?" Cari pressed her.

Kirsten didn't speak for several seconds. Cari held her breath and tried to will her to share the information.

"He has a friend who runs a laundromat. There's an apartment above it. I'd bet money he's there," Kirsten told her.

"Thanks, Kirsten. You're doing the right thing," Cari assured her.

"Just keep me out of it," Kirsten pleaded.

"We never talked," Cari replied and ended the call.

She looked at the time. It was almost eight o'clock now. She figured Bob was probably finished with his haircut, so she hit the talk button next to his name.

"I'm just walking out of the barber shop. I figured you'd be in the shower by now. What's up?" Bob asked when he answered.

"I got a call from the ex-girlfriend. She thinks she knows where Samson is hiding," Cari replied and relayed the conversation to him.

"What are you going to do?" Bob asked. "I don't really like the idea of you trying to bring in a known car thief, especially if he has a temper."

"I don't like that option either. I'm going to call Gen. They need to know where he is," Cari replied.

"Sounds good. They might need a warrant if the friend won't let them enter the apartment," Bob hypothesized. "If the person is a known associate of Samson's, it shouldn't be hard for them to get it."

"Right," Cari responded. "I guess I don't need to keep you posted. You'll probably hear about it before I do."

"Love you. Stay safe," Bob said.

"Love you too," Cari said and ended the call.

She found Gen's name in her contacts list and called her next. She thought about texting, but felt like it was more urgent than that. The call connected to her voicemail. Cari ended the call. She scrolled up the list to Alex's name. She'd gotten his number the summer before when she was trying to help Bob's aunt track down an intruder. Her thumb hovered over the call button. Alex had seemed to be more open to her involvement in their cases lately. She knew she wasn't his favorite person. She pressed her thumb down and waited.

* * * * *

Genevieve climbed back into the cab of Alex's truck. Judith, with CSU, waved goodbye as she drove away with Mr. Black's toothbrush. She heard a ringing sound come over the car's speakers.

"Is that a Bluetooth call?" Genevieve asked incredulously. "You have Bluetooth now too? Am I awake?"

She pinched herself while Alex glared at her from the driver's seat.

"Your friend is calling me. I'm guessing she called you first, but you didn't pick up," Alex grumbled as he accepted the call. "Turnlyle, we're about to go interview a witness. This better be important."

Cari's voice reverberated through the cab of the pickup. "I'm so glad you answered. Are you with Genevieve?"

"We're both here, Cari," Genevieve replied.

"Great," Cari said quickly. "Are you still looking for Samson?"

"Yeah, he cleared out of his trailer and no one has seen him since," Alex told her.

"Right. I heard about that," Cari paused. "I have a source who told me where he probably is."

"I'm not going to bother asking who the source is," Alex muttered. "Where is Samson hiding?"

"The apartment above the laundromat on Grand Avenue," Cari answered. "The manager of the laundromat lives there. I was just looking up his name on my laptop while we were chatting."

"Did you find it?" Genevieve asked.

"Reid with an 'I' Chenal," Cari replied. "He doesn't have a record from what I can see on LexisNexis."

"I'm looking him up right now," Genevieve told her. "Yeah, he's squeaky clean. I'm not sure he'll let us in. Thanks, Cari. Anything else?"

"My source swears he isn't violent," Cari said slowly. "They are concerned because of the nature of the crimes, he might get hurt when you go pick him up."

"We aren't going to shoot our way in," Alex retorted. "We know how to handle Samson. Thanks for the tip. We'll take it from here."

Alex ended the call and looked at Genevieve. "Call Grusky. See if he can put a rush on a warrant for us. Probable cause. Chenal is a known associate. I'm going to radio for backup, just in case."

Genevieve pulled out her phone. She swiped the missed call from Cari away and pulled up their lieutenant's name. He answered immediately.

"Lieutenant Grusky," he said. "What do you need?"

"We need a warrant," Genevieve told him. "We have reason to believe Samson is hiding out in an apartment on Grand Avenue."

She explained the details and gave him Chenal's name.

"Okay, got it. I'll call the judge now. If he signs off, I'll send it electronically to your phones," Grusky said. "What else?"

"Runimoss is requesting backup. We don't see him as a violent offender, but we don't want to lose him if he takes off either," she informed him.

"Okay. Roger that. I'll be in touch," Grusky responded and ended the call.

"I asked dispatch to send a couple units to the side streets near the laundromat. I don't want to spook him," Alex said.

"Good call. Let's go see if we can find him," she said and put her phone back in her coat pocket.

Alex put the pickup in reverse and backed out of the parking spot. They'd been parked next to the floral shop, waiting for it to open or for Dunleavy to arrive for her shift so they could intercept her and talk to her. A white SUV entered the lot and parked next to them. Genevieve watched as they drove past to see if it was Dunleavy in the driver's seat. A much older woman with salt and pepper hair stared back at her. Genevieve looked away. She figured she must be the shop owner and turned her attention back to finding Samson.

"It might take Grusky some time to convince the judge to sign off on the warrant. Do you want to try talking Chenal into letting us search the place for Samson without it?" she asked Alex.

He frowned. "As much as I'd like to just go in and get him, I think it's better if we give Grusky a chance with the warrant first. Chenal can't say no to that."

"True. So, we sit and watch the laundromat until we hear from him?" she asked.

"Yeah. Maybe the judge will see the logic and we'll have a warrant by the time we get there," he hypothesized. "Or maybe we'll have to beg Chenal to give Samson up."

"We can always threaten him with aiding and abetting," Genevieve suggested.

"True," Alex agreed.

It took them about fifteen minutes to reach the laundromat. They parked across the street and used binoculars to look into the windows. Two people were inside putting clothing into machines. The lights were on, but the blinds were closed in the apartment above the business. Genevieve had her phone out and kept refreshing the app for her work email.

"Anything?" Alex asked after putting the binoculars down again.

"Nothing yet," she responded. "It's only been twenty minutes. It probably took him close to ten just to get the paperwork together."

"True. It would have taken me longer," Alex remarked.

"You'd barely have the man's name on it at this point," she laughed and pantomimed hunting and pecking on a keyboard with her index fingers.

"Not everyone is good at typing," he argued.

"Clearly," she said with a grin.

She refreshed the app again. A little number one appeared next to the word inbox. She clicked on it. "We got it. Let's go get Samson."

Alex turned off the truck and they unfastened their seatbelts. "Our vests are in the backseat. I know they say he isn't violent, but we should never assume."

"Agreed," she said and reached into the back of the cab to get the smaller vest.

They took off their coats and strapped the vests on. Genevieve always found them uncomfortable and was glad they rarely needed them. She tightened the straps and pulled her coat back on.

"Ready?" she asked him.

Alex picked up the radio. "Be advised. Runimoss and Viacorte are approaching the apartment. Watch the front entrance for Samson exiting."

"Unit one, copy that."

"Unit two, copy that."

"Ready," he said and opened the door. "The apartment entrance is probably in the back. See the stairs on the side of the building?"

She looked at the laundromat. A metal staircase ran up the side of the brick building. There was a small landing at the top.

"The black door is the entrance to the apartment?" she asked him.

"I assume so. There might be an entrance inside too, but I'm sure it's harder to access," Alex remarked.

They crossed the street and started to climb the staircase. Genevieve could feel the cold of the metal railing through her gloves. The stairs were slick from the snow melting and freezing. She could see a puddle near the entrance to the apartment and wondered if there was ice on the landing too. They reached the top and Alex pounded on the door.

"Brenington PD. We have a warrant," he announced.

Genevieve tried to listen for signs of life inside the apartment, but the wind was howling too loudly. The door had a metal handle instead of a knob. She saw the handle twitch as though someone had gripped it on the other side. Seconds later, the handle dipped down and the door swung open toward them. They had to take a step back to keep from getting scraped by it. A man in a grey sweatshirt and jeans stood in front of them.

"Mr. Chenal?" Genevieve asked and held up her badge. "Detectives Viacorte and Runimoss. We're looking for a friend of yours. George Samson."

The man's eyes flicked over his shoulder and back to hers. "I'm Reid, yeah. Uh, did you say you have a warrant? I don't want any trouble."

She took out her phone and held up the screen for him to see the electronic document. "We're only here for Samson."

Chenal stepped back so they could enter. "He's asleep on my futon."

Genevieve and Alex walked past Chenal and into the apartment. They found themselves in the kitchen. It opened up to a hallway on one side and a living room on the other. Samson was blinking himself awake as they approached. Chenal remained in the kitchen. Samson's eyes bored into Chenal as he sat up.

"What the hell, Reid? Why'd you tell them I was here?" Samson grumbled as he stood up. Genevieve was relieved to see he was fully dressed, minus socks and shoes.

"They have a warrant. What was I supposed to do? I only said you could crash here, not that I'd hide you from the police," Chenal told him.

Alex locked a cuff around Samson's right wrist. "George Samson, you're under arrest for grand theft auto, specifically, the theft of a 2017 Toyota Corolla—"

"I already told you! I didn't steal that car!" Samson yelled.

"You have the right to remain silent," Alex continued.

"This is a frame! I didn't steal a car. I didn't do it!" Samson shouted some more.

Alex finished the Miranda warning as he clamped the other cuff onto Samson's left wrist in front of the man's body. Genevieve looked around the room for Samson's footwear, but didn't see any shoes.

"Mr. Samson, where are your shoes today?" she asked.

"I think I saw them in the bathroom with some socks," Chenal said from the kitchen. "Should I get them?"

"I'll join you," Genevieve replied. "Which way?"

"You're going to help the cops escort me out of here? Some friend you are," Samson said and spat in Chenal's direction.

"Hey! What the hell? That's disgusting, man," Alex said as he dodged the spittle. "No more spitting."

Chenal led Genevieve down the hallway to the bathroom. Just as he'd said, a pair of old sneakers and dingy white socks were on the linoleum floor. Genevieve pulled a pair of gloves from her pocket and then picked them up.

"Shoes and socks, Mr. Samson," she said as she placed the items on the floor in front of him.

"How am I supposed to put those on with these cuffs?" he whined.

"I think you can manage," Alex said as he helped Samson sit on the futon again.

Samson awkwardly struggled into his footwear. Alex pulled him to his feet. Samson was wearing a green and black flannel shirt over some sort of rock band t-shirt. Genevieve couldn't see the whole name.

"That's his backpack on the floor by the futon too," Chenal pointed out.

Samson's eyes grew wide. "Are you for real right now?"

Chenal shrugged. "Your mess, your problem."

Genevieve picked up the grey backpack and unzipped it. It had a laptop, a power cord, and some crumpled papers inside. There was also some sort of electronic device and a small cardboard box. She opened the box. Inside were black key fobs. She held the box up for Alex to see.

"Look, he has his own little fob factory in here, Runimoss," she said with a grin.

"Be careful with that. It's expensive!" Samson snarled.

Genevieve slipped it back into the backpack and zipped it up. She could still hear the wind and realized Samson wasn't wearing a coat again.

"Do you have a coat, Mr. Samson?" she asked.

"I got my flannel. It's fleece-lined," he responded.

"Okay. Let's go. Mr. Chenal, a copy of the warrant will be mailed to you for your records. Thank you for your cooperation," Alex said as they passed the man in the kitchen. Chenal only nodded.

They got Samson into the back seat of Alex's truck and buckled him in. Genevieve joined him on the passenger side. Alex took out his phone.

"Hey, LT," he said. "We got Samson back. Thanks for the help with the warrant. We'll be at the station shortly."

Alex slid his phone into his pocket and climbed into the driver's seat. "Like we told you, you don't have to talk to us. We were hoping you'd tell us where you found the Corolla last week, though."

"What's it worth to me?" Samson asked.

"The way it stands right now, you're the last person who saw the man in the trunk alive, so you're probably going to get charged with murder too," Genevieve explained. "Personally, I don't see you as a killer, but I've been wrong before."

Alex shook his head. "She's almost never wrong."

Samson frowned. "Who ratted me out?"

"We're not going to tell you that," Genevieve responded.

"I bet it was Jet. He's such a coward," Samson grumbled. "What kind of deal will you give me if I tell you where I got the car?"

"That's up to the DA," Alex told him.

Samson remained silent and looked out the window. Genevieve realized it had stopped snowing while they were in Chenal's apartment. Maybe the sun would come out soon. She kept her eyes on Samson. He turned from the window and looked at her.

"Fine. I'll tell you where I got the car, but I want the DA to take some time off the auto theft charges," Samson said.

Genevieve locked eyes with Alex when Samson said the word charges in plural. She wondered if they were going to discover more car thefts when they looked at his laptop.

Samson started talking again. "Also, did you say 'grand theft auto' when you cuffed me? I didn't use a gun or force. I'm not a monster."

Genevieve suppressed a smile. "Mr. Samson, grand theft auto is a lesser crime compared to carjacking, in which the assailant uses force or threatens bodily harm to the owner who is present at the time of the theft."

"Oh, news to me," Samson remarked.

Alex pulled into the parking lot at the precinct. "We'll get you set up in an interview room. Is there a lawyer you'd like us to call?"

Samson shook his head. "No. Just get the DA here. Tell them how cooperative I'm being."

Chapter 11

Samson seemed much more relaxed in the interview room than he had the previous week. Genevieve and Alex watched him through the two-way mirror. He drummed his thumbs on the table and bobbed his head along to a song only he could hear in his head.

"He waived his right to counsel. We can talk to him. I want to know where he got the car," Alex told Genevieve.

"True. I feel like he's less angry today too. Let's see if he'll give us the address where he found the car," she replied.

Alex opened the door just as Genevieve's phone vibrated with an incoming call.

"It's Green," she said as she swiped her thumb across the screen to accept it. "Dr. Green?"

"Detective Viacorte. Caught you away from your desk. I have good news for you, bad news for Mr. Black. We have identified our victim," Dr. Green reported.

"Okay, wow. Thanks for running that so quickly," she said and ended the call.

"It's Black. He's the vic. Let's see if we can get Samson to admit to finding the car at the park 'n ride. Maybe there's blood in the parking lot still," Genevieve said to Alex.

"We need to notify his wife too," Alex reminded her.

"That will have to wait. I'm sure she isn't expecting to hear from us a few hours after we were at her house," Genevieve hypothesized. "Let's talk to Samson first."

They walked down the hall to the interview room. Samson sat up straight and stopped drumming when they entered the room.

"DA here?" Samson asked.

"Not yet. We are recording your time in here, so anything you say to us, they can review later," Alex explained. "We've identified the body; we need you to tell us where you found the car."

"Sorry. I'm not talking until the man in charge is here to listen," Samson said and tried to cross his arms across his chest.

"This doesn't feel like cooperative behavior to me," Alex remarked. "Did you steal the car from a park 'n ride?"

Samson's face clouded. "A park 'n ride? Stop. I'm not talking without the DA here. Stop wasting my time."

"Our crime scene unit is reviewing the surveillance footage from the parking lot. If we see you stealing the vehicle, any hope for a deal is going to go out the window," Genevieve cautioned him.

Samson rolled his eyes. "Do you hear my words? I don't know anything about some random parking lot. If a car was stolen from there, then it wasn't me who took it."

Genevieve sighed and left the room with Alex. She closed the door and made sure it locked.

"Do we wait for the DA or go inform the wife?" Genevieve asked.

"Let's do a little more research first. You know my rule. It's always the spouse," Alex reminded her. "We need to know a little more about her before we question her about her husband's murder."

"Agreed," she responded. "Maybe the DA will get here before we go. I'd hate to make the wife feel like we suspect her of murder when it was really something that happened far away from here. She seemed really shook when we mentioned the dead body."

"Yeah, the cat too," Alex quipped.

They returned to their desks. Genevieve logged into her computer and accessed their database. She entered Reginald Black into the name boxes and Brenington, New York, as his place of residence. Their victim's name was the first one on the list.

"Okay, so this tracks with what we know. He's a paralegal. He's worked for the same firm for about a decade. He is a virtual student at one of those online universities, so it sounds like he is trying to finish law school," she informed Alex. "His record is clean. He's never even gotten a speeding ticket. Huh."

"What?" Alex asked.

"It says he isn't married," she replied. "I guess the woman we talked to never identified herself as Mrs. Black. I thought she called him her husband though, right?"

Alex scrunched up his face. "We definitely referred to him as her husband. She never corrected us. Maybe they just live together?"

"What was her name?" Genevieve asked.

"We called her Mrs. Black. She never said anything to the contrary," Alex replied.

"Rats. I wonder who she is. Something about her seemed so familiar when we were talking to her," Genevieve said again.

Genevieve's desk phone rang. She looked at the caller ID and saw it was Bob on his CSU line. "Hey, Bob, get anything from the parking lot cams?"

"I don't think you're going to like it, but we've reviewed all the footage from Tuesday evening through Wednesday morning. No blue Corollas show up," he informed her.

"Weird. Thanks, Bob," she said and put the receiver back in its place. She looked at Alex. "The Corolla never parked in the lot. It wasn't there Tuesday night or Wednesday morning. Either she lied to us or Samson carjacked him between his home and the park 'n ride. We need to figure out who she is. Did the missing person report give a name for his emergency contact?"

Alex sifted through the papers on his desk. "I took some notes when dispatch called. They forwarded me the report, so it's probably in my email…here's my notes…let's see. No, I didn't write down a name. Let me pull up the report."

He unlocked his computer and clicked on the email icon. "Here's the report. They didn't give the name of the contact either."

"Rats. I feel like we know next to nothing about both of them," Genevieve remarked. "I'll look up a reverse address search and see if her name comes up. I'd really like to know more about both of them before we do a notification. My gut says she lied to us."

Alex ran a hand over his face. "I can't believe I'm saying this, but get Turnlyle to do some research on this guy. Talk to his co-workers. You're right. People are more apt to talk to a reporter than they are to one of us. They feel like they're snitching if they say something bad about their friend to the police, but they're just gossiping a bit if they tell it to the journalist."

Genevieve raised her eyebrows. "You're like an entirely different person. This is the second time you've suggested we collaborate with Cari. Where is the real Alex and what have you done with him?"

"Funny. I'm serious. We're almost a week into this thing and we just identified the victim. We need all the information we can get, so let's get Turnlyle to dig up some more dirt for us. She has resources we don't have," Alex retorted.

"I'm not arguing. Let me text her," Genevieve said quickly.

She pulled out her phone and composed a text to Cari. After hitting send, she opened a new window in the database. She entered Black's address into the appropriate field and hit enter.

"I knew I'd heard her voice before," Genevieve told Alex.

"What?" he asked.

"Black's girlfriend or whatever she is. I talked to her yesterday. She's one of the people I called about the stolen Corolla. She said her name is Paula Atwood. I think her dad owns the Corolla or maybe he was the original owner. The name I crossed off was a Miles Atwood," Genevieve explained.

"Interesting," Alex responded. "And odd that she didn't mention talking to you already."

"You said Black owned the Corolla though," Genevieve said in confusion. "He wasn't on my list."

"Oh, I did say that, but that's just what the employer reported when they called about a missing person. They said he drives a dark blue Toyota Corolla. They didn't say he owned it," Alex clarified. "We just assumed he did."

* * * * *

Cari's phone buzzed with a text.

ID'd the dead guy. Reginald/Reggie Black. Office called him in as missing. DNA matches. PS Thanks for the tip on Samson.

She smiled. "Reginald Black. Who are you?"

"Turnlyle! I thought we were on the same page here!" Ollaman said as he burst into the newsroom from the elevators.

Cari rose from her desk. "Sir?"

"Jet spent the whole weekend in lockup. How could you let that happen?" Ollaman asked. His face was red and his eyes were angry.

"Was he charged with something?" she asked her boss quietly.

"Aiding and abetting a criminal," Ollaman barked. "That Samson fellow. They're saying Jet let him stash stolen cars at his lot."

"I haven't found anything that contradicts that narrative, Mr. Ollaman," Cari replied gently. "Jet went to high school with

206

Samson. I don't think they were close exactly, but they definitely knew each other."

Ollaman looked over her cubicle wall at her desk. "Who is Reggie Black? Is that the real killer?"

"No, this is the victim from the trunk. I'm doing a deep dive on him. I'll let you know what I find," she promised.

"I can't believe Jet's in jail…" Ollaman muttered as he slunk off to his office.

Cari rolled her eyes. She pushed Ollaman from her mind and went back to the name Reggie Black. She logged into LexisNexis to figure out where he worked. Beechman, Bortles, and Stowe. She hadn't heard of them, but quickly figured out it was a law firm. Black was a paralegal. She wondered if he had a secretary or someone he worked closely with.

"Only one way to find out," she said to herself.

She locked her computer and collected her things. She hoped the snow had let up. The law firm wasn't too far away. In the summer, she might have considered walking, but with slick sidewalks and a biting wind, she had no intention of arriving on foot. She pressed the button to call the elevator and the doors opened immediately. She rode it down to the parking garage and hurried to her vehicle. She tossed her messenger bag into the passenger seat and started the car. The vents blasted her with cold air, so she hit the button to turn the fan down until the car was warm.

Cari took her phone from her bag and plugged in the address for the law firm. It was about four blocks away. She realized she'd driven past it almost daily and they had a parking garage attached to their building too. She put her car in reverse and backed out of her spot. It took her less than five minutes to repark her car in the law firm's garage. She got out of the car and put her phone back in her messenger bag. The wind cut across the open-air garage and she wrapped her arms around herself to stay warm. She was able to park on the same level as the entrance. She hurried through the garage and sighed in relief once she was inside.

"Can I help you?" the receptionist asked her from behind the large desk. She was close to Cari's age with a reddish-pink streak in her hair. She'd braided the streak alongside some of her dark hair, which sort of made it less noticeable. Cari wondered if the firm didn't like the custom color job. The woman looked to be of Asian descent and wore rimless glasses with pink earpieces. She also had on a headset with a microphone.

"Yes, I work for the Beagle. I understand Mr. Black hasn't been at work for several days?" Cari asked as she approached the desk. "Is this a normal behavior for him?"

The woman narrowed her eyes. "Who told you he wasn't at work?"

"A source," Cari said with a smile. She'd let the detectives inform Black's employer of his death.

"Slow news day?" the woman retorted.

"It happens," Cari said noncommittally. "Do you know Mr. Black?"

"Mr. Black is an exceptional employee of this law firm. We sincerely hope he is found unharmed so he can continue completing the excellent work we have come to expect from him," the receptionist replied as though she were reading from an official statement.

An older woman came out to the desk from the wood-paneled wall. Cari hadn't realized there was a door in the wall until it opened. The woman looked at Cari and then handed a large envelope to the receptionist. Cari read the return address on it. The older woman whispered something to her while keeping her eyes on Cari.

"If one of Mr. Black's co-workers could spare a few minutes to tell me about him…" Cari added before the other woman walked away.

The older woman paused. "Did they find Reggie? Is that why you're here?"

The receptionist rolled her eyes. "She's with the newspaper, Gladys."

"Oh, I thought maybe…never mind," Gladys replied.

"Do you work with Mr. Black…uh, with Reggie?" Cari asked.

The older woman glanced at the receptionist and then retreated through the wooden door. Cari pulled out a business card and placed it on the receptionist's desk.

"If anyone feels like talking about Reggie, please have them call me," she requested.

The receptionist looked at the card but didn't take it. Cari turned around and walked back out to the parking garage and her vehicle. She realized the law firm employees were probably well-versed in not talking to the press or the police. She needed to regroup or try calling his direct line. That might get her connected to his secretary. She got back in her car and turned it on to stay warm. She looked up the law firm's website and found the division she'd seen on the envelope in the older woman's hands. Intellectual Property. She looked at the phone number and then scrolled down to another division to see if the phone number matched.

"Perfect," she said as she scrolled back up to Intellectual Property.

She touched the number and it pulled it up in her phone app. She hit the call button and waited for it to connect. After two rings, she got an automated message.

"You have reached the intellectual property office of Beechman, Bortles, and Stowe. Please enter your party's extension if you know it now. You can press zero to speak with our administrative assistant at any time."

Cari pressed zero on the number pad and heard the ringing sound. A woman answered.

"Intellectual Property at BBS, this is Gladys. How can I help you today?"

"Hi, Gladys. My name is Cari Turnlyle. I'm a journalist with the Brenington Beagle. Do you have a moment to answer some questions about Reggie Black?" Cari asked.

"Oh, you're the woman who was just here. Um, well. I suppose…can this be off the record?" Gladys asked.

"Of course," Cari assured her.

"Well, Mr. Black is one of our paralegals. Don't get me wrong, he's a great employee. He writes very well and helps our clients get everything they need and more," Gladys told her.

"But…" Cari prodded her.

"Well, his office is closest to my desk. I often hear him yelling at his…I think she's his girlfriend. I don't think they're married, or maybe she just didn't take his name?" Gladys hypothesized. "Anyway, he really tears her down and says awful things to her. Then half an hour later, he'll call back and apologize. He'll ask me to order flowers to be delivered or chocolates. He'll promise to never do it again…that if she were just less sensitive…well, I think they call it gaslighting? Is that right?"

"Sounds like the right word," Cari agreed.

"Oh, I have to go," Gladys said quickly and ended the call.

Cari looked at her phone screen for a moment and then found Genevieve's name. She touched the call button and waited for it to connect.

"Cari! That was fast. Did you find something?" Genevieve asked her.

"I just spoke with his secretary. She described some phone conversations between him and his live-in girlfriend. It sounds like, at the very least, he was verbally abusive to her," Cari informed her friend. "Have you looked up his background? Any domestic violence calls?"

She heard Genevieve typing. "Hmmm…I've got a few calls from their neighbors complaining about noise. Loud arguments. No citations though. There's a note here…we sent some officers to the house. It was quiet when they arrived. Resident answered the door and assured them everything was fine. They'd dropped a cup of hot chocolate and it shattered…burned the female inhabitant on her left forearm. It was already bandaged. That's it."

"Do you really think you could hear someone drop a mug of hot cocoa from next door?" Cari asked in a skeptical tone. "I'm going to go talk to the neighbors. If they've called, then they have stories to tell."

"Keep me posted. We're waiting for the DA to arrive so we can finish interviewing Samson," Genevieve told her. "This information makes me want to go talk to the lady of the house again. I think she may have spun us a tale when we were there before."

"Talk to you later," Cari said and ended the call.

She opened her internet browser again and logged into LexisNexis to find Black's address. It wasn't too far away. She made sure her phone was linked to the Bluetooth and got the directions pulled up on her car's dashboard screen. She hoped Black's neighbors were home and would talk to her.

* * * * *

The assistant district attorney, Emily James, finally arrived. Alex and Genevieve spent half an hour bringing her up to speed on the case. She was new to the office and they hadn't presented a case to her yet. Genevieve wondered if she was someone who wanted an airtight case before bringing charges.

"What's your theory?" James asked them. "You still have a lot of gaps to fill in from my perspective."

"Samson has been adamant from day one that he didn't kill anyone. I'm inclined to believe him," Genevieve admitted. "It is possible he's escalated from grand theft auto to carjacking, though."

"Is he dumb enough to leave his prints and the dead body where they'll be easily discovered just a few hours later?" James asked.

"Just to recap, we know Black never reached the park 'n ride, so he was either killed at home or somewhere between there and the parking lot," Alex pointed out.

"We have a source who has overheard Black talking to his live-in girlfriend and felt like he was verbally abusive," Genevieve added.

"That falls under he-said, she-said," James argued. "What else?"

"The noise complaints. The Blacks' neighbors called a couple times about loud arguments. We only sent units once and it turned out to be nothing," Genevieve explained. "When you couple that with the phone conversations, it does make you wonder."

James nodded. "Okay, let's go see what Samson will give us."

They walked to interview room one and Alex unlocked the door. He held it open and then followed his colleagues inside. Genevieve joined the ADA at the table while Alex leaned against the wall.

"Mr. Samson," James began. "I'm ADA James. I understand you'd like to make a plea deal. Would you like to have a lawyer present?"

"Nah. I don't know any lawyers. Don't trust them. No offense," he replied.

"None taken," she assured him. "Now, we have a dead body in the trunk of a 2017 Toyota Corolla found with your prints at a used car lot. Explain to me how your prints got on the vehicle. Dishonesty will end this conversation. Got it?"

Samson's eyes widened. "What kind of deal are you going to offer me? Immunity?"

James' face remained neutral. "Mr. Samson, I think we both know that was never on the table. I'm prepared to offer you leniency on your sentence in exchange for your full cooperation."

"Like time served?" Samson asked.

"You're trying my patience, Mr. Samson," James said crisply. "From our perspective, you were the last person in contact with the deceased last Tuesday night. Unless you can shed some light on the circumstances, I'm prepared to charge you with murder."

Samson's eyes shifted from James to Genevieve. "Whoa, hold up. You're not trying to pin that on me now too, are you?"

Genevieve glanced at James before responding. "We're here to listen to your side of the story. You said you didn't kill anyone. Tell us what happened. How did your prints get on the car? Where did the car come from?

James remained silent, but Genevieve saw her hand tighten on the pen hovering over the notepad in front of her. She hoped she didn't offend the woman. Samson chewed on the inside of his cheek for a moment and then licked his lips. He finally let out a sigh and opened his mouth to speak.

"I didn't kill anybody. I took the car. I'd seen it a few weeks before. It's older, which makes it fit into my demographic better," Samson told them. "It's worth less, so it's a lesser charge in the long run."

Genevieve nodded in understanding.

"Anyway, I knew it was an older model Corolla. I watched the owner's habits with it for two or three weeks. He always got home by six o'clock in the evening. He never left before six in the morning. That gave me a good twelve hours to sneak it off his property," Samson said, counting on his fingers.

"Last week, I waited until it was dark. There was a new moon and it was cloudy, so it was extra dark. I got to the guy's house at about eleven, maybe eleven-thirty. I could see the VIN on the windshield, so I used my box and made myself a fob for the locks. Opened it up and hit start. Easy as pie," Samson said somewhat proudly.

"So, you removed the VIN at some point?" Genevieve asked.

Samson lowered his eyes for a moment before responding. "I have to. I need it to be hard to trace if someone finds it before I get it to my guy," Samson explained.

Genevieve started to ask a question, but James nudged her leg under the table, so she stayed silent.

"And the location of the vehicle?" James reminded him.

"Oh, right. Uh, it's over in the kind of mid-range neighborhood on the west side of town. I'm not sure I know the exact address, but I could show you on a map," Samson replied.

Genevieve pulled out her phone and opened her maps app. "Is this the area?" she asked as she enlarged a neighborhood.

"Yeah, that's it. Is it okay if I touch the phone?" Samson asked.

"Go ahead," Genevieve nodded.

She noticed an incoming call flashing on the top of the screen. She didn't recognize the number, so she swiped it away and then tilted the screen so Samson could access it. Samson zoomed in on the area a little more until he could see specific streets. He shifted the map to the left a bit and then down. "There you go. It's the one with the blue-green door."

Genevieve felt goosebumps rise on her arms. James seemed to sense Genevieve's response and put her left hand up to signal she wanted to speak. "Perfect. Thank you for the information. My clerk is currently going through your laptop. You kept very good records of the vehicles you…shall we say 'processed' over the last year or so. I think I should be able to talk the district attorney into cutting a few years off of your sentence for your help here today."

A voicemail notification pinged from her phone as she delivered the news to Samson.

Samson's face clouded. "You tricked me! This is entrapment! I only admitted to taking one vehicle! I want a lawyer now."

"That's within your rights. Who would you like us to call?" James asked.

"You said you could appoint someone to me. How does that work?" he asked.

"You're asking for a public defender?" James asked for clarification.

"Yeah, one of those," Samson confirmed.

"I'll make some calls. Pleasure doing business with you," she said and stood up from the table. "Before I go, you mentioned you have the name of the guy you deliver these vehicles to. I might be able to broker a deal for you if you'd be willing to share his name and location with us."

"What kind of deal? Immunity?" Samson asked.

"Are you saying you're interested?" James asked him.

"I don't want to go to prison. Yeah, I'm interested. Can you still get me that lawyer? I don't want you to try to pull another fast one on me," Samson requested.

James nodded. "Let me talk to legal aid and we will get someone over here for you ASAP."

"I still think it's garbage that you tricked me into confessing. I want a lawyer who can get that thrown out!" he exclaimed. "Oh, and I don't want the same guy you sent over last week. He was trash."

"I'll see what I can do," James replied glibly.

Samson glared at the three of them as they exited the interview room. Genevieve didn't feel the least bit guilty for ambushing him with the extra charges. He was a criminal; he deserved to be punished.

* * * * *

The Blacks' neighborhood was quiet when Cari arrived. She drove past their house and pulled along the curb. She didn't want to interview the victim's girlfriend; she wanted to talk to their neighbors. Genevieve said there had been noise complaints; Cari just needed to find out who was lodging them.

She reached into her messenger bag and turned on her digital recorder. It was just after three in the afternoon. She wasn't sure if she'd find anyone at home, but it was still worth a try. She locked her car and walked up the sidewalk to the Blacks' next door neighbor's house.

The neighbors had a camera attached to their alarm system, so Cari knew they'd been alerted to her presence by the time she reached the front step. She pressed her gloved finger against the black circle and watched the white light brighten around it.

"No soliciting unless you have a permit," a voice said through the doorbell camera system.

"I'm not a solicitor," Cari responded. "I'm a journalist. I'd like to ask you some questions about your neighbors, the Blacks."

The wind gusted. Cari turned her face to the right to avoid some of the chill. She heard footsteps inside and a deadbolt releasing. A woman in her late fifties opened the door and stepped back to let Cari inside. The woman had on neon pink fuzzy house slippers, black leggings, and a white oversized knit sweater. Her short curly hair was mostly grey with the occasional strand of black. She had brown skin and big brown eyes with crow's feet at the corners of her lids.

"I know you," she said as Cari entered her home. "You're the Turnlyle woman. The writer for the Beagle who helps the police department solve murders. Was someone murdered?"

"Hi, I'm Cari. And you are?" Cari asked her.

"Larissa Nosten, N-O-S-T-E-N, but the t is silent," Larissa explained. "Would you like something to drink? Hot tea?"

"That sounds perfect," Cari agreed.

"Join me in the kitchen. I just put my kettle on before you rang the bell. It should whistle soon. I think there's enough in it for two cups," Larissa told her.

Cari followed her into the kitchen. It was decorated with black and white tiles and neon pink towels. She wondered if neon pink was making a comeback from the eighties.

"Have a seat," Larissa said and pulled out a chair.

The table and spindle chairs were painted black. A square white lace tablecloth hung perfectly over the table with each point ending at one of the four chairs. Cari took a seat while Larissa took another mug from a cabinet.

"Do you take sugar or lemon in your tea?" Larissa asked.

"Just plain is great. Thanks," Cari responded.

"You wanted to talk to me about my neighbors. Reggie and Paula, right?"

Cari nodded. "Are they married?"

Larissa shook her head and gave her a conspiratory look. "No! I thought they were when they first moved in, but neither of them wears a wedding ring. I asked Paula about it once…I didn't mean to be nosy. I think it hurt her feelings."

"What do you mean?" Cari asked.

"I think she was embarrassed to be living with Reggie when they weren't even engaged. She told me they'd been together for a while, but Reggie wanted to get his law degree before they got married. He has a multistep plan, I guess," Larissa explained.

Larissa seemed eager to share every detail she knew, so Cari pressed her for more. "Do they seem happy to you?"

The tea kettle let out a shrill whistle, which made them both jump. Larissa got up and poured the hot water into the two mugs. She added a tea bag to each one and set them on a silver tray. She placed the tray on the table and handed one of the mugs to Cari before sitting down in her chair again.

Larissa took a sip before meeting Cari's eyes again. "When I first met them, I would have said yes immediately, but the longer they've lived next to me…well, I don't think it's all roses and champagne over there."

"Say more," Cari requested.

"I hear him yelling at her a lot. Several months ago, I heard her shriek in pain. I swear to you, I heard it. I called the police that time. They told me she'd dropped a cup of cocoa on her arm and burnt it. Felt like a full-on lie to me. I think he hit her. She used to rarely wear makeup. She went natural, but lately, she has it caked on. She wears long-sleeves year-round, even when it's over ninety degrees out. It's not normal. It's what someone does when they're trying to hide the scars of abuse," Larissa insisted. "I'm not the only one who's noticed. Phyllis Mendelez, who lives on the other side? She asked me about the same thing just a week ago. She thought Reggie was hitting Paula."

Cari felt her stomach drop as the woman's words poured out. What a terrible situation to be in. She'd never known a victim of abuse. "How awful," she said finally. "Have you tried to talk to her about it?"

Larissa's shoulders slumped. "I've thought about going over there and confronting her…offering her an escape. Every time I'd get my courage up to go over, *he'd* be there. I didn't want to get hit too. I called the police a few times. I thought they might be able to intervene."

"You have to look out for yourself too," Cari agreed.

"You never answered my question," Larissa remarked. "Was someone murdered? I noticed Reggie hasn't been home since Tuesday. I haven't seen Paula either. Oh my goodness. Did he kill her? Is that why you're here? This is all my fault."

"Larissa, no. Paula is fine. No one killed her," Cari said and patted the woman's hand.

* * * * *

A white Lexus was parked in the Blacks' driveway when Genevieve and Alex returned to the house. She made a note of the license plate in her notebook. The sun was shining now; the driveway was wet in places from the dusting of snow that melted in place. She was glad the roads hadn't frozen over and it hadn't snowed for hours and hours. She looked down the street and saw Cari's tan Camry parked along the curb.

"Who do you think is visiting this afternoon?" Alex asked.

"Could be anyone. Maybe she needed a friend to sit with her after learning Black might have been murdered," Genevieve suggested. "I wonder if Cari is getting anything useful from the neighbors."

"Who was calling you during the interview?" Alex asked.

"Ugh," Genevieve groaned. "An apartment complex. Eric needs me to co-sign the lease."

"Risky business: family and money," Alex remarked.

"Tell me about it. Maybe I can get away with just doing it for a month. I don't really want to ruin my credit if he flakes on the rest."

"Good luck with that," Alex replied and then gestured to the Blacks' house. "Shall we?"

They walked up to the front door and knocked again. Genevieve heard a heavier set of footsteps approaching the door. It swung open. An older gentleman in a brown cable sweater over a pale blue button-up shirt and dark khaki pants stood before them. The sweater seemed too large for him, hanging past his wrists and covering half of his hands.

"Detectives?" the man asked.

They held up their badges for him to see.

"And you are?" Genevieve asked.

"Miles Atwood. I'm Paula's father," he told them. "Please come in. I take it if you're here, you don't have good news for Paula."

"Is Paula home?" Alex asked him.

"Yes, she's in the living room," Atwood replied and stepped back so they could enter.

Paula Atwood was seated on the love seat next to Jasper, the tabby cat. She offered them a half smile as they entered the room. Her father tried to shoo the cat off of the furniture so he could sit next to his daughter, but the cat ignored him. He sat on the arm of the love seat instead.

Genevieve sat in one of the upright chairs, but Alex remained standing. "Ms. Atwood, we've received confirmation from our medical examiner. The DNA from Reggie's toothbrush matched that of our victim. We're very sorry for your loss."

The woman's eyes filled with tears. She blotted at them with a tissue. "He was in the trunk of the car?"

"I'm afraid so," Genevieve said and nodded.

Mr. Atwood tried to lean over the cat to drape his arm over his daughter, but the cat swatted at him with its claws out. He got up and walked to the other side of the love seat.

"Can you think of anyone who might want to hurt Mr. Black? Someone who had been threatening him?" Genevieve asked.

Tears continued to fall from the young woman's eyes. She blotted at her face repeatedly, but couldn't keep up.

"No, I can't. Reggie had a lot of boundaries. I don't know his co-workers; he never talked about them. No one ever called and yelled at him or anything though," she explained and sniffled.

"Do you have any suspects?" Mr. Atwood asked.

Before they could respond, the young woman let out a wail. Her shoulders shook as she sobbed. She tried to blot at the tears before they hit her cheeks, but Genevieve was certain she was smearing her makeup in the process.

"Let me get you a glass of water," Genevieve offered and stood up.

The kitchen was just behind the living room in a somewhat open floor plan. The cabinets wrapped around the space with an arched entrance just past the love seat. She walked up to the cabinet nearest the sink and opened it. It was filled with all shapes and sizes of cups and glasses. She grabbed a large plastic one with "UCONN Huskies" printed on the side and filled it with water from the tap. The toe of her boot nudged something. She set the cup on the counter and bent down to look at what she'd bumped. A small dark turquoise pottery shard was under the lip of the cabinets. Genevieve felt the hair on the back of her neck lift; the ceramic bit represented the puzzle piece that made everything else fall into place. She took a photo of it with her phone and then pulled a glove from her pocket and picked it up. She didn't have an evidence bag on her and she wanted Alex to see it.

"Alex, I'm too short to reach the glasses. Could you come give me a hand?" she called out to him.

"Be right there," he responded.

The Atwoods didn't seem to register her request; the father was still comforting his sobbing daughter. Genevieve held the piece of pottery out to show Alex when he reached the kitchen. He stepped closer.

"That looks like what Green found in the victim's pants cuff," he agreed. "Reggie Black died in this kitchen on Tuesday night."

"But who killed him?" Genevieve whispered.

Alex raised his eyebrows. "Let's go find out."

Genevieve wrapped the glove around the shard and slid it into her coat pocket. Alex grabbed the cup of water and they returned to the living room.

"Here you go. Have a drink," Alex said when they'd returned to the living room. "Take a deep breath."

"Maybe you should come back later," Mr. Atwood suggested. "I don't think she's going to be very helpful right now."

"I'm afraid we can't do that, sir," Alex responded. "Mr. Black was killed almost a week ago."

"She's distraught. She doesn't know anything," Atwood insisted.

The cat hissed at Alex. He glared at it.

"Again, we're very sorry for your loss. We just have a few questions," Genevieve said gently. "When did you last see Mr. Black?"

Paula dabbed at her eyes one more time and then put her hands in her lap. Her mascara was smeared under her eyes, which were red and puffy.

"He came home from work on Tuesday. Then he decided to leave early for the ski trip, like I told you earlier," Paula insisted.

"He left after dark?" Genevieve asked.

"I tried to talk him out of it, but he wanted to get an early start on Wednesday," Paula explained.

"What time was that?" Alex asked.

"I'm not sure. Maybe eight or eight-thirty?" Paula offered.

Alex nodded. "Was anyone else here with you when he left?"

"No, it was just me," Paula answered. "We don't have any children. We're not married. Reggie wanted to wait until he finished law school and passed the bar exam."

"It's good to have a plan," Genevieve agreed.

"Do you think someone killed him to get his car?" Mr. Atwood asked.

Alex turned to look at the older man. "Isn't it really your car, Mr. Atwood?"

The man's face paled. "I guess it's technically still registered in my name. The kids needed a car and I couldn't get much for that old Corolla. I offered to let them drive it around until they could afford one of their own. No crime in that, right?"

"Did you watch Mr. Black drive away from the house?" Genevieve asked.

Paula shook her head. "Why would I watch him drive away?"

"Are you saying someone killed him in her driveway?" Mr. Atwood asked.

"I'm stuck on a few things," Genevieve admitted. "We have a time of death between eight and nine o'clock on Tuesday evening. This is around the same time you claim Mr. Black left to start on his vacation early. You also told us you didn't hear from him again once he walked out that door. It seems like he might call or text to let you know he made it safely to his destination."

"I told you, the service is bad up there," Paula repeated.

"Unfortunately, Ms. Atwood, I know you're lying to me," Genevieve explained. "Someone stole your vehicle from your driveway on Tuesday night. Isn't that correct?" Genevieve asked.

"Now hold on here," Mr. Atwood rose to his feet. "She's the victim here. She just lost a loved one. What are you saying?"

"Mr. Atwood, please don't interrupt. If you continue to do so, we're going to have to ask you to leave the room," Alex said firmly.

Atwood glared at Alex. He was making friends left and right today.

"Someone stole our car?" Paula asked with a confused look.

"Someone confessed to stealing the Corolla from your driveway between eleven and eleven-thirty on Tuesday night, so Mr. Black could not have left in that vehicle to go skiing two or three hours before that," Alex stated plainly.

Paula winced at his words. "What are you saying? Maybe Reggie came back and the thief killed him so he could steal the car."

"I'm sorry, but we're going to need to bring you in for formal questioning, Ms. Atwood," Genevieve told her.

"You can't do that!" Mr. Atwood exclaimed. "She's a victim as much as he is; she's not lying. She's in shock. She must have given you the wrong times."

"I think we all know that isn't exactly true," Genevieve said quietly and pulled the pottery shard from her pocket.

Paula's eyes grew wide. Her father patted her shoulder, but didn't speak.

"Our medical examiner found a piece similar to this in the cuff of the victim's pant leg. I feel certain the paint and material will be an exact match to this piece," Genevieve said. "Mr. Black's face was so badly beaten, we couldn't identify him. Several of his teeth were knocked out. His jaw was broken. His skull was fractured in multiple places. We believe someone hit him over the head with a large ceramic vase, a dark turquoise vase much like the color in my hand. Then they hit him repeatedly with something else until no one could recognize him. Somehow, Mr. Black ended up in the trunk of his car, after which another man arrived and stole the car without realizing he was transporting a dead body too."

"Don't say anything," Mr. Atwood instructed his daughter. "She wasn't here. I did this. I did it to protect my daughter from that…that monster. He hit her for the last time."

"Daddy—"

"Don't say anything, Paula," Atwood hissed. "Look at her. She probably doesn't even weigh a hundred pounds. You think she can swing a vase hard enough to take out a grown man and then pummel his face into ground beef? You think she could lift his body and put it into the trunk of a car?"

Paula burst into tears again. "Daddy, please."

Genevieve looked at Alex and then turned to Mr. Atwood. "Mr. Atwood, could you lift the cuffs of your sweater, please?"

"Why?" he growled.

"We need to see your knuckles," Alex told him.

"They've already healed. I've always been a fast healer," he said and crossed his arms.

"He's lying. He wasn't here," Paula said quietly. "I'm sorry, Daddy."

Mr. Atwood's eyes filled with tears. "Why?" he whispered.

Genevieve's heart sank. The young woman seemed so broken and so afraid. Something bad had happened here and she hadn't heard the whole story yet.

"I'm going to read you your rights, Paula. We have to bring you in and get an official statement," Genevieve promised. "Please stand up."

Chapter 12

J ust as Cari turned on her car, her watch pinged with a reminder.

Pick up Hilary!!!!

"Oh no!" she said aloud.

She wasn't sure how far she was from Hilary's middle school. She should have set the reminder to go off earlier, then she would have definitely been on time. She unlocked her phone and looked up the address of the middle school. It was 4:15 now. Her maps app estimated the school was thirty-two minutes away.

"Shoot, shoot, shoot! I'll never get there on time," she grumbled as she flipped a U and drove past Alex's pickup.

She gripped the wheel tighter out of frustration and spoke to her phone.

"Siri, call Bea."

Sure. Calling Bea.

The call rang twice before her sister answered.

"You forgot about Hilary," she said. Cari could hear the frustration in her voice.

"I didn't forget. I just didn't realize I'd be on the other side of town when my reminder went off. I'm headed that way now, but I'm going to be about fifteen minutes late," Cari admitted.

"They get really frustrated when people pick up their kids late," Bea complained.

"I'm sorry. I'm doing my best. Is there a neighbor who could drive you over and get there sooner?" Cari suggested.

Bea sighed. "If there were, don't you think I would have asked them already?"

Cari hesitated. "Can you call the school or the teacher and tell them I'm running late?"

Bea groaned. "I'll give them a call. Talk to you later."

The call ended as Cari steered her car toward the middle school. She felt guilty for letting Bea down. She had forgotten to pay attention to the time. Picking up children from school activities just wasn't on her radar at all. She was so used to going wherever she wanted to go without concern for anyone else. Even when she tried to do something nice for people, she failed at following through. At least Bob got his suit back from the cleaners in time.

An incoming call disrupted her thoughts.

"Mr. Ollaman, I'll be back at the office soon. I need to pick up my niece and then I'll come straight there. I'm going to be working late today," Cari told her boss.

"They charged Jet. This is terrible for us," Ollaman complained.

"Sir?" Cari asked in confusion.

"Jackson's Used Car Lot is our biggest supporter. The business won't survive without him and we'll lose their annual ad subscription. They buy our weekly full-page ad package as well as social media ads. This could do us in," Ollaman told her.

"Haven't they already paid for this year?" Cari asked him.

"Yes, but we'll never be able to replace them with an equally dedicated sponsor," he said and groaned. "I don't know how we're going to keep our doors open. It might be time to start sending out resumes, Turnlyle."

Cari blinked. He couldn't be serious. "Surely it isn't that catastrophic, sir."

"No one buys the paper anymore. We've become old news," Ollaman said sadly.

The call ended before Cari could say something encouraging to her boss. She knew the newspaper business needed a facelift to stay relevant, but she couldn't believe people would stop reading the news altogether. Printing the newspaper must cost a lot of money between maintenance fees and supplies. Maybe it was time to go fully digital. She looked at the display on her dashboard as she pulled to a stop at a red light. It showed her recent call history. Alex and Genevieve were both near the top of the list. She cringed. She needed to tell them what she'd learned from Gladys.

She scrolled to Genevieve's name and clicked the call button on her steering wheel as the light turned green. The call rang once before Genevieve picked up.

"We just got back to the station, Cari. Did you learn anything new about Reggie Black or his significant other?" she asked.

"She's a victim of abuse," Cari blurted out. "Her next-door neighbor never saw him hit Paula, but she is certain it was happening."

"I'm inclined to believe the neighbor," Genevieve admitted. "What I don't understand is why she tried to cover up his death along with her bruises. I need to chat with Alex and our lieutenant. Thanks for the update."

The call ended as Cari pulled into the parking lot at the middle school. The messy investigation just got messier.

* * * * *

A call came in on Genevieve's cell before she could put it away. *Eric.*

"Hey, Eric. I'm right in the middle of closing my case. Can this wait?" she asked him.

"I found an apartment in my price range, but since I haven't gotten a paycheck yet, they need someone to cosign with me. They said they tried to call you," Eric explained.

Genevieve sighed. "They did, but I didn't have time to take the call. I'm working."

Eric groaned. "I just need a little help…and not money! I just need you to sign a document. I'm a responsible adult now, Gen. Can't you just trust me? I have a good job. People like my cooking. I'm really good at it."

"What time does the leasing office close?" Genevieve asked.

"She said they could hold the unit for me until seven tonight. Can you be here before seven?" he asked earnestly.

She checked her watch. It wasn't quite five o'clock yet. "I'll make it happen. Wait…why aren't you at work?"

"I told you; the restaurant is closed on Mondays. I did all my paperwork this morning and then went back out to look for an apartment," he explained.

"I'll see you before seven. Text me the address," she requested.

"Consider it done," he replied.

Genevieve rejoined Alex in Grusky's office after taking Eric's call. Both men looked her way as she took a seat.

"I'm fairly confident Paula Atwood was being abused by Reggie Black. I think if she washed off her makeup, we'd see that she has a black eye, maybe two. What I don't know is if she killed him by herself or if her father was involved," Genevieve stated.

"What evidence do you have to place the father at the home?" Grusky asked.

"Nothing. He tried to confess, but she refused to let him. I don't know what happened at that house on Tuesday night, but the result was Reggie Black ended up dead in the trunk of a Corolla," she said.

"Which was later stolen by our local car thief," Alex added.

"So, we can establish a timeline between the time of death and the time of…theft," Grusky remarked. "Let's get a warrant for their phone records. See if she called her dad in for help. I'll get the ball rolling on that. Go talk to her. The ADA is still here. Have her listen and see what she thinks."

"By the way, I took a glance at the mantle above the fireplace when we were there. She had one pewter candlestick on the shelf. The shelf was pretty dusty. I noticed a dust-free circle right next to the candlestick. I think it's supposed to be a set of two and one is missing," Alex pointed out.

"You think she clobbered him with the candlestick after the vase broke?" Grusky asked.

"It's a theory," Alex admitted.

"Well, go talk to James," he repeated.

"Got it. We'll keep you posted," Genevieve replied.

They walked down to the break room and found ADA James drinking a cup of coffee. She had a file open in front of her and was highlighting portions of the text on one of the pages.

Genevieve cleared her throat. "ADA James?"

The woman looked up. "Please, call me Emily. What can I do for you?"

"We have a person in interview two who's probably good for the murder of Reggie Black. There's also some evidence she's a victim of domestic violence," Genevieve explained. "Could you listen in on the interview and let us know your opinion once we wrap it up?"

"Of course. I'll be right over," she said and closed the file.

They walked down the hallway to the interview rooms. Emily peeled off to watch from the A/V room. Genevieve unlocked interview room two and opened the door. Alex followed her inside.

"Ms. Atwood, tell us about your relationship with Reggie Black," Genevieve requested.

"Where is my dad? You said he couldn't join me in here, so where did you put him?" Atwood asked, her voice rising in pitch.

"He's in the family waiting room," Alex told her.

The woman took a breath and let it out. "Okay, good. Uh, Reggie and me. We met in a park one day. We were both jogging and going the same pace, so we ran together for a few miles and just talked. I hadn't realized we'd run so far at first; the miles just flew by as we chatted. He was funny and kind. He was so interested in everything I talked about. We exchanged phone numbers and he called the next day to ask me on a date.

"He took me to a lovely little diner and was such a gentleman. I could tell he was nervous and trying to do everything right to impress me, which completely worked. We started meeting to run before work in the mornings regularly…" she paused. "I've never been in better shape than the first few weeks I knew Reggie. He told me how he was a paralegal who was also in law school and how he had all of these big dreams to make partner one day at the law firm. I only have my associate's degree in nursing. I'm not a registered nurse, so I can only do certain things. I've thought about going back to school and getting licensed, but once Reggie and I were together, he told me I didn't need to do that. He was going to make the big bucks once he got that law degree.

"I believed him too. We moved in together about three months after we met. I know it seems fast, but I was so in love with him. He got terrific grades in most of his classes. He had to retake a couple, which was really frustrating. Reggie said the professors were attendance sticklers and with his full-time job at the law firm, he couldn't always make it to class. It made his long-term plan a little longer every time that happened. We were sharing a car, well, it was my dad's car as you know. It got to be a real struggle for me to get to work and him to get to work or home for class, so when he suggested I take a leave from the hospital while he finished school, I couldn't really argue. His job was a lot better than mine," she said and nodded her head.

"How long ago was that?" Genevieve asked.

"Since I quit my job?" Atwood asked.

Genevieve nodded.

"About a year and a half ago. All my certifications expired after a year, so I would basically have to start over at this point if I wanted to return," she told them. "After I quit, Reggie got more clingy. He wanted to know what I did all day while he was working or learning. He told me I couldn't go to coffee with my friends anymore because we'd lost my paycheck and couldn't afford it. We have a joint cell phone plan and he tracked my phone. Any time I left the house, he'd call to see where I was going. I thought it was sweet at first. I thought he was worried about me. Then, he started acting jealous if he saw I'd walked to the park or the library. He'd question me about who I saw and who I talked to. One of my girl friends told me I needed to confront him. She said he was a big red flag and I shouldn't put up with it."

"Did you confront him?" Genevieve asked her.

Atwood's eyes dropped. "Not directly. I told her he was a good guy. She said I should meet her at the coffee shop one day and just buy a drip coffee…you know, the cheapest thing on the menu. She argued that he was buying signature coffees from the kiosk at his office, so why couldn't I have a real cup of coffee every now and then too. I didn't think he'd mind. It was one time after months of only being at home.

"I'd never seen him so angry. He slammed the door to the house so loudly when he got home. He accused me of spending his money without permission. I couldn't believe he was treating me that way. He'd always been so nice and thoughtful. I talked back to him. I shouldn't have done that. It was his money; I had no income," she said quietly. "He took a mug out of the cabinet and filled it with water. Then he stuck it in the microwave for three minutes. He kept saying how he could make me coffee if I wanted coffee. He'd paid for the coffee at the grocery store so I could drink coffee at the house. The microwave beeped and he scooped some grounds into it. I was sitting at the table. He came over with this boiling cup of water and coffee grounds and he slammed it on the table in front of me. The mug shattered and the contents splashed toward me. I put my arms up to shield my face. The boiling water hit my skin and burned it. He grabbed what was left of the mug and threw it at me. It hit me in the head and cut me behind my ear."

She stopped speaking and pulled her hair away from her ear. "I have a little scar. It bled a lot, but he wouldn't let me go to the hospital to get it stitched. That was the beginning of the terror. He told me it was time for bed and I was so scared. I wasn't sure what else he was going to do to me, but he just got ready for bed and I laid next to him without sleeping all night. The next morning, he saw the blood on my pillow from the cut and he was devastated. He apologized and got me flowers on his way home from work. He was sweet again for a week or two. Then I burned the dinner. And it happened all over again. I kept making mistakes and making him angry. I couldn't do anything right in his eyes. My dad invited us over for dinner and Reggie told me I better not say anything stupid in front of him."

"Your dad lives in the area?" Genevieve asked.

Atwood nodded. "He's only twenty minutes away. He moved closer to me after my mom died last year."

"You and your dad are close," Genevieve prompted.

"Very close, even before mom…" Atwood trailed off and picked at her cuticles for a moment. "Anyway, my dad had asked me if everything was okay a few months ago. He said it seemed like I always had a new bruise on my arm or a scrape somewhere. He was worried, but I told him everything was fine. I lied to him," her eyes filled with tears and she angrily swiped them away.

"You think he knew what was happening?" Genevieve asked gently.

"Maybe. I'm not sure he believed my story, but he didn't ask again. I think he was afraid Reggie might overhear our conversation and take it out on me later," Atwood explained.

"What happened on Tuesday?" Genevieve felt like Atwood was ready to finish her story.

Atwood sighed. "It started out mostly normal. I got up early and made Reggie breakfast. He had a big meeting with his advisor from the law school. He's supposed to graduate in May, but you have to have all the right credits, of course. Anyway, it was a virtual meeting…everything is virtual with his school. If everything was as it should be, he would graduate in May and sit for the bar at some point this summer. He was certain it was going to be a quick meeting and the guy would sign off on everything for him. I wanted to celebrate; it's a big accomplishment. I decided to cook a roast and potatoes…bake a cake, the works! We didn't have any of the groceries for that and I don't have a car, so I made a delivery order. It costs a few dollars extra. Reggie got the alert of the charge right before he got home from work.

"The roast had just come out of the oven. I put on a nice dress and did my hair and makeup to look pretty for him. He barged inside with so much rage. At first, I thought he was upset because the meeting didn't go well. I met him in the hallway and asked if his graduation was still on for May. He slapped me and said I didn't respect him. He said I never believed in him. I backed into the kitchen as he yelled at me for paying a delivery fee for groceries when we have a perfectly good car to drive to the store to buy groceries. He pulled his fist back and punched me in the eye. It almost knocked me out, but I saw him coming and pulled my head back enough to avoid most of the force. That just made him angrier. We had a vase out…" she laughed in a sardonic tone. "We always had a vase out. He got me flowers almost every week to apologize for one thing or another. Anyway, it was tall and slender and empty. It was the closest thing to me. I grabbed it and swung it at his head. It stunned him and knocked him over. The vase shattered and I knew if I didn't hit him again, he was going to get up and kill me. I grabbed one of the candlesticks from the mantle and slammed it into his head over and over and over until my arms couldn't swing anymore. I knew he was dead. I have enough nursing experience to see that.

"I had blood and who knows what else in my hair and on my face. I was frozen with indecision for a few minutes. I thought about calling the police, but I was scared no one would believe my story. I grabbed a tarp from the garage instead and dragged Reggie onto it. We have a ramp from when my mom was in a wheelchair and she couldn't navigate the porch steps. I figured the top of it would be close enough to the height of the trunk that I could get him in it without too much trouble. I got the keys out of his pocket and went to work. I just kept doing the next thing and before I knew it, Reggie was in the trunk. And it was over."

"Until the car disappeared," Genevieve said quietly.

Atwood hung her head. "Yeah. That complicated everything. I called my dad at that point. We went back and forth on reporting the car and Reggie as missing, but I was afraid. I thought since I waited, maybe it would make things worse for me. I kept hoping no one would connect us to the car. Then you called. I knew it was really over then."

A knock sounded at the door. Alex opened it and ADA James stepped inside the interview room. Her makeup was a bit smeared; her face was somber. She pulled out the chair next to Genevieve, sat down, and reached across the table to grab one of Atwood's hands.

"I'm so very sorry for all you've endured."

* * * * *

Cari listened as Genevieve retold Paula Atwood's horrific story on the phone Monday evening. She'd felt confident early on neither Jackson nor Samson was guilty of murder, but they had struggled to find any other suspects. She'd never suspected the victim was really a monster, a person who'd been killed trying to attack someone they supposedly loved.

"This is all on the record?" Cari asked when Genevieve finished speaking.

"You can write it up and put it in the Beagle," Genevieve responded. "I need to go finish my paperwork."

"Talk to you later, Gen," Cari said and ended the call.

"Everything okay?" Bob asked when she joined him in the kitchen.

"I guess you already heard how the case closed?" Cari responded with a question.

Bob set the spatula down next to the stove top and walked over to Cari to give her a hug. "I did. It's awful. No one should have to live like that."

He kissed the top of her head and went back to the stove. She opened the fridge and took out a bottle of white wine.

"Gen didn't tell me what the district attorney is going to do," Cari said. "Want a glass?"

Bob nodded. "They're having a meeting about it tomorrow. I think the new ADA is pretty sympathetic to victims of domestic abuse, and it's clear the Atwood woman falls in that category."

"Good. I can't imagine her being punished after everything she's already been through," Cari remarked and poured two glasses of wine. "I'm glad we found each other, Bob. I'm glad we can trust each other to never be hurtful like that."

Bob took the glass of wine from her outstretched hand. "Me too. The whole thing is really eye-opening. You never know what others are going through."

Cari rubbed her locket and then picked up her glass of wine to take a sip. "I was late to get Hilary today. I was on the west side of town when my reminder went off…just too far away to get there on time. Bea was pretty upset with me."

Bob smiled. "Don't feel too guilty. At least you called before you were late. You didn't just ghost them or something."

"I guess. I feel bad. Bea asked me for one thing. Normally, her kids ride the bus to and from school, so they don't need a ride, but this was an extra thing. Sometimes I feel like I have good intentions but my lack of follow-through is more destructive. I almost made you late for court last week because I forgot I took your suit to be cleaned. If I hadn't done anything, your life would have been less stressful," Cari said sadly.

"Hey. My life is always better because you're in it. Never forget that. I love you. Forever. You're stuck with me, Turnlyle. And just in time too," he said with a grin. "I joined the family before your grandmother offered to take the clan to Hawaii. I kind of like to think it's my charm and handsomeness that inspired her to plan the trip."

Cari wrapped her arms around him. "Definitely. I love you, Bob Hursley."

The End

Ready for more Cari and friends? Book 9 will be here before you know it. Cari is out for a run with Bob when she spots what looks like the back end of a car protruding from the lake. They call it in and the vehicle is extracted from the icy waters. A body is slumped over the steering wheel, which brings Genevieve and Alex to the scene as well. The victim is the younger son of a local wealthy businessman known for getting into trouble and constantly being out of money. Did his debts finally come to call?

Find out in Book 9 of the Cari Turnlyle Series! Coming in the summer of 2026!

Thank you for reading "Shattered Links"! Please leave a review on Goodreads or wherever you obtained your copy. For more information on my books or to subscribe to my e-newsletter, please visit my website at https://leslieapiggott.com.

Acknowledgments

While this novel is entirely fictional, domestic violence is a painful reality for many. My deepest respect goes to those who have endured it. If you or someone you know is experiencing abuse, please call 1-800-799-7233 or visit https://www.thehotline.org/. You are not alone.

Thank you for your grace with loose interpretation of LexisNexis and the information you can glean from it. I've never used the program and am limited to using Google to search for its features. If I've made it more powerful than it actually is, I apologize.

As always, thank you to my amazing editor, Jennie Rosenblum! This series would be lost without you.

Another *huge* shoutout to my beautiful friend Desiree. Thank you for reading each manuscript first and finding all my mistakes. All the love for you!

A big thank you goes to Indies United Publishing House and all its authors! Thank you for your support and for sharing my book with your readers too.

About the Author

Leslie A. Piggott lives in the Austin, Texas area with her husband and their two children. She is a scientist-turned-mom who received her doctorate in Biomedical Sciences from the University of Texas Health Science Center at Houston. In addition to writing, she also enjoys running marathons, quilting, knitting, singing in the church choir, and watercolor painting. She has previously published two watercolor and poetry books, both in 2021: *Poems in the Pandemic*, and *Art in Words*. Her first novel, *Rising Pressure* was published in January of 2022. She began publishing her first mystery series with *Chasing the Edge, book 1 of the Cari Turnlyle Series* in July of 2022. To sign up for her newsletter, you can visit her website at https://leslieapiggott.com.